# INTO THE ATTIC OF THE WORLD

## JOSEPH MAZERAC

MILFORD
HOUSE

an imprint of Sunbury Press, Inc.
Mechanicsburg, PA USA

## MILFORD HOUSE

an imprint of Sunbury Press, Inc.
Mechanicsburg, PA USA

For information about special discounts for bulk purchases, please contact Sunbury Press Orders Dept. at (855) 338-8359 or orders@sunburypress.com.

To request one of our authors for speaking engagements or book signings, please contact Sunbury Press Publicity Dept. at publicity@sunburypress.com.

FIRST MILFORD HOUSE PRESS EDITION: June 2025

Set in Garamond | Interior design by Chris Fenwick | Cover by Joseph Mazerac | Edited by Chris Fenwick.

Publisher's Cataloging-in-Publication Data
Names: Mazerac, Joseph, author.
Title: Into the attic of the world / Joseph Mazerac.
Description: First trade paperback edition. | Mechanicsburg, PA : Milford House Press, 2025.
Summary: Charles Miller and his closest friends join Captain Kid's mission to find a missing fairy and a villainous girl from the captain's past. To Charles, the quest is the most epic adventure imaginable, but he strongly suspects it is smarter to stay home.
Identifiers: ISBN : 978-1-62006-229-6 (paperback).
Subjects: YOUNG ADULT FICTION / Fantasy / Contemporary | FICTION / Fantasy / Action & Adventure | YOUNG ADULT FICTION / Fantasy / Epic.

Designed in the USA
0  1  1  2  3  5  8  13  21  34  55

*For the Love of Books!*

*This book is dedicated to my children, William, Dylan, Layla, and Malia, who keep me young at heart; to my beloved wife, Johanna, who has constantly supported my creative endeavors; and to my writing friends at FCCW—We did it!*

Drawing by Connor Poovey

# CHAPTER 1

# CHARLES MILLER

I was barely a teenager when magic first touched my life. Those days were so much like dreams, with their strange wanderings and incredible wonders, it's difficult to believe they happened. Most of the time, all I wanted was to forget, but the past is like a lion in the way it patiently hunts for the present.

A few months ago, I bought my old childhood home, and that's when the ol' lion caught up to me. The memories came back stronger than they have in decades. Even as I write this, when I close my eyes I'm visited by visions from other worlds, of the broken bones of shipwrecks sunken in sand and drifting shapes of ghosts too scared and wayward to face judgment. I recall the stolid face of a king on his blue throne and the radiance of a girl so beautiful I fell in love just by looking at her.

I suppose I can deal with that, but today is a good day. On the bad days, I see dead friends and a terrible black unicorn with his horn dripping blood. Through the rational eyes of adulthood, I know what I remember is impossible, but here's the paradox: even impossible things can happen when magic cuts holes in the world.

I'm trying to prepare you, but in a way, I'm doing a disservice because this story isn't about unicorns. It's not about ghosts, shipwrecks, or kings. It's not even about falling in love. Most of that comes later. This story is about me as a boy and how I became first mate on a crew of kids, led into another world by…well, the captain. You'll meet him soon enough. Before I introduce you to him, however, I have to show you around my old neighborhood.

In the summer of 1990, my family lived on a long, skinny lake with townhouses built on one side and a wetlands forest on the other. This was in Florida, so the waterline was constantly visited by wildlife, mostly ducks and other more exotic looking birds like egrets, but also the occasional deer or alligator.

On one of those warm summer mornings, I was on the back porch, sitting in a chair that looked like wood but was really made of plastic. You know the ones, beachy-looking things with low sloped bottoms. There were no deer or alligator that morning, just ducks waddling along the paved lake-side path.

I was not interested in ducks. Instead, I sat watching the water, letting my mind drift out like fishing line. Then I saw something interrupt the bright blue sheet of reflected sunlight. What was it? I couldn't tell and wouldn't be able to for several hours.

I took a mental note that breakfast had passed, and lunch was still a ways off.

My mother leaned out the sliding door, saying something, but I ignored her. Not that I meant to do that, it's just concentration is tricky for all boys and even more difficult for a thirteen-year-old. It seemed every moment I was thinking of a dozen things at once or nothing at all. Either that or my brain—every gooey gray wrinkle— focused one hundred percent on a single subject, all interruption banned forthwith upon pain of death.

She waited for an answer. "Well?" she asked.

I groaned, "Victor said he saw Bigfoot again. I said it was bogus, and he started crying."

"Be nice, Charles. Every time he goes home crying, I get a phone call."

"That's not my fault."

"It is if you're not being nice." She waved for me to come to her. "I bought that shirt for school next year. You're going to ruin it." She pulled me inside the house. "Change your clothes. And I want you to read a book today. Your brain's turning to mush."

"Aww, do I have to?" But I was already darting up the stairs. As I changed into an old T-shirt, I looked out my bedroom window. On the distant side of the lake, I spotted again that strange disruption. This time it was closer, or maybe my angle was better to see it, because I could make out its shape, vaguely triangular, and its size, roughly the same height as my bedroom door. I stepped closer to the window, peeking out the open blinds.

Was the shape moving? I thought it was.

A knock came on the back door, which set my dog, Chimney, barking up a storm. I raced down the stairs to find one of the neighborhood boys, Ozzie Ernesto, pressing his greasy forehead to the glass. I'd hoped to see William, but Ozzie would have to do. Mom gripped Chimney by the collar as I pushed through the back door. I had to get out of the house before she gave me something to do. She'd already threatened me with a book.

Unlike my best friend, William, Ozzie shifted the focus of his friendship between me and my little brother, Tommy, every few years. He'd started out as my friend back in our dinosaur phase, but had followed my brother into He-Man, stuck with him for a short while into Star Wars, and ditched that to play backyard football with me. I suspected he was about to switch loyalties again because he was into video games and my brother had a Nintendo in his bedroom.

Maybe not, though, because one thing Ozzie and I had in common was our love of baseball. Ozzie's favorite player was Jose Canseco, a Cuban-American like himself. Mine was Mark McGuire.

Where was Tommy when all this was going on? I can't remember, probably upstairs preparing an epic conquest of the Galactic Empire. He had a million action figures—including the previously mentioned He-Man barbarians—but more than anything else, the boy had stormtroopers, great armies of them.

So, without Tommy and William to entertain us, Ozzie and I played out on the back lawns. We threw the football around and, later, played that stupid hand-slapping game. We stood facing one another, our palms touching. Ozzie would give me a false-start fake-out and then *Whack!* He was a crazy-fast slapper. By the time I dodged him, and we switched positions, the back of my hand was fiery red and stinging.

After that, Ozzie and I just wandered around arguing over the merits of Victor's Bigfoot sightings. In my view, Victor was only ten, an unreliable witness and a crybaby to boot. I didn't believe a word he said. Ozzie, on the other hand, liked believing a seven-foot-tall, hairy monster lived in the forest behind the lake. He said it would be like *Harry and the Hendersons* or something, but if he wanted to convince me, he should have referenced Chewbacca instead.

At some point, Dawn joined us. She was breathtaking when she was young, blonde hair with curls and big brown eyes like pools of honey—that sort of thing. I was infatuated with her, and so was everybody else. I tried not to be a jerk about it because, along with being pretty, she was one of my best friends.

She had a little sister, Layla, but Layla was six and mostly rode her Big Wheel up and down the pathway, her plastic wheels knocking against the spaces in the pavers. *Tock-tock-tock-tock-tock-tock-tock*—I still remember that sound.

Then after a while, we returned to my porch. Ozzie and I lounged in the beach chairs while Dawn stood over us, the three of us chatting about who-knows-what. Then out of the blue, the plastic tires of Layla's big wheel screeched to a halt and she shouted out, "It's a boy!"

That phrase, *it's a boy*, brings to mind a delivery room, a doctor in blue scrubs holding up a slimy, crying baby. That's not what Layla was referring to, but in a sense, the boy's arrival was a lot like a birth because, until that very morning, I'm not even sure he existed. At least, not in our world.

He piloted a raft across the lake. The triangular shape I'd seen from my bedroom was its sail. To be clear, ours was a skinny lake, not much good for boating, and the only other watercraft we'd seen on it were boats from the wildlife service. Their people came out when neighborhood mothers complained about alligators. But the wildlife service hired men with beards, not boys, and they took to the water in johnboats with gas engines, not little rafts with sails.

The boy stood alongside his sail, one hand gripping the mast post. The raft itself was barely visible above the waterline. A breeze washed across the lake, and the sail billowed, catching the air like a kite in the wind. The boy took the sail by its lower cross member, leaned back, his right leg stretching to dip toes in the water. The raft turned, one of its corners peeking up into the air like the face of a curious fish.

No one spoke. We only watched, amazed.

As the approaching craft slowed, the boy lifted his hand into the air and waved to us. I waved back. We all did. When the raft came near to the bank—perhaps ten feet from land—the stranger loosened a cord on the mast and the sail dropped limp against the post like a flag on a windless day.

The boy seemed so efficient in his sea-faring duties. In a minute flat, he had the sail removed and folded into a box. Then he lifted the mast from its mount in the floor, turned it side-ways, and out slid a staff, slim like a broomstick. He laid the mast across the wooden deck and used the smaller staff to guide the raft in slowly turning circles in the shallow water.

When first I thought about this as an adult, I compared it to a dream, but later I concluded that watching the boy drift circles through the sunshine reflections was less like a dream and more like an old Disney movie, like the kid in *The Jungle Book* floating down a river on the belly of a bear; half like that and half Peter Pan drifting in through an open window. I almost expected to see a fairy alight upon his shoulder, sprinkling his shirt with fairy dust.

The boy peered into the water, his prodding stick rippling the surface. Then the slow *tock-tock-tock* of plastic wheels over pavers lifted the scene out of the cartoon realm and onto the familiar face of reality. Layla stopped her Big Wheel in front of me. She sat astride the three-wheeler, arms resting across the handlebars and her knees bobbing side-to-side. Her left knee was scraped, and she wore her white church shoes. I don't know why I remember that so clearly.

The boy on the raft looked like a Hummel figurine come to life. His skin was porcelain-white with cheeks so rosy they look painted. His eyes were a perfect caramel-gold, and his auburn hair, although messy, waved and tumbled with friendly indifference. He wore trousers rolled up to the knees, a plaid, short-sleeved shirt, and a khaki vest with all kinds of peculiar patches sewn onto it. Plus, he had a knife in a leather sheath on his belt. The thing had a handle made of bone. To me, that was most impressive and very interesting but also a flag of warning.

By this time, Ozzie, Dawn, and I were all standing near the water. Ozzie piped up, "Who are you?"

The boy on the raft looked surprised by the question. He placed an innocent hand across his heart. "Me? Some people call me Captain Kid, but I'm nobody, just a boy on a raft."

"Where'd you get it?" Ozzie asked.

"This ol' thing?" The boy tapped the wooden floor with his staff. "I didn't *get it*. I built it—you know, from logs and such."

Amazement colored Dawn's voice. "You built that? Can I ride it?"

"You bet," the stranger replied.

"Now, hold on," I said to Dawn. "A raft built by a kid will sink, I bet." I looked at the boy with suspicion. "What school do you go to?"

"What do you mean?" he asked.

"You know—Argyle Forest? Orange Park? Did you move from outta state?" My hands had become fists, and I wasn't sure why. "Where do you go to school? It's an easy question."

Then Ozzie, speaking as if the boy wasn't standing—or rather, floating—right in front of us, said to me, "He probably goes to elementary."

I looked to the seafarer. "Well do you?"

"Do I what?" he asked.

"Do you go to the elementary school?"

"That foul place? I'd rather fight a dragon than go there." He brought the staff up, whirling it between his hands in mock battle. His stomping feet cast the raft about wildly, but it didn't tip over or sink. In fact, it looked rather well made and would support Dawn easily, or all of us, for that matter.

From her seat on the Big Wheel, Layla said with perfect certainty, "There's no such thing as dragons, and any boy who doesn't go to school will be dumb as a post." Not a bad retort for a six-year-old.

The boy on the raft spun the staff between his fingers, gripped it in the center, then drove it down onto the decking. "Quite right, my dear. That's why I insist on the finest education possible."

"Where do you go to school then?" Dawn laughed.

"Why," the boy replied, "out in the deepest jungles of Africa, for starts. Then off to Burma, New Guinea, and West Texas. I was even tutored by a mummy once." He spoke with such enthusiastic confidence it was hard not to buy into the lunacy.

"So, world traveler," I motioned to the lake, "what brings you to these humble waters?"

The boy sighed. "I'm glad you asked. By chance, have any of you earned merit badges of late?" He looked at our blank faces. "You know, patches?" He presented the many patches sewn onto his vest for evidence.

"Like from the Scouts?" Dawn looked to each of us before admitting, "No, we haven't. I was in the Girl Scouts, but that was years ago and—"

"No, no," the kid cut in. "Not from the Scouts. What about besides that?"

Still, we shook our heads.

The boy rubbed his chin. "As suspected. *Hmmm.* What new skills have you learned?" He waited for our answers.

Dawn pointed to her little sister. "Layla can ride a bike with no training wheels."

"That's something," the boy said. He pointed to me. "What about you?"

I shifted my stance, feeling like I'd done something wrong. Out from my mouth popped the first thing I could think of. "I learned to tie on fishhooks."

"How many times do you twist the line around itself before running it back through the loop?" he asked.

Was this a quiz now? "Seven times," I said, triumph lifting my voice.

"That should do it." The boy paced the short length of the raft. Then snapping his fingers, "We need snacks to clear our heads!"

But what the boy considered snacks I thought of as a picnic feast. That was the first time I ever ate lobster.

Consider the scene and pay attention because there are a few important details I don't want you to miss. First, the food truck. Had anyone called it? No. Were visits to my subdivision part of its route? Never, yet, it pulled up to the neighborhood gazebo just as us kids settled in around the shaded picnic table. And the truck was no ordinary taco stand on wheels. Oh no, it was some kind of reconfigured military vehicle. A Mercedes. It had no business on the North American continent, much less in our little subdivision.

Also, the men who drove it and made the food had skin as dark as black coffee and spoke with accents too thick to understand. I thought they were *islanders*, although, what gave me that impression I'm not certain. Maybe it was something in a movie I'd seen.

They shoveled out the food for us, as much as we could carry on paper platters: lobster tails and shrimp, little rolled up taquitos, and fried sugary treats on sticks. Lots of fruit, too. And firecrackers. I suppose the firecrackers were their version of Happy Meal toys.

The boy paid the food truck islanders with large coins from a leather pouch. This could be wrong, but I think the coins were Morgan silver dollars.

By this point, I was amazed by the kid. How could I not be? But here's the second detail to take away from the encounter before we get into the matter with the patches: Captain Kid had a way of making a person look at himself with a critical eye. And not necessarily in a good way, which I suspect contributed to the way he made enemies. Any two people get in a room together and they'll draw comparisons. My friend, Captain Kid, set the bar too high. Some people just couldn't accept their abilities being so meager next to his. I know that's not a good way of looking at it, but it's human nature. So, when I saw him usurping my position as the leader of our little neighborhood gang, I didn't like it. That was my weak spot, my pride, the chink in my youthful armor.

But let us not linger in negativity because my mistrust of the boy was not motivated entirely by selfishness. I loved my friends, and trust is earned. Now, enough of that—come with me and learn of the patches.

# CHAPTER 2

# PATCHES

Captain Kid sat cross-legged atop the picnic table. The rest of us were gathered around him on the benches, our fingers sullied and smelling of the juicy seasoning in the lobster tails.

Looking down at the many patches sewn upon his vest, the captain asked, "Honestly, you don't know of these? Whenever you do something new, like something extra special or hard, you earn a patch from the Patch Fairy. She leaves them under your pillow."

He looked to us for confirmation, checking to make sure we weren't playing a trick on him. To him, earning patches must have been as obvious as getting French fries at McDonalds or presents at Christmas. But when he saw our unknowing expressions, he understood that wasn't the way of things in Jacksonville, Florida. His eyes squinted suspiciously then softened as he tapped his chin. He looked each of us over, fixing his amber eyes on me last. "No merit patches for you either? Not ever?"

Turning a Black Cat firecracker in my sticky fingers, I said, "No, with all seriousness."

"But you use pillows at night—that isn't the problem, is it?"

I smirked, "We use pillows, just no patches."

The young captain scratched his head. "I don't suspect you *look* for the patches if you've never heard of them...but even without looking, you'd come upon them eventually."

Dawn gestured to the boy's chest with the fried, sugary stick in her hand. "The Patch Fairy gave you all those?"

"She did," he said, "and many more than just these."

She pointed. "What's that one for?"

The captain examined a square patch, deep blue with a snarling bear embroidered onto it. It was one of his more menacing patches.

"It's for facing a grizzly bear at night and keeping my wits." He fingered the circular patch next to it. On it, a river flowed left to right in the shape of a swooping letter *S*. "This is for learning all the major rivers of the world, their names and the countries they cross." He moved to the next one, an old-fashioned feather pen and ink bottle. "That's for calligraphy." Then the next. "This one is quite rare, I'm told." The patch was thinner than the others and tall, a blue line with a little red at the very bottom. "For helping catch a very wicked person."

He looked up at Dawn, then to the rest of us. He had a somber look, neither smiling nor frowning.

Dawn must've sensed something wrong because she touched his knee. "What is it?" she asked.

He looked at her hand, then forced himself to smile. It wasn't a happy smile, but a brave one. "The Patch Fairy is missing. I'm afraid something bad has happened, but I don't know where to look for answers." He climbed down off the table, and turning toward the lake, he propped his hands on his narrow hips. Holding the pose, he stood that way for what felt like a long time. At last he said, "This lake looks familiar… I wonder…"

"What?" I asked.

The captain looked to me. "Does the path go all the way around the lake?"

"No," I said. "It leads to the pool and basketball courts."

He nodded. "What if you're not going to the pool or basketball courts, does it continue around the lake and into the woods?"

"Sure. There's a walkway that goes over the creek to another part of the neighborhood. My mom and dad go that way on their bikes."

At the mention of my parents, the captain—how can I describe it? We were kids, which meant we were his kind of folk, but having parents meant we were also quite different. It was as if he expected us to be orphans or some other version of humans in a world without grownups, never mind the people in the food truck were middle-aged men.

After taking in this new bit of information like a sea captain adjusting for a change in wind speed, he turned again to the lake and said, "We should go that way and see if the shuttle's still there. Might

be gone, though. Or stolen. Or sunk." Then to me: "You didn't happen to see a shuttle in the woods, did you?"

"What, like a bus?"

Rather than answering my question, what he said next withdrew
our invitation to go with him. "I'll check if it's still there. Maybe Marshal Rayban borrowed it." Then his mood brightened. "I guess I'll
see you later. I'll be back tonight if I'm able." Without another word,
he waved a quick goodbye and left us to clean up the mess we'd made
of the picnic table.

Even in the summer, on weekdays my bedtime was 9:30, so after
dinner, I was in a rush to get outside. Something new was happening.
Something special. I could feel it, even if I didn't understand what it
was.

So, out onto the backyard lawns I rushed to meet my friends. This
time, my little brother Tommy came, too. My best friend, William,
was waiting for us by the lake. Heather and Asa came out next, Victor
and Diego a little later. Others trickled out as soon as their dinners
or chores allowed it.

Earlier in the day, they'd heard about our morning visitor, and
now they wanted to see him for themselves, possibly even take a ride
on his sailing raft. And if nothing else, they came to crack off the
fireworks we got at the captain's picnic. Kids came and went. Along
the pathway, grownups passed by walking their dogs, but, other than
looking up and shaking their heads when the fireworks exploded,
they paid us no mind.

The kids who'd gathered to meet the mysterious sailor waited a
long time, but eventually wandered off, certain we'd made up the
story out of boredom. My little brother and Victor—he was the Bigfoot spotter—were the first to go back inside. Layla headed in around
8:00. I understood why she left, she was so young, but Ozzie gave up
on Captain Kid just after she did.

William, Dawn, and I stayed on my back porch until our parents threatened our lives if we didn't give up the night watch. So, like the rest, we surrendered and went inside.

As I pulled the sliding door closed behind me, I felt like I was closing myself off to a world of wonderful possibilities. The door, sealing out the night, alerted me to how noisy the evening air had been, when before I'd thought of it as quiet. Confined to the stillness of the living room, with my dad looking up from the couch, a remote in his hand, and the TV muted, I realized what real silence was.

"Charles, I was calling you for ten minutes." Dad never had a bad temper. He wasn't that kind of guy. But upsetting him at bedtime could mean early to bed the next day, or chores, or even getting yelled at.

"Sorry, Dad," I said.

He looked to the glass door. "Close the blinds, it's like living in a fishbowl." As I tugged the verticals shut, he asked, "What were you guys doing out there?"

I shrugged. "Dunno. Talking, I guess." Not a good excuse, but at dinner, something had stopped me from mentioning the boy and his raft. The same thing was happening now. Captain Kid's arrival felt like a secret, something not intended for adult minds. Grownups couldn't handle it, wouldn't believe it anyway. Even I was questioning the reality of our morning picnic. Might have been a group hallucination brought on by exposure to pesticides or some such.

Why hadn't the boy showed up again to prove to our friends we hadn't lost our marbles? Maybe something happened to him, the same way something happened to his Patch Fairy friend.

After saying goodnight to Dad, I went upstairs, brushed my teeth, and climbed into bed. Not ready for sleep, I tried flipping through an issue of *Beckett*, but my effort to read was no good. In the dim glow of an Autobots night light, my tired and distracted eyes refused to focus on the tiny columns of names and numbers. Anyway, the baseball cards I cared about I'd already looked up. I stashed the price guide under my bed and lay back on the pillow.

The way I positioned myself, I could see the lake through slots in the blinds. In a little while, my mom came to tuck me in and say our prayers. She didn't do that every night, but often enough I knew what to do when the time came. I said something about having a good day and for God to help me stay out of trouble, but made no mention of Captain Kid, not in front of my mother.

Afterward, Mom sat with me, stroking my hair and humming softly. I resisted sleep. I always did that, but I could feel my eyelids giving up the fight.

If I didn't say something, I'd fall asleep, so I asked, "Is Tommy sleeping?"

She brushed hair from my forehead. The weight of her hand, her fingers in my hair, it was like raking leaves of consciousness into a pile so she could bag them up and carry them away for the night.

She leaned over and kissed me. "Sweet dreams," she said and got up to leave the bedroom. As she closed the door behind her, my eyes fixed on the moonlight reflections on the water. Then, into the dancing white light of the moon, floated a familiar silhouette. The boy on his raft. Though he was easily a hundred yards away, and I was hidden in the darkness of my bedroom behind glass and the white slashes of the blinds, through all of that he saw me. He straightened to attention, brought a hand up to his forehead, and whisked it away in a casual salute. *As you were, soldier.*

So, it wasn't all in my head. He was real. Something new *was* happening, something different. I could feel it in the air swished about my bedroom by the ceiling fan, in the moonlight shining on the water outside, and in the droning cricket songs and bullfrog croaks.

Something special was about to happen. It wasn't for grownups with their complicated lives, and it wasn't for children, but it was for people like me, caught in the middle. Yes, because at *about-to-be* fourteen, I could believe in the simple, innocent magic of my bedtime prayers, and I wasn't bogged down in the quick-dry cement of grownup reality. My friends and I were teens, but really we were just kids, plain and simple. And that's exactly what was needed.

As Captain Kid drifted, his shadowed form faded into the surrounding darkness. I closed my eyes. The boy wasn't missing like the Patch Fairy, wasn't a figment of my overactive imagination, either. He had seen me from his raft and waved. That felt important.

Then an inspiration came to me—I felt under the pillow. My hands searched the covers. But, no. There was no patch hiding there to reward me for my hopefulness. It seemed like there should be. At that moment, for the first time, I had a vague notion of what the captain must've felt like when the patches he earned never came.

Another inspired impulse came to me then, or maybe this was what the first one was about. I balled up a fist, raised my hand to my lips, and breathed out a prayer, catching it between my fingers. I held it tight, else it might fly away, and slipping my hand beneath the pillow, I hid it there. Jacksonville didn't have a Patch Fairy, but we were not completely without magic. There was still a God to pray to at night. Always him, overlooking everything, everywhere. My parents had instilled that belief way back in earliest childhood. God could find my prayer—my secret wish—even if the fairy could not.

What had I, that restless and youthful version of myself, prayed for on that enchanting summer night? That Captain Kid would find his fairy, and I would help him do it.

# CHAPTER 3

# INTO THE LAKE WE GO

The next morning, we found the boy's raft tied to a tree. Ozzie first spotted it secured along the wooded side of the lake. There was no walkway on that side, and we rarely went that way. Too thick with briers. Also, there were snakes, bad ones like copperheads and water moccasins. On occasion, a group of us would cast off such concerns in favor of adventure, but always someone returned with a blood-sucking tick hiding under their clothes.

Ozzie asked, "You think he's in the woods?"

I looked at him. "Like camping? Maybe."

Dawn grimaced. "You think he spent the night out there? The bugs would carry him away. He'd have spiders crawling in his hair and—" she shivered. "Ewwww!"

William grinned wickedly. "Or a gator would grab him by the head and drag him underwater."

She swatted his arm. "Shut-UP. That's mean."

"I'm gonna check it out," William said. He looked to me. "Wanna come?"

I eyed Ozzie. We both shrugged, *Why not?*

Dawn crossed her arms. "I wanna go."

The three of us boys eyed her skeptically. She wasn't invited because she was a girl and a pretty one at that. She might get scratched, heaven forbid, or even come upon a bug or ten. Already, she'd voiced that concern. Worse yet, possibly a snake could slither out of the briars.

Excluding her would be a jerk move. I knew that, but also, I knew sometimes boys needed to feel braver than girls. I came up with the compromise. "Okay, but William leads the way." That satisfied everyone, although, it wasn't like we could stop her from going any more than she could stop us.

With eyes hidden behind the glossy black lenses of his sunglasses, William examined the raft in the water, the tree the craft was tied to, and the overgrown ground between. He proceeded. With black hair combed back and in a plain white T-shirt and blue jeans, he looked like a kid from the 1950s. Of our little gang, he was the coolest by far and would've been the leader, without question, but he was too shy for that.

Ozzie followed him to the edge of the thicket. Ozzie was in a baggy pair of gym shorts and a grungy tank top. Also, that summer he was never without his shredded Oakland Athletics ball cap.

Dawn looked to me, and I gestured for her to go ahead. She smiled, advancing proudly in her flip-flops and cut-offs.

Into the thicket, the four of us marched, until we reached the raft moored to the trunk of a crepe myrtle full of pink blossoms.

"That's pretty," Dawn said.

Oz reached up, shaking the branches, and tiny pink petals rained down onto the dirt and into the water. William ducked beneath the tree, his sneakers grinding the fallen flower petals into the muck. When I saw the impressions left by his shoes, I looked along the strip of sandy soil at the waterline. There were the broad, forked tracks of waddling ducks, and other divots left by something smaller, but no human tracks other than William's.

I pointed. "Where're his tracks?"

The others studied the ground. *A mystery.* Any number of rational explanations could explain what we were seeing—rather, what we were *not seeing*—but Dawn said, "He's hiding on it someplace." She was looking at the raft.

That made no sense. The raft was a floating floor. No walls or partitions of any kind. As the boy had said, it was made from *logs and such* strung together. Though, as I examined the raft more closely, even with it still well away from the bank, I could spot bits and pieces that were less rudimentary.

"Pull it here," I said.

William tugged the rope, but the raft wouldn't budge. "Must be anchored," he suggested.

I shaded my eyes. I could see no rope for an anchor, only the one William held. So, why was it stuck? I tested the rope for myself. It gave up a few inches of slack and then nothing. The raft would not move. "Must be anchored," I agreed.

"Or stuck," Ozzie said, although, I saw no obstructions in the water.

Dawn shook off her flip flops. "I'm going out there." Then she dug in her back pocket for a hair tie. With her hair pulled back out of her face, she stepped boldly into the water.

William, Ozzie, and I just watched. She went first into the shallows, but then deeper. In her blue jean cut-offs, the splashing water only wet her bare legs, not her clothes. When she reached the raft, she was standing in water halfway up her thighs.

She turned to us and smiled, her hands lifting victoriously into the air. "See. Easy." Then she tested the raft, pushing down on a corner. It wouldn't move for her, either. "Seems solid to me," she said.

I looked at my pants, then to William and Ozzie's legs. Ozzie was in shorts—shorts, yes, but much longer than Dawn's—and William was wearing jeans, same as me. "I guess we're going in," I said.

As William and I took off our shoes and socks, Ozzie kicked his Reeboks into the air and charged gracelessly into the water, splashing so much that not only were his shorts soaked, but also his shirt. He was so wet, he might have dived in. It made us all laugh, including Dawn who he drenched, falling on her and groaning like a mummy in a *Scooby-Doo* cartoon.

By the time William and I joined them in the water, they were already climbing aboard.

As I climbed onto the raft, I saw how sturdy it was. The logs fit so tightly together I couldn't see water between the cracks. Also, all the middle logs were smoothly split so the floor we stood upon was flat and without splinters.

Dawn felt with her wet foot at a rounded bracket set into a floor plank. It was a hefty bit of hardware, polished brass, one of the pieces not made from material harvested from the forest.

"The sail goes in there," I guessed.

Hands on her hips, water dripping down her neck, and black dirt speckling her arms, Dawn traced a large rectangle along the floor with her toe. The purple paint on her toenails was flaking off.

"Look," she whispered.

She was focusing our attention on a shape cut into the rough planks. Our youthful, detective minds identified the purpose at once—a secret compartment.

Then Dawn's words came back to me, *he's hiding on it someplace*. As it turned out, she was right.

# CHAPTER 4

# DOOR IN THE FLOOR

Aside from the few refinements—the brass mounting bracket and a bundle of black, square-head nails—the raft was as the boy claimed: made of logs. The logs forming the perimeter were notched, fitted together, and secured with ropes. The whole thing sat low in the water, mere inches above the surface. With the four of us on it, it should have rocked and swayed terribly, but it didn't. It felt as steady as any pier I'd walked on. A part of me wondered if it was the same raft we'd seen before. For that matter, was it a raft at all? Maybe it was something different.

Whatever it was, it was small. If I laid down, I could've touched all four sides at once with some part of my body.

I took a knee and felt at the rectangle on the floor. Perhaps if I had a knife like the one the boy captain wore on his belt, I could have used it to pry the thing open—if it opened at all—but I had no knife, and my fingernails weren't strong enough.

Ozzie leaned over me. "What's this?" He pushed a circular knot in the wood. It sank into the plank, popping up again with a *click* as he released it.

The knot was some kind of handle. We all looked at each other. My friends' faces, mixing with varying levels of trepidation and curiosity, urged me forward, to open the secret door. I looked down at the raised wooden knot. The vertical surface had a smooth groove carved around it for gripping. I touched it cautiously—*What if it's a trap?*

Slowly, I pulled the knot, and the door tilted open on hidden hinges. It creaked and my arm stiffened, but I kept going. As the door eased open, the sunlight streaming in did not reveal a simple compartment for stowing trinkets, but an entire lower cabin, and a large one at that.

Captain Kid reclined below us in a hammock strung between a pair of bookcases. He squinted against the inrushing sunlight. Shading his eyes with a hand, he leaned over and trimmed out the flame of a red lantern hanging from a hook on the wall. The walls of the cabin were logs, like a log cabin out in the woods. Impossible to think such a large room, especially a wooden one, existed beneath the waterline below the tiny raft floor.

I looked from the open door past the edge of the raft and saw nothing in the water but mucky brown vegetation and blue-green tinted sand. No cabin at all, unless it was invisible from the outside.

William leaned over the edge of the raft. I could tell by the expression on his face he saw nothing beneath us, either. "It's cloaked," he said, "like a Klingon Bird of Prey."

He was referring to the enemy warships on *Star Trek*, and he was exactly right.

Then I heard Dawn's breath catch in her chest. When I looked up, both she and Ozzie were frozen in place. Dawn reached for my arm and stepped back. I had to catch her from falling backward into the water. William went for the hole in the floor, lifting his glasses onto his forehead. When he looked into the shadowy space, his eyes widened, his face hardening. That was his fighting face.

I glanced at Dawn. She was clinging to me. Then as boldly as I dared, I looked again into the impossible space beneath. At first, I only saw what I'd noticed before, the boy on his hammock, the bookshelves, the red lantern on the wall, but as my eyes adjusted to the dimness I could see farther into the dark corners.

There in the shadow, sitting in a rocking chair was a man. A broad-brimmed cowboy hat hid his face, but I could faintly make out the rough silver of his beard. He wore a black duster, dirty, scuffed, and ruffled from long use. The hard, triangular tips of his boots clipped the line of sunlight at his feet like black mountain peaks. Most importantly, however, was the shape of a rifle propped across his lap. Even with the gentle morning breeze blowing over the lake, I could smell the oiled steel. The man was the most menacing creature I had ever laid eyes on, as hard as a boxer's fists and twice as mean.

I knew at once, there sat the reason the kid's Patch Fairy stopped delivering merit badges. She'd fallen victim to that monster. He'd killed her or was holding her ransom, and now he had Captain Kid. Us, too, if we weren't careful.

My eyes shot to William. He'd slipped a foot under the upturned lip of the open door. With the slightest nod from me, he'd kick it shut and the four of us could spring into the water before the villain lifted his gun, much less fired a shot. My heart raced.

Then I felt Dawn's arm brush against me. Her hands balled into fists. She looked ready to—not just to fight but to murder the no-good outlaw where he sat. What would she do, pounce down on him like a lunatic badger, wild-eyed and nails thrashing? Seeing her like that, I found my strength.

I looked down on Captain Kid again. The relaxation I'd observed on his face before was a mistake. He was lying in a hammock, true, but his eyes were weary and blinking, his jaw muscles tense, his whole body as tight as a bowstring. He looked scared, tired, and angry in equal portions. I didn't know the young captain well, but I doubted he was often so out of sorts.

With a thick voice, I asked him, "You okay?"

"I've had some bad news," he said.

*Bad news*, was that what he called strange gunmen?

I looked to the shadowy figure, and out of the corner of my eye, I could see William's leg muscles flex, ready to fling the door shut. But Captain Kid did something strange, he waved for us to climb down as if the Big Bad Wolf wasn't waiting there to devour us.

The captain followed my eyes. "I'm okay," he said. "Marshal Ray-ban's a friend."

When the cowboy tipped back his hat, the face I saw was not a monstrous wolf's grinning, gray muzzle, but looked instead like the world's toughest grandpa. He looked like a man who'd spent twenty years in the Marine Corps and then enjoyed his retirement on beat cop duty in a crime-ridden inner city. Only, instead of the crisp blue uniform of a police officer, he dressed like a bounty hunter in a western movie.

"Marshal?" I asked. "Is that your name or…"

The man folded back his duster. There on his shirt, a tarnished metal star. He spoke with a voice as dry as the dust on his clothes. "Edward Rayban, U.S. Marshals service."

At that, a breath rushed out of me as relief poured in. I felt like I'd been the opposite of snake-bitten, like poison was being sucked out rather than squirted in.

Ozzie teetered and swayed. "Awe, man! You guys were freakin' me out." In an exaggerated motion, he wiped his forehead with the back of his hand. Then, bending to take a better look down at the basement-dwellers, he propped his hands on the soaked legs of his shorts. "You guys are something, you know that?"

The cowboy looked to Captain Kid. "These the ones you told me about?"

"I told you they would find us." The captain scrutinized our faces. "Except...who are you?" He was talking to William.

"He's with me," I said, "my best friend."

The cowboy smiled. "Let him speak for himself, son." His rust-colored eyes focused on William. "Well, young man, the good captain asked you a question. I'd hear your answer."

William pushed his sunglasses a little farther up onto his forehead, his young face mirroring more of the man's hard menace than I thought possible. "I wasn't home yesterday—" He looked to the kid. "—when you were here before." Then he raked fingers through his hair, sighed, and hung his thumbs in the front pockets of his jeans. "My name's William Gazack. I live down the street. What is this place, some kinda magic trick?"

"Something like that," the young captain said.

"Uh-hu." William's mutter was the sound of skepticism and I wholeheartedly agreed. The *magic* seemed true, but the *trick* did not. *Something like that.* The captain and his marshal did not feel like prankster magicians. These were no Penn and Teller, not at all. But the clear, empty water beneath the raft *had to be* an illusion...using mirrors, or... I didn't know, but not real magic. Surely not. That would be crazy.

"We can come inside?" Dawn asked.

The captain nodded. "I hope you will. But leave the door open. It's stuffy in here."

Oz was the first down the ladder. He seemed eager to go. I followed him, only a little reluctant because…well, I had prayed for something like this, prayed to help the captain. Now, this was happening. Dawn came down after me. The room was huge for a raft, which had no business having a lower cabin at all, but with the five of us inside, it felt crowded. My back was to a wall lined with fishing rods, Dawn standing close at my left. To my right, William was coming down the ladder.

Captain Kid sat up in his hammock, crossing his legs. He stretched out a hand toward William. "I'm Captain Kid. Welcome."

They shook hands.

I looked to Ozzie, who was standing between a dresser and the marshal, eyeing the long gun laid across the cowboy's lap. Down in the small room, the smell of the gun was stronger, and now I could also smell his dusty leathers. An armoire and desk occupied the space between Marshal Rayban and Dawn. Atop the desk, an aquarium glowed blue, casting ghostly shimmers onto the wall. River rocks lined the bottom of the tank, across them scooting the reddest little crab I'd ever seen.

After taking in the scene, "Are you gonna tell us what this is about?" I asked.

Then Dawn, "You said there was bad news?"

The little captain nodded. "Remember I told you the Patch Fairy is missing? Turns out, she's kidnapped." His eyes flicked to the marshal then back to Dawn. "I intend to rescue her."

"You do?" Her whisper brimmed with admiration.

The captain looked my direction, and whatever he hoped to glimpse in my eyes, he probably didn't see it. To me, the crime didn't seem real. Not even close. For that matter, the fairy herself was an open question. At the moment, I was more interested in trying to figure out how the cabin fit under the raft.

He smiled at me warmly. "What do you think of my boat?" He leaned back in the hammock and tapped the log wall with a knuckle. "Neat trick, right?"

Was it a trick?

"How is this possible?" Dawn asked, her eyes dancing between wonderment and fear.

The cowboy answered. "It's not possible, young miss, not nor-mally. But the good captain ain't from around here." He squinted, peering over at the kid. "They don't know about the decks, do they?"

"Not yet," the captain said.

The marshal felt in his pocket. "Are you going to explain it, or should I?"

# CHAPTER 5

# THE REALITY DECKS

Captain Kid got to his feet. After gathering up the hammock into his arms, he deposited the bundle into a basket on the floor. Then he donned a white captain's cap, twisted a wooden peg on the wall, and folded a long tray table down between the shelves where his bed had been.

He looked to William. "Hand me that chair, would you?"

William found a metal folding chair tucked behind the ladder. He handed it over, and the cowboy marshal offered the captain two packs of playing cards from a coat pocket. Captain Kid sat at the table, slid the cards from their boxes, and lined the decks neatly side by side. He turned, looking each of us in the eye. His mood had changed, not as weary as before. Not as angry, either, but he was still very serious. Whatever he would show us, he only wanted to do it once.

He turned again to the table, his youthful hands settling over the cards, one stack blue, the other red. His thumbs fanned through the decks, seeming as familiar with playing cards as my dad, who was my family's all-time shuffler. As the captain's thumbs lifted the neighboring corners of the decks, the opposing pressure of his hands drove the cards down in rapid patter against the tabletop. He moved the corners of the decks together, the red and blue cards just missing, then brushing together as he fanned them, then falling with overlapping edges.

With the corners of the cards interlaced, he adjusted his grip then moved the stacks together so only their white borders touched.

He lowered his head to examine the gently steepled stacks. Satisfied, his mood brightened. "Reality is like two decks of cards shuffled together. They meet in the middle, like this." A waving dip of his hand guided our eyes. "There's a red side and a blue side, and they have layers." His voice had the rare quality of a teacher who marvels over a favorite subject. "See there, the little gaps between the cards?" Where the decks met, cards from one stack made spaces in the other. "Reality is like that, gaps between the levels, but they touch."

Captain Kid was in his element. The way his voice smoothed into a calm, concentrated whisper and his expression softened, it seemed as if talking about the cards was therapeutic to him. His fingers moved over the decks with such care. "We're right about... *mmmm*... here, I'd say." Squeezing the pad of his finger down with a thumb, he pointed with just his fingernail to a card very near the top of the blue deck. He and I met eyes. "Understand?" he asked.

I nodded.

He looked at me long enough to make me uncomfortable, but when he was satisfied, his eyes moved on to my friends. They also nodded.

The captain looked at the cards again. "It's possible to move between the layers, but you have to be in the middle where the cards meet. Another thing to consider, reality has its own kind of physics— easier to go down a deck than up. That's called Reality Gravity." Once more, his eyes checked to make sure we were keeping up. We were.

Dawn looked around at the cabin. "Is this room in our world, or yours, or somewhere else? I don't understand how a door in a little raft opens up to this place. Are we on another card—like in another layer of reality?"

"Not exactly," the kid said.

The marshal's gruff and rumbling voice offered a more complete answer. "This is magic. Like the captain said, it's a trick. If reality is divvied up into thin slices like a deck of cards, this room is in the space between the layers."

We all looked at him.

"This place is unusual magic." Marshal Rayban said this with a measure of reverence.

Dawn's attention returned to Captain Kid's folding table. She was looking at the two decks, one side red, the other blue. "Where do you think the Patch Fairy is?"

The captain's lips pulled to one side. "Mmmmaybe one level up."

William locked his arms across his chest. "What happened to her? How do you know she's kidnapped?"

The captain eyed the adult in the room.

Marshal Rayban propped his rifle against the wall and leaned forward with elbows on his knees. "I'd heard talk the kids weren't getting their patches but thought nothing of it till someone found her cart in ol' New Orleans. When I got there, I knew something was wrong 'cause her wagon was already turning to dust."

A smile tugged the corner of Dawn's mouth. "Fairy dust?" she asked.

"Sounds funny to you, I guess..." The marshal took a labored breath. "What I found there, tweren't nothin' funny about that." He leaned back in the rocking chair, the soles of his boots scuffing against the dry planks. His coat opened, revealing the worn grips of revolvers, one at each hip.

I wondered what other armaments he was carrying, maybe a sawed-off shotgun or dynamite. Even though he was a marshal—presumably a *good guy*—intimidation rolled off him like smoke from a burning tire.

As he spoke, I could hear wiry whiskers along his lower jaw scratching the raised collar of his duster. "The cart was outside an old house. Neighbors said the place was rented by a little girl. No parents. And the day before the cart arrived, the girl invited them over for a recital. She'd learned to play something special on the piano, something by Frédéric Chopin. It was very pretty, they said."

After listening to the cowboy's thunderstorm voice, Ozzie sounded like a squeaky five-year-old. "That's why the Patch Fairy came—to give her a patch for learning a song?"

The marshal sniffed. "That's what I suspect."

"And the girl?" Dawn asked.

"I'm getting to that." The marshal rocked in the chair, the heels of his boots pushing against the floor in creaking rhythm, no doubt timed to the second hand of his pocket watch. It made me feel dizzy. He growled, "I knocked on the door, but no one answered, so I picked the lock and went inside. The house was dark. I flipped the switch, but nothing. Either the breaker tripped, or she hadn't paid her bill."

Until this point, I had pictured the story taking place in another world before electricity. He'd said *New Orleans*, but I didn't think he was talking about our version of the city. No one in our world rented houses to kids without parents. At least, I didn't think so.

His rusty eyes flickered. "In a bedroom, the one that looked lived in, the bed was all a shambles. Beneath the pillow, I found a looped cable. It ran down the bed to a heavy spring and a foot pedal."

To the left of me, Dawn's hand rose to her mouth.

William gave voice to her fears. "It was a trap, for when the fairy gave her a patch."

The dusty cowboy stroked his mustache. "Yeahhhh."

I got the feeling that he was leaving something out, like the blood he'd found on the cable. Then it was the captain's turn to speak. "The Patch Fairy is more than just a fairy. She's a daughter of the king of the Blue Realms."

"She's a *princess*," Dawn said.

"Yes." Captain Kid sat as tall as he was able. "I have to find her— to free her if I can."

William asked, "Can we help?"

Captain Kid smiled. "You're brave. I was hoping you would ask that."

I shook my head. "No offense, but we're just kids. We can't save a princess." I gestured to the gunslinger in the rocking chair, he with his hard features and years of experience, not to mention all his weapons. "Take him. He could do it."

Captain Kid and the marshal exchanged looks.

The marshal said, "I would... *maybe*... but I can't, outside my jurisdiction. I'm a U.S. marshal, and up there..." He motioned with his thumb. "That ain't America—no version of it. I don't go there."

The captain looked to me. "It's not for grownups anyway."

"Why not?" I asked.

"Just isn't." Captain Kid gestured to the marshal. "He'll go left into the Red Deck. We'll go up."

"Why not go down?" Ozzie asked. "You said down is easier."

"I came from *down*. So did Marshal Rayban."

I asked, "What if she went up again—and again—all the way to the top?"

"No," Captain Kid said with confidence. "Not that far. Trust me, one level's high enough." He adjusted his hat. "But you should know, monsters live in the Attic of the World. Great things, too, but even they are dangerous."

The great things didn't concern me, but monsters... "What kind of monsters?" I asked.

The marshal answered. "Spiders with faces, dead kings of darkness, the terrible black unicorn, Nightmare, with all of his minions." He dusted off his pant legs. "I should be off." He stood, towering over us. "I'll leave you the rifle. If I happen upon her trail, I'll send the hawk. You know where to find the Upward Facing Door?"

"It's close," the captain said, "but my compass is going nuts." He took a brass compass from his pocket and handed it to Marshal Rayban.

The marshal examined it. Beneath the glass, the little red needle was bouncing, first one direction then another. When he shook it, the needle spun circles. "Where's the button to select the door you want?"

Captain Kid grinned like a boy caught doing something funny but wrong. "It broke off."

The marshal raised an eyebrow, handing it back. "You should get that fixed."

"I will. It levels off when I'm closer to the mark."

The grizzly cowboy scratch beneath his chin, eyeing me and my compatriots. Then to the captain, he asked, "You sure about these little ones? They're awful green."

"They'll do," the captain assured him.

Marshal Rayban propped his hands on his pistol grips. "I reckon I could show you to the shuttle. It's a bugger to find with no guide and a busted compass. When you plan on setting off?"

"Now," the captain said.

I scoffed, "NOW? What will we tell our parents?"

"I hope you won't tell them anything." Captain Kid shouldered a backpack that looked like something a soldier would carry into war, except, no ordinary soldier and no ordinary war, either. It was army-green canvas, bulging with pockets, but the shoulder straps were leather decorated with beads and dangling shark teeth.

"We can't just leave," I said. "When will we be back?"

Then Dawn asked, "What about Layla? She'll want to come."

Captain Kid shrugged. "Layla isn't here. Sorry. I called, but she didn't answer."

"What is that supposed to mean?" Dawn was close to tears.

"I can't explain it," he said. "You found me. She didn't. It's not her fault. She's probably too young."

The marshal stepped between Dawn and I. "Trust the captain. No one knows the decks better than him." With that, the old cowboy climbed the ladder, disappearing with the flourish of his coat out the open hatch door. We followed, although, if we knew what we were getting into, Layla wouldn't have been the only one to stay home.

# CHAPTER 6

# THE WAY

We had thirty minutes to gather our things, which was the right amount of time: not enough to think of everything we needed, but that meant we would travel light. Also, thirty minutes meant we were too busy packing our book bags to think of how reckless we were being. We were gearing up to follow a strange kid with a magical raft and a grizzled cowboy with revolvers on his hips, follow them into the forest, no less. That sort of irresponsibility could end with our pictures on the sides of milk cartons. What's more, we were leaving the magic raft behind.

When I'd packed my bag, I took a moment to peek into my brother's room. Tommy was squatting by his bed, arranging stormtroopers into battle positions amidst his sheets. From around his pillow, the stormtroopers' movements were being watched by a small contingent of rebel soldiers, chief among them Luke Skywalker in his Hoth snowsuit. The Jedi had a lightsaber in one molded plastic hand and a blaster in the other.

"Tommy," I said, "wanna go on an adventure?"

Oh, how I wanted him to say, *yes*, but he scarcely even looked up. "Nah," he mumbled and went right back to playing. Although he was years older than Dawn's little sister, Layla, he was still only eleven. Maybe that was too young to hear the captain calling.

My shoulders slumped. "See ya later." Then closing the door behind me, I left him to his own alternate version of reality.

I'd half expected the marshal to lead us into the forest from atop a horse. That's not how it happened, though. He walked with us, the heavy heels of his boots coming down on the pavers like clopping hooves.

The old cowboy's holstered pistols brushed against his marching legs. Captain Kid walked beside him, the cowboy's long rifle slung over one shoulder and carrying his war-time rucksack on his back. Why no one stopped us—*or called the police*—must've been more magic.

Ozzie was darting ahead, running and stopping. He wore a Jose Canseco jersey and had an aluminum baseball bat. He'd swing the bat, spin around, and take off running, all the while spouting make-believe play-by-play commentary. William ran ahead with him, wrestling Ozzie for the bat so he could have a go. Lucky no one got knocked in the head.

Dawn walked with me. We trailed the young captain and the cowboy marshal. Dawn had changed out of her cut-offs and into long pants. Her backpack was red like her father's Corvette, and her hair was the same color as the car's tan interior.

And then there was me, feeling the weight of the backpack on my shoulders, something I hadn't felt since school ended. There was a different kind of weight, too, because I knew what we were doing was dangerous. Yet, we were invincible, barely teenagers with our whole lives ahead. What could happen to us? And, truly, we were caught up in the moment.

Dawn nudged me with her elbow. "Think they're really from other worlds?"

"I don't know."

She nudged me again, this time in the ribs and a lot harder.

"OW!" I pushed her away.

She laughed, "C'mon, ya big baby. Are they from other worlds or not?"

I grumbled, "How am I supposed to know?"

Then we were walking so close our arms brushed together.

She looked me in the eyes. "Just guess. What do you think?"

"I think—Like, they almost have to be."

"I think so, too." She smiled brightly. "This is fun, right?"

"Sure," I said, but to me, it didn't feel fun at all. It felt *right*, like it was the right thing for us to do, but that was well short of feeling *fun*. I looked to the marching figures ahead of us, to the boy and man who'd set us on this journey. Did they have any idea of the strangeness of what we were doing? If so, they didn't show it. For that matter, neither did William and Ozzie. Dawn was the only one showing any anxiety at all.

She conspired in a hushed voice, "They might be crazy."

"Might be, but...I don't know," I said again and looked back along the lake, at our houses disappearing into the distance. "The raft was pretty amazing. Like magic," I admitted.

"*Rare magic*," she said. "And what about the monsters?" She took my hand in hers. That felt...well...it helped me think of the adventure as a good idea, I can say that much. But then she let go of my hand to grip the straps of her book bag. "C'mon," she said, and then we were running to catch up to the others.

Where the walkway divided, Marshal Rayban took the lead, guiding us away from the pool complex and basketball courts and toward the forest. After a short distance, near the thick growth of trees, the paving stone walkway ended at a raised boardwalk. I had walked upon those weather-treated boards with my father several times, but even then, the pathway had an eerie feel. Old trees shaded the curving path with canopies sagging with moss. Spiders, big ones like silver and yellow orb weavers, spun webs high in the trees—high enough to walk under—but sometimes lower, down around face-level where boys would walk into them if they weren't careful. The cowboy, however, did not intend to use the established trail.

Captain Kid took out his compass. Still, the needle bounced. "Which way?" he asked.

The marshal stepped left onto the grass and fallen leaves. Past him, at the edge of the forest, was a tall broad gate of rough-cut timbers. A long-horned bull skull decorated the crossbeam. How we managed to pass this way so many times without noticing such an obvious landmark, none of us could say, but there it stood, looking decades older than the neighborhood itself.

The marshal took out a revolver, spinning the cylinder to check the bullets, then holstered it again. He spoke to us, his voice dry and irritable like a thirsty bear. "Ever been in these woods, kids?"

We all nodded.

"Good," he said, "then you know how thick it is." He opened the gate. "Step high and keep moving. When I say so, we'll stop and check for ticks."

"Mister," I said. Then pausing, I gave myself time to form my feelings into words. As I looked to my friends, each of them looked to me. I was not the leader of this rescue party—that was Captain Kid, or maybe the marshal—but I was still leading my friends. I would lead them home if necessary.

"What's up?" William asked. "You don't wanna go?"

I looked from William to Dawn, to Ozzie, then to Captain Kid in his vest full of patches, and last, up at the marshal. Marshal Rayban's face was like leather, his beard silver wires, his eyes beads of rusty glass. He was well over six feet tall and strong even though he was old. Walking into a forest full of ticks, spiders, and snakes to find a kidnapper was just his thing, what he was built for, but I was in a T-shirt, not a duster, sneakers, not cowboy boots, and I had a folding knife in my pocket but no guns.

"Where are you taking us?" I asked.

The marshal rolled his bottom lip. "I told you, son, to the shuttle."

"What's that?" I still didn't know.

"It's how you get to the level above this one, the next card up in the deck." He was smiling a little, amused in a way that scared me. He eyed Captain Kid, then looked to me again.

I didn't know what to say, but I knew I wasn't about to follow this creepy stranger into the woods without more information. "Why?" I asked, realizing each of my questions was shorter than the last.

"Why what?" he rasped.

Then speaking quickly, I said, "Why up? Why not some other way?"

Then Ozzie, *God bless him*, added, "How do you know the Patch Fairy isn't around here someplace?"

"Because I followed her trail," the marshal growled. "Not hers—you cain't track a fairy—but I tracked the girl who stole her."

Finally, we were getting somewhere. "Why can't you track a fairy?" I asked.

"Charles," the cowboy studied me, "that's your name, right?"

I nodded.

"Charles, if a fairy is unconscious, you could fold her up small enough to fit in a matchbook—Just keep folding her." He said that like it was obvious. "Cain't track that, but I can track the gal who's carrying her. I followed her here and sent my hawk to get the captain."

Captain Kid said, "That's why I first came to your world."

Then the cowboy, "I got here first and looked for her. You might've seen her yourself, a girl about your age with black hair streaked blue. She has blue eyes and pale skin..." He paused. "You seen a girl like that?"

Dawn spoke quietly. "I did when I was walking Pepsi." That was her dog's name.

The marshal nodded. "Aye, and did you speak to her?"

Dawn shook her head.

"Why not?" he asked.

Dawn's hands balled up at her stomach. "She felt wrong—gave me the chills—and Pepsi started barking at her. He never does that."

Marshal Rayban looked at the rest of us. "Any of you seen her?"

We hadn't.

He hooked his thumbs in his gun belt. "She wouldn't stay here. Too much unwanted attention. I reckon she's on her way up the deck."

"But how do you know that?" I asked—more than *asked*, I pleaded. "Even here, people go missing all the time." It was true. The show *Unsolved Mysteries* was all about missing people.

The cowboy sniffed the air, his nostrils expanding over the silvery tusks of his mustache. "There's no scent of her in the air. She smells like candy and smoke."

At that, Dawn recoiled. Apparently, she'd also smelled her.

The marshal adjusted his hat. The brim was wet with sweat. "It's all right, little miss. She ain't around here anymore. That's what I'm telling you. She left. I'm sure of it. My hawk looked for her trail and came up empty. That settles it in my mind."

"She went up," Dawn whispered.

Captain Kid shrugged. "Or into the Red Deck, but probably up."

"And we'll chase her," I said.

The captain nodded, the faintest smile upon his lips. "That's right, Charles. Chase her. And catch her. And rescue the Patch Fairy." He nodded toward the forest. "But to do that, we need the shuttle. And it would help if the marshal could lead us to it, wouldn't you agree?"

I did, of course, and the lightness of his tone made me feel better, but still, I was not ready to commit myself and my closest friends to the hunt. My final question came to me then. "Do you know the girl who stole the fairy?"

Captain Kid's eyes looked to the bouncing compass needle. "I think I must," he said, his voice showing no sign of heaviness. "But walking helps me think, and her name is difficult to remember. Will you let me think about it on the way?"

How could I argue? Looking to the agreeable expressions on my friends' faces, I relented, and into the forest we went, following in the marshal's broad footprints.

.

# CHAPTER 7

# A RING OF STONE

We followed Marshal Rayban and the young captain into the undergrowth, shoving ourselves into the thick of it. Every bush we touched had thorns. In a different month, it would've been a great place to pick blackberries, but now all the berries were past ripe, their leaves turning from green to ash-gray.

Every which way, vines tangled around trees. It was rough going because, like the bushes, the vines also wore thorns. Eventually, the hard ground and thicket gave way to muck and tall grass. That made movement easier, but then I became certain that one or all of us would wind up snake bit or gator chomped.

When we came to a stream, Captain Kid took off his scuffed loafers and hopped across barefoot, balancing on the larger rocks just below the surface of the water. The marshal went next, managing not to slip on the slime-covered rocks, even in his smooth-soled boots.

Once we were across, William walked with me for a while. "Feels like we're in a movie," he said. "I bet we get gold medals if we save the Patch Fairy. Or at least a wicked patch to sow on our jackets—I don't see me wearin' a vest."

I eyed him doubtfully. "If she's real. Could be totally bogus, ya know."

"To the max." William swatted a mosquito. "Maybe not, though."

Considering the otherworldly cowboy trudging ahead of us, I reassessed the situation. "Might find out it's *all* real, including the monsters."

"Might." William grinned. "But the marshal's got guns. *Bang, Bang, Bang.*" He blew invisible smoke from the barrels of his fingers.

I groaned, "He's not going with us, remember? He's got his own deck to check out."

"Oh yeah, the red one..." William shot a glance at Dawn then leaned toward me. "Think it's smart bringing your girlfriend?"

I rolled my eyes. "She's not my girlfriend, dummy."

"Whatever. You're practically going steady."

"Shut up, barf bag. You're just jealous that girls know the truth—that I'm awesome and you're a walkin' butt-wipe."

"Ha! Good one," William roared. "PSYCH! I make you look like a soup sandwich with a fart stain on the bread." He smoothed back his hair. Then, looking to me, his expression became an exaggerated frowny face. "She just feels sorry for you cause when you were a baby in diapers, Mama dropped you on your *swoft* *wittle* head."

I couldn't help but laugh. Then, mere inches ahead of the marshal, a turkey burst into flight. The cowboy yanked out a gun and fired before I had time to form a single cohesive thought. He stretched forward, his right arm reaching out, the gun barrel extending away from his hand like a wizard's wand. His movements had come so incredibly fast, his reaction speed like that of a mousetrap. I'd never seen a man move so quickly. And yet, he'd missed.

The cowboy grumbled, "That could've been my dinner." Then muttering to himself, he slipped the revolver back into the smooth pocket of his holster.

Only then did I realized Captain Kid had also acted upon the unexpected rousing. He had the marshal's rifle unslung and lifted to his shoulder. But then he raised the gun point into the air unfired. "That thing was fast," he said.

The marshal eyed the captain's vest pocket. "What's your compass say, now?"

Captain Kid took out the instrument, flipping open the brass lid with his thumb. We gathered around to see the needle bobbing between two points.

Marshal Rayban lifted off his hat. "Another quarter mile, I'd guess. Everybody check for ticks. Do it quick. We'll check again when we get to the shuttle."

I found one sneaking up my pants and another on my belly. *So gross.* I always hated ticks with a passion, but no one else found any.

We came to a place in the forest where a huge wall blocked our way. The blockade stood, perhaps, nine feet high and spread out to the left and right, a weathered wall of dead gray and living green, the colors of concrete reclaimed by nature. What was the purpose of this barrier? I had no idea. How far did it go? Again, unknown. Through the dense growth of trees, I could see no corners. For all I knew, it walled off the entire forest. And a more important question: what was on the other side? A secret government base was one option presented by my imagination.

Then I remembered the Berlin Wall so recently torn down. I could still hear President Reagan's booming voice, *"Mr. Gorbachev, tear down this wall."*

I stared up at the barrier. The structure was dreary looking and old, but from my limited viewpoint, I saw no lookout towers nor gunmen walking the perimeter, with the exception of Marshal Ray-ban and the captain.

I looked to the left. The wall—unless I was mistaken—had a slight curve to it. I checked right. Yes, the wall curved.

William pressed his hand to the concrete. I did the same. The wall was cool to the touch and rough against my palm.

The cowboy stood over me. "I'll lift you up." His fingers laced together in front of him, the implication clear.

I eyed William then the marshal. "What's on the other side?" I asked.

"Climb up, and you'll see." He lowered his linked hands.

William shook his head. He wasn't telling me not to do it but was sharing my frustration in the constant lack of useful information. Why couldn't the man just tell us what we wanted to know?

The cowboy's face was a leathery, grinning, contemptuous mask, his eyes dark beads in the shadow cast by his hat. If he thought this was funny, maybe he was a villain.

Captain Kid's curious look was only slightly less irritating. To him, this whole operation seemed to be some kind of amusing test, only we couldn't know the rules because it was more entertaining to keep us in the dark.

*Why did I offer to help this guy?* I was trying to remember.

Seeing no better course of action—and because everyone was waiting for me—I took off my backpack and lifted my foot into the cowboy's mighty grip. Then I braced my hands on his shoulders. As he hoisted me into the air, I reached to grasp the upper lip of the wall. My fingers clung to the edge, the rough concrete biting into my skin while patches of slick, wet mildew threatened to spill me onto Marshal Rayban's head. I didn't slip, though, and with reasonable confidence, I swung up a leg.

When I stood, I saw I'd smeared my pants and shirt with blackish-green, moldy streaks. "Awwwe, man." I pawed at my clothes, but as I turned around, I forgot about the mess I'd made of myself.

Whatever I'd expected before it was not the scene set before me. I was looking at a huge, circular pond of murky water. It was not a lake, but some kind of manmade pool. Also, I realized how massive the concrete structure was. The wall I stood upon was eight feet thick and stretched away from me in an even, flat arc, forming a perfect circle the width of a football stadium. And, yes, the inside of the circle was filled with water up to the top.

My best guess, totally unsupported by evidence, was this strange construction was a water treatment facility. What that meant in practical terms I hadn't the foggiest idea, only that the place was unreasonably big, and it looked long abandoned.

"Well, Chuckles, what the heck is it?" Ozzie stared up at me with twisted, befuddlement on his impatient face.

"I'm not sure what it is." That was the truth.

The marshal growled at me, "What do ya see?"

"The world's biggest, dirtiest swimming pool," I said.

I could tell by the slump of his broad shoulders that he wasn't pleased.

Captain Kid went to him. "It's filled with water. Too much rain, I guess."

"Nah." Marshal Rayban took off his hat and scratched his forehead. "Drain must be clogged. I'll see if I can find the pump." He shot irritated glances at each of his companions. "Check yourselves for ticks again. I'll holler when I find something." Then he stomped off, following along the base of the wall in search of the pump.

I looked back over the water. Strange to see such a massive body of liquid forming a perfect, unbroken circle. "If this thing's deep at all, it'll take forever to drain."

"I wanna see." William took Ozzie by the shoulder. "Help me up."

My friends took turns boosting one another and tossing up the book bags. Captain Kid came up last. Lying on our bellies, William and I caught his hands when he jumped and hoisted him to the top.

Investigating the inky water, Dawn asked, "How deep is this thing?" She addressed no one in particular, but we all guessed—all but the captain, who had nothing to say.

After a few minutes of speculation, we began to walk along the top of the wall. Birds chirped in the trees, and insects made their clicking communications. The water in the pond gave off a stagnant musk, and the air was miserably humid. Sweat dripped down my back, and the sun cooked my neck. But we were moving, and our interest was up, so it wasn't boring in the least.

Several minutes passed before hearing the marshal's thunderous call. "OVER HERE."

We jogged toward his voice, and when we found him, he was standing beside an old metal building. From the building sprouted two metal pipes, each broad enough for a skinny person to crawl into. They stretched away from the side of the outbuilding and disappeared into the base of the wall we were standing on. Unlike the place where we climbed up, here there was a ladder bolted to the concrete. Opposite that, on the inside of the ring, a rickety, rusted stairway dipped down into the water.

As we watched from above, Marshal Rayban rolled back a door on the side of the shed. Then I understood, the shed wasn't a building at all, but everything below the corrugated roof was part of a machine. It was a gigantic pump house.

The marshal lifted a panel and turned a key. *EEEE-Vrom-Vrom-Vrom*, and the pump sputtered out. He adjusted the choke and tried again several times, but it wouldn't start. All the while, he muttered curses to himself.

"Check the gas," Captain Kid suggested.

The marshal wiped a panel of gauges with his thumb. "Shows full."

"It's probably a weak battery," the captain surmised.

The marshal leaned on the machine with his hands, his head hanging down, the toe of his boot kicking at the dirt. "Your machines will be the death of you, you know that?"

The captain snapped his fingers. "Could have a pull start in case of emergency."

Marshal Rayban straightened. Then sticking his hand into a dark gap in the machinery, he felt around, bringing out a pull cord.

With hands propped on his hips, the captain offered, "Do I need to come down there?" If he meant that as a taunt, I wasn't sure, but that's what it sounded like to me.

The cowboy tugged the cord, a mighty pull to be sure. The motor turned and sputtered. He tried again, and *POP*, the cord snapped off, sending him sprawling to the ground. He jerked up, roared a series of obscenities, and kicked the frame of the machine. The pump house shuddered. For a second, I thought he would shoot it full of holes. I half wanted him to, but he settled for tossing the broken handle at Captain Kid, who was laughing at him.

"Funny—sure!" the cowboy yelled. "You start it then."

The captain went to the ladder bolted to the concrete circle, and lowering his legs over the side, he slid down. After a brief exchange with the cowboy, they decided starting water pumps was work perfectly suited for four strong boys and one equally matched young lass.

So, Marshal Rayban wished us luck and shook our hands. Then he left through the woods to find his own secret door, a door he said needed to be opened at dusk.

We watched him go. I did not like the man—not at all—but with the only adult gone, the forest felt darker, our predicament more serious, and our position seemed deeper in the wilderness than it had a moment before.

The young captain appeared unaffected by the marshal's departure. Whistling to himself, he took off his backpack and from a zipper pocket produced a bundle of rope. He unspooled it, tying one end to the broken pull cord. We joined him, looped the rope in our hands, and yanked at his command. After a dozen tries, the machine came alive. The engine made a chugging sound. Pipes gurgled, then whooshed. We could hear the flow of liquid then saw the lowland pooling with water darkened by the decay of fallen leaves.

# CHAPTER 8

# THE SHUTTLE

From atop the wall, we watched the water level recede in the stadium-sized circle of concrete. At first, a shiver went out across the surface. Then, ever so slowly, the water began to rotate. This we could only tell by the motion of leaves floating along the edges. Still, there was no way to know its depth, the water was too black.

When the waterline sunk near the level of the forest ground, I expected to see a floor appear through the thinning murk, but it did not. Instead, what I saw was a single, little, white bump emerge in the middle of the receding pool. The bump was not much bigger than the backs of the turtles peeking up out of the water. Soon, this bump was revealed to be the tip of a metal post. Still, there was no bottom to be seen. Not yet.

The water continued to drain, past the ground level, and when it was thirty-five or forty feet below us, we saw the post was fixed to a heavy framework of steel beams. Even then, I had no idea what we were looking at. Over the next hour, the retreating water revealed more buried secrets.

In the center of the gigantic concrete pit, the metal framework stood out from the surrounding water like a tower, almost like an offshore oil derrick. Beside it was what I took to be an orange, pointy-topped silo, like a grain silo. To each side of the silo, white cones appeared in the water.

After that, between the cones, fixed to the side of the larger orange structure, a black dome emerged. That was when I started to understand what I was looking at. Not a grain silo, nor any kind of silo. The orange cylinder was a fuel tank, the smaller, white, rocket-shaped cylinders were just that—*rockets*.

The cowboy had taken us to a shuttle—not like a bus. The blackened dome was the nose cone of a *space* shuttle, and the metal framework beside it was its launch tower. We were looking down on it, far down. Then I realized how deep the hole must be.

Already a sense of vertigo seized me when I came too close to the plunging concrete cliff. Where this shuttle had come from, who could say? I was sure all the shuttles were accounted for, and no space shuttle ever launched from my neighborhood. I was certain of that. A shuttle launch was visible from hundreds of miles away, so if one took off within walking distance of my house, even I couldn't miss that.

We watched the water withdraw, and the sunken spaceship was revealed in the bleak depths. Water poured off it, dead leaves speckled its white surface, and snake-like vines strung its wings. Slime caked the windows and the whole thing had a haunted look. Only a fool would think it still capable of flight.

Turtles slipped down off the launch pad decks, splashing into the water. I followed one with my eyes, its bobbing head disappearing into a large pipe set into the wall. Turning around, I notice the forest drowning in water. The huge concrete ring was an island in an ocean of swimming trees. Outside the ring, the forest was flooding, and inside was a circular precipice.

Captain Kid put a hand on my shoulder to settle my nerves. Whistling, he went to the dilapidated, very narrow stairway leading into the subterranean grounds. I followed him, William coming after me, and Dawn and Ozzie bringing up the rear.

The walk was long, and all the while water drained from the chasm. We could see the whole shuttle by then. All the space shuttles looked the same to me, and this one looked like all the rest. The only difference was, this example...*well*...it looked fake. For one thing, water was pouring out from between the metal panels on its wings, jetting out of the little door up near the cockpit, and streaming from the massive bay doors. A *real* shuttle would have to be airtight. If this thing were in space, all the air would suck out instantly.

And it wasn't just the cracks in its skin, but the whole thing looked slightly *off* somehow. It looked like a fantasy version of the real space shuttle, but a fantasy from the early 1900s. The basic proportions were right, but the thing was made all wrong. A space shuttle should be aluminum except for the ceramic heat shields. This one looked like heavy steel bolted together. All down the white rocket boosters, exposed bolt heads pocked the curved metal panels, not smooth at all. And another thing, the seals around the windows, although dirty, were brass. I was sure of it.

As the stairway led us winding down the towering perimeter wall, I could read the moniker stenciled in black on the shuttle's right wing. *Nautilus.* The name was somewhat familiar to me, but I couldn't place it.

Dawn provided the answer. "Wasn't the Nautilus the submarine in *20,000 Leagues Under the Sea?*"

"You're right," I said. "I guess that makes sense because real shuttles are named after important real-life exploring ships."

"Yeah," William agreed. "So, why not name a fake underwater shuttle after a make-believe submarine?"

"It's not make-believe," Captain said, and we all kept walking.

The hole we were in—I was thinking of it in a new way, like it was the barrel of one of those massive nuclear cooling towers—smelled of sewage drains after heavy rain. Everything was wet, including us, owing to the Florida summertime humidity and the still air inside the subterranean facility. All around us, everything dripped with condensation. The stairway creaked, ducks flew over our heads, squawking, and below, the turtles were trying to figure out where their lake had gone.

We reached the bottom of the steps and I looked up. How odd the sight was, the dark grey walls towering far above to a perfect circle of bright blue sky. Again, the dizziness came to me, with the curving walls looming large overhead. The proportions were so unusual to my vision, it was hard to look at.

Standing atop the ring filled with water, I had guessed the structure to be a little over a hundred yards across, but now the circle of sky looked no wider than a dinner table. I supposed, if comparing the walls of concrete to a building, they were the height of a skyscraper, only built downward instead of up. We were in the deepest basement I had ever heard of, especially in Florida where the water table is so high. That explained the pumps and all the drainage built into the place.

With my feet planted on the ground—finally, the floor I'd been looking for—I could consider the Nautilus space shuttle and its purpose. "What is this place?" I asked.

Captain Kid turned to me. He, too, had been staring up at the circular patch of sky. "The shuttle is how we get to the next level."

"Like a video game," Ozzie said.

Dawn was gripping the shoulder straps of her book bag like a nervous parachute jumper. "We're going to ride that thing?"

I could tell in her shaky voice, she was remembering the same thing I was: the real space shuttle, the Challenger, blowing up in the sky just a few years prior. The whole country had stopped to observe the disastrous explosion in reverent, horrible, awe. A TV had been wheeled into our classroom so kids could watch the liftoff. Then it happened. Had we known what was coming, my teacher could have turned it off. Of course, she didn't know, and the event brought home the stark reality: space travel was a risky business.

"Isn't that dangerous?" I insisted, but Ozzie was grinning like an idiot and William not far behind.

Captain Kid followed a sidewalk to a line of windows set into the wall. When he reached a yellow door, he tried the handle. He jiggled it. I heard Ozzie make a screeching sound, but too late, the captain was already twisting the knob. The door shot open with a roaring *WHOOSH* as a tidal wave engulfed him. He rocked backward, water erupting around him. Had he not kept his grip on the door handle, he would've been washed away down the drainpipes like the turtles.

When the room was empty, Captain Kid spat out a mouthful of murky water. He was soaked, his auburn hair streaking over his eyes. Then he laughed, "Should've seen that coming."

"I tried to warn you," Ozzie said. "A fish swam by the window, but—"

"That's all right. I needed a bath anyway." Captain Kid rested his rifle against the wall and let his huge, sodden army backpack—the one with the shark teeth dangling from its leather shoulder straps— fall in the puddle at his feet. With his clothes drenched and clinging to him, I saw how skinny he was. He went to the open door, rubbing his chin. "I doubt any of these computers work."

As he said this, I noticed the sign above the door: *Mission Control.* We went into the open room. Just beyond the threshold, a catfish flopped on the floor. William scooped it up, pushed past Dawn and Ozzie, and chucked it into a pool still disappearing down a drain. With that done, we returned our attention to the control room. Inside were row after row of computers all set up to allow users to face the algae-tinted windows.

Ozzie went to one, running his fingers across the keyboard. "It's fried. I guarantee it."

He was right. The whole room looked salvaged from the bottom of the ocean. No way the computers worked.

Captain Kid rolled a chair out from behind a desk, plopping down in the wet-sponge seat. He tried a Power button on a CPU. There was a *click*, but nothing else.

He scooted his chair to the left and tried another with similar results. "Doesn't matter. We'll make our calculations the old-fashioned way." At that moment, he looked even younger than my little brother, so it was strange to hear him speak with such authority. "I won't lie to you, this will be dangerous, but moving up the decks often is, especially this close to the top."

He looked beyond the open door to the Nautilus poised atop the launch pad. Huge clamps on its wings held the shuttle upright. If it looked abandoned before, now it appeared ready to leap into the air. Maybe that was only a trick of sunlight gleaming off its wet skin, but I fancied the mist beneath its engines was really smoke.

As I turned to Captain Kid again, he gestured with his chin. "It takes a heap of explosives to lift an ol' bird like that one, but if my calculations are true, and I have some good help, I'm sure we can do it." He looked each of us in the eyes. "What do you say?"

William and Ozzie were nodding their agreement, but Dawn said, "You didn't answer Charles's question—The girl who took the Patch Fairy, who is she?"

I had forgotten about that.

# CHAPTER 9

# CASTATINE

Captain Kid rocked in the office chair as the rest of us gathered around him like he was our coach, and this was game time. I suppose it was, and he would lead us, his title of "Captain" seeming to fit him so naturally, though, he looked no older than we were.

Ozzie, William, and I sat on one of the long rows of desks, computer monitors between us we were using for armrests. Dawn set her backpack in one of the swivel chairs, dug out a big bag of Skittles, and passed them out, giving each of us a handful.

I watched Captain Kid examine the colorful candies before tasting one. "Thank you," he said with a smile, then tossed the rest in his mouth all at once.

I popped a selection of purples and yellows in my mouth, noticing the candy coloring had run off onto my sweaty fingers. Captain Kid's hands, however, were totally clean. Totally dry, also. In fact, although he was as wet as possible mere moments ago, now he was almost dried out. Even the chair he sat upon looked dry, which was impossible.

He looked into the distance over our heads, his clean fingernails picking at a seam in the fabric of his seat cushion. "She's called Castatine," he said. "We knew each other a long time ago way up high on the Rooftop of the World."

"What's that?" Ozzie asked, his tone that of a boy who'd discovered some new marvel.

The captain tilted his head, his expression even dreamier than before. "It's the top of the Reality Deck. The top of everything. Remember, one side is blue. The other is red. That's why they're called the red and blue decks."

My skin was clammy. My stomach churned. "But what does that even mean?"

The captain shrugged. "You'll know better if you see it."

I wasn't sure I wanted to see it, or even if I could.

Dawn leaned in. "Explain it to us."

Captain Kid stroked his palms together. The movement seemed to produce heat, maybe even light. "At the top of reality, there are two realms, as I've already told you. The blue side, where I'm from, is ruled by the Blue King and the Blue Queen, royalty of the highest order. They are as wise as can be for any mortals—though they're practically immortal—and they're very great in law and beauty."

"Are they gods?" Dawn asked.

"No, but they have great power. But Castatine isn't from there. She's of the Red where the black unicorn reigns. Or, at least, he used to."

"What happened to him?" Dawn asked.

"I do not know, but he no longer lives in the Rooftop of the World. Now he lives in the Red Attic."

My stomach clenched. "Isn't that where we're going, the Attic of the World?"

"Yes," the captain said, "but not to the red side—I hope not, any-way."

Was that supposed to be reassuring? I watched every movement of his face. "But there are monsters in the blue side, too. I mean, isn't that what you told us?"

Captain Kid's lips tightened, his brow fidgeting, but his eyes, like amber crystals, locked on mine. "There are monsters on the blue side. That is true, but not Lord Nightmare."

Dawn brought us back to the question at hand, the main question. "Fine," she said. "We'll get back to that in a minute if we have to, but how do you know Castatine?"

Captain Kid studied Dawn's face. Then looking to the rest of us, he said, "In the Rooftop of the World, where the red and blue decks meet, in between, there is a place called the Gossamer Gardens. It's almost like—"

"Eden," I heard myself say.

The captain looked at me. "Sure, in a way it is. It's a very special place." His voice seemed to hum in my ears. "There's a well in the garden where people come from all over to draw water and tell stories. At the well, sunlight plays tricks, the air is thin, and when the wind blows across the honeysuckle vines, all of life feels like fantasy. It's the best." He rubbed his cheek.

"That's where you met her," Dawn said.

Captain Kid nodded. "But the well in the Gossamer Gardens is no ordinary watering hole. It's the Downward Facing Door, the gateway from the Rooftop into the Attic of the World. We knew the place was unusual and somewhat restricted. And it was dangerous. Kids could get lost there. Our elders told us that many times."

I watched the captain's changing expression. Boys, even magical ones it seemed, were too curious for their own good and often went places they shouldn't. I felt the same way, sitting on the control room desk between a pair of dead computers, my friends all around me. We were in a place we had no business being, contemplating heroics that would likely get us killed, and for a purpose we didn't understand.

The captain said, "Castatine and I would gather water in buckets lowered down on ropes, but also, we would look into the unknown darkness and smell its strange perfumes…and listen to its music."

William swallowed his candies. "You could hear the music from other worlds?" He always was interested in music.

The captain nodded.

Dawn whispered, "And Castatine fell in, didn't she, like Tiki Tiki Tembo down the well?"

Captain Kid sighed, giving her another of those sad smiles. "That's right. I tried to save her. I climbed down with the rope, but that was the problem. I didn't understand the doorways, that the water would take her to the Red Deck below, but the rope would take me to the blue side. And I didn't realize how difficult it would be to get back up."

Considering the green Skittles in my damp palm, I said, "You were like Jack with a pocketful of magic beans but didn't know how to use them."

"I guess so," the captain agreed. "In any case, I lost her." He sat forward, taking off his hat and hiding his face in a hand.

What could we say?

I heard the old pipes in the floor grumble. Water oozed from sagging ceiling tiles and drizzled down the walls in filthy trickles.

Dawn had moved in close to the young captain. She stood over him, and when she stroked the back of his head, he looked up at her. "What was she like?" she asked.

Dawn had seen Castatine in our neighborhood, but the fear she'd shown before—or maybe it was just a case of the heebie-jeebies—was gone now. Now she brightened with the affectation of a girl who smells romance in the air.

Dawn was probably imagining a tragic love story, a young girl with a headful of dreams, betrayed by her own sweet passions. Yet, I pictured someone entirely different. I imagined a creature of broken purpose, like a vampire. In my mind, Castatine had bloodless, pale skin and big, dark eyes. I saw white fangs behind grinning red lips. She was evil to the core. She'd tricked the young captain into using the rope. It was a trap, just like she'd used a snare to catch the Patch Fairy.

Captain Kid lowered his head again. "She was funny. I remember that. And she was pretty in her own weird way. She had deep eyes. Also, she was so carefree, everything was play to her. No matter what I said, she'd laugh. But she was..." He reached for the right word. "She was *wayward*."

"You mean, she was *naughty*?" I asked.

"I mean she had something wrong with her heart." Captain Kid sat a little straighter. "She thought grownups were all fools and made fun of everyone in authority, even the king. And she courted danger. She would climb up onto the stone lip of the well and twirl around the posts. Her little black flats were always slipping on the rocks, but that only made her giggle. When I'd tell her to stop—to get down— she'd lean back over the pit and threaten to toss herself in. And sometimes, she'd jump from one side to the other, daring me to catch her."

He'd already told us the outcome of her carelessness, she'd fallen in.

Dawn grimaced. "Did you ever find her?"

Captain Kid shook his head. "No. By the time I made my way into the Red Attic, she was already in the service of that land's king."

"The black unicorn," Dawn said.

I remembered the warning, that the Attic of the World was full of monsters. I stood up. "Look, Captain, I'm sorry about the fairy n'all. I am. But you have the wrong kids. Whatever you're planning, it's too much. We have to get home to our families." Dawn caught my hand, but I pulled it free, looking to my friends. "Guys, this is all super weird and interesting, but what will our moms think when that rocket blows up in the air and none of us are ever seen again?"

Ozzie glared at me. "C'mon! This is once in a lifetime. You're gonna ruin it."

William leaned forward, his elbows on his knees. "Maybe Charles's right." He said this as if the admonition was painful.

Ozzie threw his hands up. "Don't be ridiculous. It's not gonna blow up. Will it?"

We all looked to the captain.

"Well?" Dawn asked.

"It could," the captain admitted.

Dawn studied him. "But it's worth the risk?"

"It is," he said.

She was looking at him with an intensity I'd never seen before. "Why?"

Captain Kid got to his feet, straightening his vest. "Because the Patch Fairy is worth saving. In a world full of worries, people need to know someone good is watching." He placed a hand on Ozzie's shoulder. "Besides, haven't you ever wanted to ride a rocket?" He looked to William. "To see a world anew with all of its wonders?" Then to me, "And if monsters creep in dark places, don't you wanna know how many heads they have?"

Strangely, I did, but would it matter what we learned or what amazing sights we saw if we were eaten in the process?

The captain twirled his hat back onto his head and tugged at the glossy, black brim. "Who's with me?"

Ozzie stood at once. Then William slipped off the desk and stepped forward.

Dawn looked to me. "Charles, what about you?"

I could see in her eyes she was going, but she wanted me to come with her. What kind of friend was I—what kind of leader—if I let them go without me into danger. I looked at the captain. Undeniably, he seemed to know what he was doing. The cap he wore fit him perfectly, not only in size but in purpose. Yet, I would not go for him. Not even close. And I would not go for some unknown fairy, even if she was a princess from some high-away land. But for my friends, *yes*, I would go for them.

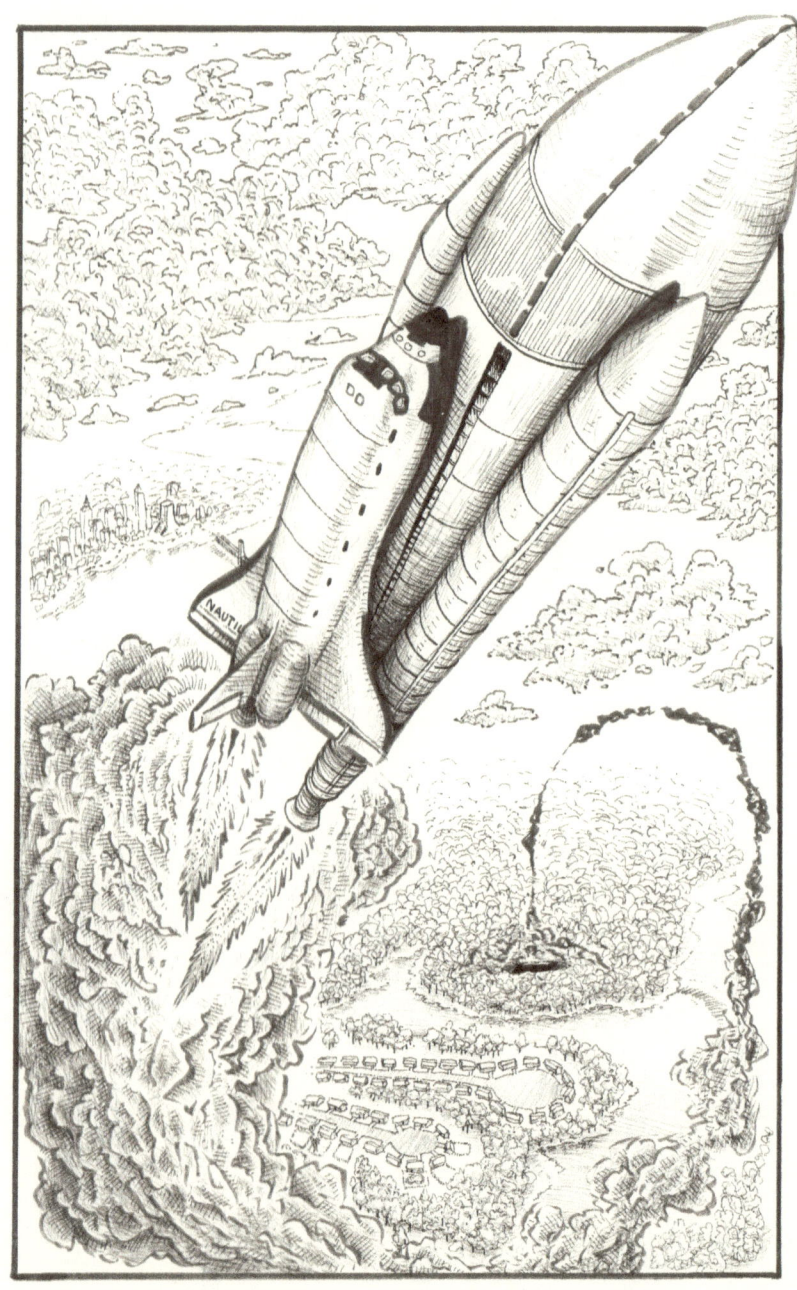

Drawing by Connor Poovey

# CHAPTER 10

# THE BOARDING

Before beginning launch preparations, the captain showed us the shuttle. It was very impressive, far bigger than it looked on television. The ship had a patriotic energy, an American flag painted on its left wing. The flag looked small from a distance, but as we climbed the stairs of the launch tower, I saw how big it was. Although, like the rest of the Nautilus, something about the flag looked vaguely out of sorts.

Ozzie was walking up the stairs behind me when he called out, "Hey, Cap, what's up with the flag—not enough stars?"

He was right. There were six even rows of eight.

Captain Kid paused, looking past the railing to the wing stretched out beside us. The wing was white, trimmed in black, and dotted with rusting bolt heads. "This ol' bird wasn't built for NASA, ya know? It's not even made to go into space."

Ozzie darted past me, gripping his baseball bat with one hand and steadying his bulky backpack with the other. "What's it for, then?"

"I already told you, it takes us up the deck." With a chipper tour-guide inflection, the captain waved a hand toward the shuttle. "A wizard named Doctor Alkatan built the Nautilus way back in the nineteen-thirties. That's why the flag's missing some stars. Alaska and Hawaii weren't states back then."

Ozzie looked back at me. "*Woah*, the nineteen-thirties." But I had latched onto another detail: the ship was built by a *wizard*.

Yet, what sort of wizard could a doctor be? Was he the gray-bearded variety with a robe and floppy, pointed hat, or was he a monster in a red cape waiting to kill us in a room made of mirrors, like the sorcerer in the second Conan movie? Whatever the case, no wizard I could think of would build a rocket ship.

As we continued up the stairs—two more flights and we'd be even with the cockpit—Captain Kid said, "This shuttle looks a lot like NASA's. I'm sure they borrowed the design, but it works totally different."

"How so?" I asked.

"For starts, it uses dynamite as rocket fuel."

"D-dynamite!" I sputtered. "That's crazy."

But the captain just went on talking. "The rockets are like giant stacks of tuna cans. Each has a few thousand sticks of dynamite inside. Kooky, right? But it works. The math is pretty simple, but the variables—wind speed, barometric pressure, weight of the passengers and cargo—can make a big difference. Too much bang and we'll fly past the door. Too little and we'll have to land the thing. And trust me, landing is the hard part."

Dawn stopped him. "What if we get it right, we don't have to land?"

"Nope," the captain said. "Our aim is to dock with the door, not to land."

"Where's the door?" I asked.

Captain Kid was climbing again. "Above us."

I leaned out over the railing, seeing nothing in the sky but shifting clouds.

When we got to the final platform, we crossed a narrow catwalk to get to the cabin of the shuttle. Captain Kid led the way. When he reached the cockpit door, he opened it by twisting a blue doorknob made of glass. Because the ship pointed toward the sky, the door was sideways, the hinges on the bottom. He had to lower the door toward himself, supporting it with both hands. I could tell the passage was designed with this orientation in mind because the inside of the door had wooden notches big enough to use as steps.

The captain looked to me, gesturing with his hand to go ahead. I approached with caution. The transition would be awkward because the opening was much wider than it was tall. I'd have to step out onto the door, duck down, and swing my legs in first. What would come after that? I couldn't guess. The interior was dark. It might be like climbing into an airliner that was standing on its tail. I'd have to walk on seat backs or bulkheads because the floor was now straight up and down.

When I put a foot on the open door, the entire vessel rocked nervously. From far below, I heard the massive wing-clamps strain, the weight of countless tons of iron binding up as it swayed. I withdrew my foot at once. The top of the shuttle teetered to the right then came back to settle against the catwalk. I tried my foot again, and this time the shuttle tilted away from me.

How unstable it felt with the groaning metal and the shuttle tottering like a stack of plates in a Bugs Bunny caper. At any moment, the thing might tip over with disastrous effect. As it drifted, the incredible gap growing between the platform and the shuttle revealed how far I could fall—doubtless to my death—should the boarding go awry.

"You'll have to jump on," Dawn said.

I could feel my temperature rising. "I shouldn't have to *jump on*. The thing should be built better than this." I eyed the young captain.

He watched the Nautilus lean, creaking, back again to touch the outstretched boarding platform. "Should be," he said, "but it isn't. Jump. It won't fall." Then, with an odd glimmer in his eyes, he added, "I promise."

Resenting my inclusion in this escapade, I gritted my teeth, swung my backpack in through the open door, and stepped with purpose onto the first unsteady step. As my weight shifted from the platform to the shuttle door, the step seemed to drop. If that was real or only in my head, I wasn't sure, but the Nautilus tilted away from the tower again. I didn't realize how far away until I looked back.

My friends were a dozen feet from me. On the catwalk, they stared with wide eyes, yelling, "Get in!" and, "Oh no!" and all sorts of useless exclamations.

As the shuttle reached the end of its pendulum sway, I pawed at the doorframe, scrambling for purchase, knowing my part in this drama could end with me cartwheeling into open air.

I stood on the door, a shelf on the side of a metal cliff. The concrete walls of the canyon curved around me. Overhead, an alien disk of blue sky wobbled. Below, the metal bindings on the wings sent moaning complains humming up through the skin of the ship. Then the shuttle was moving back toward the launch tower, moving fast, with me stuck in the middle. It would crush me. I yelled but couldn't hear my voice over the creaking metal bindings.

As the tower closed in, I dove into the ship, landing on my backpack. I looked up at the strange sideways door, expecting to see the launch tower smash into it. It didn't. The tower came into view, already slowing. The contact was almost unperceivable.

I let out a long breath, *"Vwaaaahhh,"* and sat back, an unknown lump digging into my backside. I ignored it. Something else had my attention.

The room was not as dark as it first seemed, only dim compared to the outside. Sunlight streamed in through a row of cockpit windows. Above me, silhouetted against the sun was a row of five seats, all positioned to access a multitude of control panels. Some of the panels displayed broad-faced brass gauges. Toggle switches and lifeless lightbulbs covered others. Another had levers and twistable valves. Every seat seemed to have responsibility for some crucial aspect of the flight. That made me nervous.

Then I saw William's smiling face looking in through the door. "You all right in there?"

I didn't know if I was or not. I felt a little sick to my stomach and I'd banged my knee, but more importantly, William's weight on the door was causing the ship to wobble again. "In or out," I said. "This thing feels like it's balanced on a spring."

William hopped in beside me, a quick and easy move, using one hand to steady himself as he swung in his legs. That's what I'd intended to do before my life was threatened. Next came Dawn. Her boarding was as uneventful as William's. Ozzie, however, made the thing tilt so far, I thought for sure we were going over. He screamed and laughed the whole time. I had to pull him in by double-handfuls of his Jose Canseco jersey.

When at last the captain joined us in the shuttle, I took a second to register what I was sitting on: the handle of a drawer. I was perched atop a cabinet. Dawn stood on a door. *A downward-facing door,* I noted morosely. The door was lacquered wood. The interior of the Nautilus looked like the inside of an old yacht, or maybe a fancy fishing boat, but nothing like a spaceship. That made sense if it was built in the nineteen-thirties.

Captain Kid dusted off his britches then dug in his backpack, taking out a little glass box. "There you are," he said, and sat the box in a bracket on the wall, securing it with a leather strap.

When he withdrew his hands, I saw we would have an unexpected passenger joining us.

"You remember Joseph?" the captain asked.

Joseph was his pet crab. We first saw the little guy in the basement of the raft. Truthfully, I'd forgotten about the bright red crustacean. On pointed feet, the crab scampered across the miniature habitat, looking rather happy for a creature with mandibles.

"Awwwe," Dawn swooned. "You brought him."

"Of course, I brought him. Joseph's my buddy." Captain Kid tapped the aquarium with his knuckle. Amazingly, the little crab returned the gesture, clicking with his largest pincher. The captain looked up at the row of cockpit seats. "Ozzie, climb up there and lower the ladder. Let's see if we can get the power on."

# CHAPTER 11

# PREPARATIONS

When the lights flickered on, the young captain put us to work, prepping the shuttle for liftoff. Ozzie and Dawn were assigned the harrowing task of removing the vines strung about the ship's wings and rockets. William was charged with cleaning the windows and plugging all the drain spouts around the huge, black, funnel-shaped engine nozzles.

While my friends dispersed, I assisted Captain Kid with data collection. We—mostly the captain—determined barometric pressure and wind speed using a stopwatch, an enormous protractor with a sight glass built onto it, and a helium balloon on a string. When that was finished, we set off to find the Upwards Facing Door.

Near the top of the launch tower, where the catwalk stretched out to the shuttle's cockpit door, there was a ladder. The ladder continued the upward climb another twenty feet through a framework of steel I-beams, ending at a small platform surrounded by rails. The white post I'd first spotted from atop the concrete rim was affixed to the platform. That little platform felt a long way up, especially with us already so high in the air.

I followed Captain Kid up the ladder, coming out on a floor made of slotted metal decking. Slotted, so I could see straight through, all the way to the ground. I could imagine dropping my house keys and watching them fall in slow motion, smack the deck, then slip between the cracks. *Goodbye keys,* because I'd never find them after that.

Captain Kid had recovered a collapsible brass telescope out of the shuttle. Now he used it to peer at the sky.

I looked up, shading my eyes with my hands. "What are you—"

"Quiet," he said. "I need to concentrate."

Then, from below, I heard tinkling glass. William was coming up the ladder, his right hand securing three Coke bottles to his chest. He took an upward step, adjusted his grip, then shot his left hand up to catch the next rung.

"Where'd you get the Cokes?" I asked.

"They got a machine in the breakroom—" He was red-faced and out of breath, his words coming in herky-jerky puffs. "—for the astronauts—or scientists—or whatever."

"Or for us." I smiled, reaching down to help.

When he was with me on the deck, he wiped sweat from his brow and eyed the captain. "Is he looking for the door?"

"Yeah. *Shhhh*. He needs to concentrate."

William shrugged, then we popped off our bottle caps using a squared-off corner of railing. William tossed his cap over the side. It tumbled through the air, clinked against a support beam several flights below, and disappeared out of sight.

I turned mine in my fingers. It was jagged, toothy around the edges, and bent in the middle where I'd pried it from the lip of the bottle. I stuck it in my pocket and took a drink that was fresh-out-of-the-icebox cold and deliciously sweet with a carbonated, sparkly after-bite.

"*MMMMM*. Thanks," I said.

He clicked the necks of our bottles together. "Dawn bought 'em. She must have ten dollars in change in her backpack."

Returning our attention to Captain Kid, we watched him walk little circles, the spyglass pressed to his eye and his tongue peeking out between his lips. The search took a long time. Occasionally, he'd lower the telescope, roll his neck, wipe his forehead, then go back to scanning.

Then his circular pacing stopped.

He lifted a finger into the air and said the word we were waiting to hear: "There."

"You found it?" William asked.

Captain Kid offered him the telescope. William set his Coke on the deck and traded the third unopened bottle for the spyglass.

The captain took the soda, smirked, and popped the top with the backside of the blade on his bone-handled knife.

A few moments later, with a small amount of direction from our leader, William spotted the door. "Whoa," he breathed.

"What's it look like?" I asked.

William handed me the scope, an amused look on his face.

I lifted the narrow barrel to my eye. The view was not at all clear. Beyond a thin, horizontal line of hash marks on the lens—those were for taking measurements—all I saw were clouds and blue-sky dancing around with the slightest input from my fingers. I braced my elbows against my chest and leaned back, trying to hold steady. Captain Kid stood beside me. He adjusted my shoulders and guided my aim. Then, flying across the narrow focus of the telescope, sped a dark blur.

"Breathe," the captain said.

I let out my breath, filled my lungs with new air, and let it out again, slowly. I tried to relax, but the fact that William hadn't needed such counseling was not helping me concentrate on the problem. As air passed in and out of my lungs, I tried to clear my head. At last, the elusive door came into the viewfinder, but my eyes refused to focus. Even twisting the eyepiece didn't help. I gave up and handed the scope back.

"Did you see it?" the captain asked.

"I couldn't get it to focus." The admission stung. I wanted to see it but wanting wasn't enough.

William drew meaningless circles with his hands. "Looks like a cross between a blimp and a space station. A blimp-station." He grinned and sucked down the last of his cola.

"Huh," I muttered, looking up, but if I couldn't see the flying doorway with a telescope, certainly, I wouldn't spot it with my naked eyes. I saw nothing, just fluffy clouds on their long journeys.

With the door located and armed with his measurements, the captain was ready to begin calculations. We followed him back down the ladder and over the catwalk into the ship. The boarding went somewhat better than before, but still, the topsy-turvy sway of the shuttle unnerved me. In fact, my nerves were shot. Even though it was only three o'clock in the afternoon, I was exhausted. The stress of the day, along with the march into the forest, the heat, and now all this climbing—after that, all I wanted to do was fall onto a couch and watch television.

When we boarded the Nautilus, Captain Kid got right to work, pouring over volumes of ship manuals—all handwritten—and charts of mathematical tables and formulas. I, however, reclined in one of the five upward-facing cockpit seats.

Resting there, I hardly thought of anything. Even when William, Dawn, and Ozzie climbed up beside me, their commotion scarcely registered in my thoughts. When my mind settled on any subject, it was a faint curiosity about the incomprehensible control panels in front of me or my family beyond the wild woods.

What would they think in another few hours when I still wasn't home? And what terrible thoughts would haunt them when evening set? And what after that?

There I was, my parents' oldest son, my little brother's *Big Bro*, sitting in a spaceship, getting ready to blast off to destinations unknown…and I hadn't even left a note. None of us had. Our actions were as mysterious and foreign as the shuttle's controls. And then another thought: the night before in my bed, I had prayed for this to happen. I wanted to help Captain Kid find his missing Patch Fairy. But why? Now it was coming true, and I wanted to take it all back.

Overhead, on an illuminated gauge the size of a classroom wall clock, a needle started to move. That was the first sign of life I'd seen from the abandoned, sunken ship since the lights first came on. I leaned over in my chair and peeked below to check the captain's progress. He was sitting cross-legged on the bulkhead, books open all around him. He bent over, scribbled in a note pad, erased, and then scribbled again.

"How's it going?" I asked.

"This is harder than I remember, but I've almost got it." He stuck the pencil in his teeth and flipped through a manual.

I couldn't tell if he was leading us from experience or making it up as he went. This conflict in my impression of him was like my understanding of his age, how sometimes he seemed younger than me but, also, so much older.

He stood, gathering his books and papers, then handed them up to me. "Charles, put these in that cubby, then all of you get down here. You're all in the wrong seats."

I stowed the captain's library in the bin at my feet and followed my friends down the ladder to stand in the cramped space beneath.

Captain Kid straightened his hat and vest, then stood at attention, addressing us for the first time as our real captain. "Charles, you're the first mate. That means when I'm not around, you're in charge. Can you handle that?"

I had not anticipated having a title, which insinuated I would also have responsibilities and that the captain trusted me. "I can," I agreed.

He glanced around at my friends. "When you address Charles by rank, you can call him 'First Mate,' but 'Chief' is shorter and generally acceptable." His eyes settled on Dawn. "Miss McFarland, how are you with electricity?"

Her eyes widened. "I-uh. I know it hurts if it shocks you."

Captain Kid smiled. "All right then. You'll be our electro-technical officer. Congratulations." He regarded William next. "Who's stronger, you or Ozzie?"

"I AM!" they both shouted.

The captain looked to me. "Chief, you know them better than me. Which one's strongest?"

A test, I was sure, not of them but of me. I considered my friends. William was my best friend. He was athletic, and he was bigger than Ozzie. But, if I were honest, I would have to say Ozzie was a bit tougher, if only because he was crazier.

I made my decision. "Ozzie, sir."

Ozzie beamed. "Chief Charles, my man!"

William wasn't happy.

"Very well," Captain Kid said. "Ozzie Ernesto, you will be our first assistant engineer. William, because I reckon you're smarter than Ozzie, I'm making you chief engineer."

William roared laughter, shoving Ozzie so hard they both fell over.

"Enough roughhousing." Captain Kid pointed above us to the seat farthest to the left. All along that side of the wall, heavy levers, cranks, and valves bombarded the chair. "Ozzie, up there." His finger drifted right. "William, you're next to him." William's chair sat slightly forward, presenting its occupant with countless gauge clusters.

Captain Kid placed a reassuring hand on Dawn's shoulder. "You're next to the wall on the right." Gauges surrounded her seat, but instead of round-faced instruments, hers were square and beset with antique lightbulbs and little dials. He looked at me and nodded skyward. "Take your position next to our electro-technical officer."

"Aye, aye." I climbed the ladder, noticing again our smallest crew member, Joseph in his travel-sized container secured in its wall bracket. The little red crab was digging through pebbles with strong pointed legs.

I pulled myself up into my chair. This was really happening, the lift-off. We were about to take flight in a dynamite-powered rocket. As I settled into my seat, Dawn smiled, anxiously. I returned the smile, mine no more confident than hers.

"Don't forget your seatbelt," she whispered.

"Oh yeah." I checked the side of my chair, found the belt, and clasped it at my waist.

Captain Kid came up last, pulling himself into the middle seat. After fastening his seatbelt, he handed each of us instruction manuals for our areas of responsibility. My book was red, leather-bound, and titled in bold text, *The Nautilus First Mate: A Working Knowledge of Duties and Operations*. On the third page, I found a brief description of what a first mate—A.K.A. the *chief officer*—did. I was to give training to my shipmates, a laughable thought considering my complete ignorance of the vessel. Also, I was to direct day-to-day assignments aboard the ship, ensure the ship's maintenance, safety, and the welfare of my friends, the crew.

The captain said, "Chief, what's the temperature readings in the rocket boosters?"

I blustered, "Let me see." I scanned the multitude of gauges. Their labels were all in thinnest, swirling, cursive. The writing was elegant, but to the untrained eye, it was very difficult to read. I found my answer encased in a miniature window presenting six mercury thermometers. "Rocket A is showing ninety-five degrees in Zone One, a hundred and four in Zone Two, and a hundred and eighteen in Zone Three. Rocket B temps are similar."

"What system of measurement are those temperatures?" The captain waited.

I leaned forward to study the instruments, difficult to do lying on my back. "Fahrenheit, sir."

"Are those temps within norms?"

"I have no idea. Zone three is in the red, but I don't know if that's good or bad."

Captain Kid leaned toward me but couldn't see the gauge from his position. "Is there a color beyond red?"

"Yes, sir," I said. "White."

"All right then. Tell me if it gets into the white." He drew in a long breath. His hand was resting on a T-shaped handle protruding from the right side of his control module. "In just a moment, I'll twist this handle for all it's worth." His cheeks reddened merrily. "The dynamo inside this unit will generate an electric jolt." He glanced past me to Dawn. Electricity was her area. "That will start a chain reaction explosion in rockets A and B."

"The Dynamite," Ozzie said in awe.

"That's right," the captain agreed. "Remember when I said the rockets are like tuna cans filled with dynamite? The explosion starts at the bottom and works its way up. When a can's finished, it falls away, so the ship has less mass the higher we go. That's why the calculations are so hard."

William twisted in his seat. "When will the center rocket go, the big orange one?"

The captain shook his head. "That's not a rocket. And it's not a fuel cell, like on NASA shuttles. It's a balloon. In case of emergency."

Dawn sat forward suddenly. "If the shuttle can float, we don't even need rockets."

"But we do." Captain Kid tested his grip on the T-handle. "The balloon can't lift the shuttle, not by a longshot. But it can carry the five of us if we lose control and have to abandon ship. That's not going to happen."

He referred to a scrap of notepaper in his pocket, then twisted a pair of tiny cranks on the side of his control module. The cranking action spun numbers on analog odometers. He stopped when the numbers matched the figure on his note.

"What's that for?" I asked.

He stuck the paper back in his pocket. "That, my good sir, tells us how much explosives we're using, 15,780 pounds, to be exact." He winked at me. "How are those temperature readings?"

They were still in the red but climbing.

# CHAPTER 12

# GOING UP

I watched the temperature rise, half-convinced that if the mercury climbed into the white, the rockets would detonate on the platform, as rockets are prone to do. But Captain Kid didn't appear worried.

"Zone Three on Rocket B has reached peak temperature," I reported.

"Good." The captain looked to his left. "Mr. Gazack, open the circulatory valves. Let's see if we can get those temps to even out."

William looked surprised to hear himself referred to as "Mister," but then found a series of gauges corresponding to rocket temperatures. He had a gauge for each layer within the rockets, not just the three major temperature zones. And yet, at his panel, he found no way to affect them.

He leaned to his left, studying Ozzie's instruments. "Looks like you've gotta open those valves." He pointed. "I think they correspond to my readouts."

Ozzie twisted open a stacked series of notched handles similar to outdoor water spigots.

The captain said, "When a section of rocket burns through its dynamite, close the valve and pull the lever next to it. That will jettison the can."

"How'll I know when it's spent?" Ozzie asked.

*Good question.*

"William will see a warning light below his gauge." Captain Kid turned to Dawn. "Monitor those voltage meters. If there's no power, the fuse burned out. Replace it immediately."

She looked around her seat.

The captain pointed. "The spares are in the box under your chair."

She reached between her feet and brought out a shoebox with a Nike swoosh printed on the side. The box was definitely not from the nineteen-thirties. "Men's, size ten and a half," she read. She opened the lid to find a pair of pliers and fuses the size of poker decks.

"What do I do?" I asked.

Captain Kid eyed me sidelong. "You're in charge of docking. When I tell you, pull that lever and pedal as fast as you can to extend the boom. You'll use that joystick to aim."

My control module stood on a squared-off pedestal. On each side of the pedestal were bicycle pedals. I hadn't noticed those before. If I scooted my chair all the way up, I could reach them. The joystick was within reach of my right hand. "What's the trigger for?" I imagined machine guns popping out from hidden hatches on the nose.

The captain looked at me seriously. "It operates the clamp. One shot only. Use it on my mark, or we'll have a major problem." He faced forward again. If he had any concern at all that I—or any of us, for that matter—would clam up under pressure, he showed not a hint of it. His face was serene, his posture relaxed, and if anything, he was ready to be off. His hands went to the T-bar handle, his clean, youthful fingers adjusting their grip. "Chief, if the crew is ready, begin the countdown."

I looked to my friends. Dawn took a breath, squeezed the shoebox of fuses against her body, and nodded. I leaned back in my chair, looking past the captain to William.

William shrugged.

I waited, then he nodded in the affirmative.

When I looked to Ozzie, he waved a quick salute. "Let's light this candle. We've got a fairy-thief to catch."

"Yeah," William agreed. "Like the marshal would say, we're burnin' daylight."

I grinned. They were right. My parents wouldn't understand— even I didn't—but what we were doing was important. And there was no going back now. I looked to Captain Kid. "We're ready, sir. How long should I set the timer?"

"Eleven seconds but adjust your seat now if you need to. Won't be able with the thrusters on boost."

He was right. Working against gravity, I could hardly pull the seat forward even now. But after my feet rested on the foot pedals, I thumbed the up-arrow on the dash-mounted stopwatch. "Eleven seconds," I said. "On your mark." I could feel my voice hiccup, but the others were probably too anxious to hear it.

The captain's hands tightened on the T-handle. "Begin and count us down." Even in his voice, I could hear energy bubbling over.

I pressed the start button. "Eleven. Ten. Nine." My voice grew louder with every second lost from the clock. "Eight. Seven. Six." My heart was pounding out of my chest. "Five. Four. Three." Strange tingles danced over my skin. "Two. One. LIFTOFF!"

The captain cranked the T-bar with all his might. The machinery *zinged*, and he threw himself back against the seat, his hands moving for the armrests. "Brace yourselves!"

As the words left his mouth, I heard a rumble from the base of the launch pad and felt a tremble throughout the entire ship. The rumble grew into a deafening roar. The Nautilus was vibrating like a paint shaker, us the paint. With the titanic shout of dynamite exploding in the steel confines of the rocket tubes, I felt the shove—the thrust from the explosions—pushing my seat against my back.

"We're moving!" Ozzie cried.

Glancing his direction, I saw the highest point of the launch tower—the white post—disappear out of view. Beyond that, the concrete walls of the canyon were a gray blur and then gone. We were up past ground level, past the treetops, and into the air.

Captain Kid called out, "Engineer, what's the status of those rocket temps?" A good thing, too, because William was staring out the window. Below the first two temperature gauges, warning lights glowed an angry orange.

William turned to Ozzie. "Jettison the first rocket sections."

Ozzie, already turning, spun the valves closed and yanked the release levers. I could feel the weight fall away. The next lights in the series blinked on, and Ozzie released those, too.

To my right, Dawn threw the lid off her shoebox, ripped free a burnt fuse from the breaker, and shoved a new one into place.

The arm rests on Captain Kid's seat had unfolded to reveal two joysticks similar to mine but without the triggers. He was using the sticks to control the flight—*I assumed*—but our mad explosion into the air felt totally out of control. "How are those temperatures, Mr. Gazack?"

"Holding steady," William said. "A hundred and twenty degrees except for the burning cans. They're off the scales." Between the flash of warning lights and the ejection of rocket canisters, William and Ozzie worked in tandem. William called out section numbers and temperatures as Ozzie opened and closed coolant valves to avoid a meltdown.

In front of the captain, a glass dial—like a free-floating billiard ball—spun in its housing. "I'm having trouble holding it steady," he said. "Charles, how much dynamite's left?"

The little odometers he'd cranked to over fifteen thousand pounds were turning with rapidity on their descent back down to zero. "Just dropped past twelve hundred. Maybe another twenty seconds."

To the sides of the ship, spent rocket sections—indeed, looking very much like gigantic tuna cans with the lids cut off—fell away, their rims flaming. This time, I not only felt the added lift, but the roar of the rockets was growing louder, the vibrations threatening to tear the ship apart. My teeth chattered so hard I thought they'd crack. Another set of rocket sections broke free. I could smell explosive vapor seeping into the cockpit, like gunpowder smoke soured by the fragrance of an industrial chemical factory.

Dawn reset the fried circuits, the oily pliers in one hand, a handful of fresh fuses shiny and new in the other.

The rockets were almost done, and still, I hadn't seen the space station. Were we off course? Had we passed it? No way to know.

The rocket-fuel odometers tracked the last few hundred pounds of explosives.

"Chief," the captain's hands gripped the control sticks, "when it zeros out, hit the master release switch."

I found the switch beneath the odometers, an intimidating lever as broad as my hand surrounded by yellow and black checkered warning paint. I seized it, paused for the last second of thrust, and pulled. A crack sounded along the length of the floor and the remaining rocket sections fell away, including the tall, white nose cones.

Where they might land—on someone's house for all I knew—was a concern for another day.

With the rockets freed, the ship fell into relative silence. Now it was only the *SHHHH* of rushing wind. However, I still couldn't see the docking station.

The captain spoke through clenched teeth. "Start peddling, Charles. Be quick about it."

No need to tell me twice. I rowed the pedals as if my life depended on it, and perhaps it did. Strange, jarring resistance communicated through the pedals into the soles of my shoes. I ignored it, cranking at the gears with all the strength in my legs. Mechanisms were moving in the floor; I felt them.

A moment later, through the curved bank of windows, I saw a peculiar, open, two-fingered claw extend past the nose of the ship. The thing's talons were shiny and thin like on the arcade-game claws that drop down to paw at stuffed animals, only this one was big enough to grab a station wagon. As my feet worked the pedals, the reach of the claw lengthened on an extendable arm. Then, past the gleaming curves of the docking claw, I saw, at last, the target of our trajectory.

# CHAPTER 13

# THE CROSSING

At first, the Upwards Facing Door was but a speck. As our momentum carried us higher into the sky, the doorway, which William had described as a cross between a space station and a blimp, grew in size and detail.

The thing was not actually a space station—not even in space—but was a turning ring of zeppelins that floated in the upper atmosphere. Tethered nose to tail, the zeppelins made a circular chain like ponies in a carrousel, and spokes connected each blimp to a central hub. In the center of the hub was the door itself, looking like the front door of a house, blue and cheerful with a little diamond-shaped window. It wasn't like an outer space airlock at all.

Captain Kid angled a control stick to the right, and our upwards trajectory spiraled.

My head pressed to the side, and I felt my guts mashing into my ribcage. "Wwwwwhat are you d-d-doing?" I slurred through numb lips.

The captain's eyes narrowed, his voice tight but under control. "Matching the spin. Get ready with that trigger."

My index finger prepared to squeeze. *One shot only.* The docking claw was fully extended, its silver arcs reflecting sunlight as the sky whirled around us. "W-w-w-what am I-I-I aiming for?" I saw nothing made for grabbing, no designated anchor point, just a mess of cables and the door itself.

"At the base of the door, there's an opening." The captain made tiny adjustments with his hands. "Chief, on my mark."

My vibrating eyes strained to focus. Below the door's threshold, I could faintly make out a wide dark line. A shadow.

"Chief," Captain Kid said, his voice calm beyond reason.

We were like a pop-fly baseball at the crest of its flight. I watched the gleaming fingers of the claw approach the station. I pulled up on the joystick, then to the right, then down. Just below the Upwards Facing Door, the open mouth of the docking claw disappeared into the shadowy slot—

"NOW!" the captain yelled.

My trigger finger squeezed. I felt contact, metal-on-metal. Our ascent reached its climax. For the briefest moment, my guts felt weightless, and if the claw grabbed anything at all, I couldn't tell. The shuttle dipped, paused, then swayed, the docking arm scraping the housing below the door. The sound was terrible, a slow, shrill scrape. I thought for sure the claw would let go—the claw games at arcades always slipped off their prizes—but it didn't. It held.

The Nautilus settled, moaning. I heard a sharp pop. Then realizing my eyes were pinched shut, I reopened them to find two of the windshield sections cracked. Beyond the broken glass, waiting for us like a blue invitation, was the Upwards Facing Door in its hub surrounded by a web of steel cables. At the outer ends of the cables, encircling us, were the bright, floating blimp-shapes.

All around me, my friends let out the most wonderful sighs of relief. Ozzie started laughing. Then William. Then we all cheered.

Unbuckling his seatbelt, the captain swung himself upright to sit on the back of his chair. "Splendid flying." He opened and closed his fists. "My hands got a workout. Ozzie, so did yours, by the look of you."

Ozzie lay back in his seat, his arms dangling at his sides, his hair and clothes wet with sweat. Captain Kid dropped onto the floor below. The rest of us followed, and a moment later, we gathered with our things, including Joseph the crab, at the open cockpit door.

Amazing to think how brazen we were to take to the sky in that antique deathtrap. And more amazing still, using nothing but a grappling hook retrieved from the captain's pack, we climbed up to the nose—*on the outside!* Wind whirled around us, the whole thing bobbed and swayed, and the steel cables linking the hub to the circle of blimps made metallic *twang* sounds. If we fell, there was no one to catch us. No safety net. Yet, we didn't fall, and we pressed on even though we were terrified. Even Ozzie was scared. I could tell by the shrillness of his cackles.

With only enough room for us to crouch between the nose of the Nautilus and the strange blue door, my friends and I clung together in desperate triumph. All around us, sights indescribably wondrous. We were so high above the face of the earth I could see its curvature, all of Florida, Georgia, and Alabama laid out before me. As the dock rotated, I gazed out across the Atlantic Ocean. It turned more, and I was looking down on the Gulf of Mexico.

William gripped my shoulder. "See. What did I tell you, a blimp-station."

The chain of silver-skinned blimps encircled our incredible position in the sky. Then he looked up, reminding me of the purpose of this flight. Above us, the blue door with its little window seemed to watch us like a cyclops with a diamond-shaped eye. It felt alive, and its orientation, horizontal rather than vertical, was all wrong. And yet, huddled with my friends and the young captain on the black nose of a make-believe space shuttle, I witnessed an even stranger sight. Captain Kid grasped the handle of the Upward Facing Door, turned it, and when he tossed it open, we were looking in on another world.

The sky through the door was brightest blue, cloudless, dry, and oh-so-hot. Even from the windswept nose of the Nautilus, I could feel desert heat. Shifting sand poured out of the opening, carried away by wind to dust our awestruck faces. Then a lizard darted into view, standing on the doorframe to peer down at us. The reptile had a scaly, angular face and it held its black-and-white banded tail in an arc above its body, perhaps to save it from the heat of the sand. The strange lizard opened its mouth as if to say something—at that moment, I was ready to believe anything—but then scampered off without a word.

William was the first to stand. I watched as the desert sunlight hit his face. Then I stood beside him.

*Another world, oh yes.*

I looked out at a barren land, so starkly contrasted to the green and blue world below. Sand and tiny rocks of every sun-bleached hue covered the ground. Standing in the distance, I saw the strange poses of huge cacti, their arms held up in surrender. Beyond, in every direction, the horizon was cut by the hard teeth of lifeless mountain tops.

William pulled himself up into the sandy gravel. "People live here," he said.

I climbed up to see what he had found: two worn boards nailed to a post. The boards were cut into points, serving as arrows. One was illegible, too long out in the sun, but the other had some paint left. It read, *Salvation Mountain, 3.5 miles.*

*Thataway*, I mused.

I turned to see the captain, Oz, and Dawn climbing out of the rectangular hole in the ground like vampires emerging from a grave.

When the captain was on his feet, I asked, "You know that place, Salvation Mountain?"

"I think I must," he said, but he'd used that line before. He offered his hand to Dawn and helped her onto the surface of the desolate world.

Then I watched with sudden, cold terror as Ozzie, without a thought as to the consequence, lifted the old blue door with his foot. I tried to stop him. My hand reached out, my mouth opened, but I was too late. The door fell shut. When I picked it up again, there was nothing beneath but sand, and the door in my hand was nothing but a piece of discarded trash.

I kicked the dirt.

William slid down beside me on his knees. His hands shoveled at the ground. "There's no way back, is there?"

The captain gazed off toward the hills. "There is, but not by digging."

Dawn dropped her book bag. "Then how do we get home?"

The captain took off his white cap. "There are rules. In the Blue Deck, to move down a card you use a special elevator, or a stairway—sometimes a tomb—something unnatural that goes down."

William got to his feet, his hands balled into sandy fists. "Then why can't I dig to it, that's unnatural?"

"You just can't." Captain Kid rolled his lips. "Maybe you could if you were a wizard…" He took out his compass. "Remember the needle? It points to the doors." He popped the lid, studied it, and looked in the direction of Salvation Mountain. "The closest door is that way—probably. But may I remind you, we're not looking for a way home. We're looking for Castatine and the Patch Fairy."

William walked past the captain, turning circles. "Where are they, then? I don't see anybody. This place is a wasteland. We'll get lost and die out here."

"You're being rash." Captain Kid unslung his rifle and took off his pack. "But now that we're here—and as you so keenly pointed out, *here* is an inhospitable wasteland—we should inventory our supplies." He looked to Dawn. "You got any more Skittles?"

William turned hard in his tracks, his face red with fury. I grabbed him by the shoulders. "Captain," I said.

The captain went on digging through his backpack.

"*Captain!*" I repeated, this time with force.

He looked up to see me restraining my friend.

I leveled my tone the best I could, but on the inside, I felt much the same as William. "We need to know that when the time comes, you won't leave us here. You'll get us home to our families."

Captain Kid brought out his pet crab, holding the miniature aquarium in gentle fingers. "Chief, report to the crew that their captain is not in the habit of forsaking those who risk their lives to help him."

I wanted to believe him. Really, I did. "I don't know that, *sir*. We just met you." It hurt to say, but it was true.

The captain met my eyes, and now his look was cold. "Then you're relieved of duty." He eyed Dawn. "You're the new chief. Charles can be the electro-technical officer." He stuck the crab back into his bag. "Chief, have the men give you an inventory of their supplies. I'll be back in a few hours." Then shouldering his rifle, he walked out into the desert.

Dawn called after him, "Shouldn't we stick together?"

"Just work on those inventories." He kept marching.

She threw up her arms in frustration. "But where are you going?"

"To make sure we're not being watched." Then he disappeared into the desert willow scrubs, and we were alone in the wilderness to think about the trouble we were in. And, *oh yes*, to work on those inventories. Chief Dawn would see to that.

# CHAPTER 14

# THE DESERT ROAD

I was lying on the ground, my extra pair of pants rolled up beneath my head for a pillow. Above me, the night twinkled with a universe of stars and the silver-white glow of a moon that was nearly full. A little earlier, when the captain returned from his walkabout, he wanted to press on, to spend the night at the mountain, but I suppose he could see in our faces we were not in the mood for more travel. The day had been a long one, tiring both physically and mentally. All we wanted to do was lie down and absorb the meaning of the day.

As I lay there, my mind returned to the way the captain so unceremoniously demoted me. Before that, I thought I was special, that I was chosen for this mission for a reason. But lying in the sand with my head on a pair of rolled-up jeans, I had my doubts.

William had not spoken in hours. He sat on the ground near me, tracing lines in the sand with a stick. What thoughts were running through his mind? I couldn't imagine.

Ozzie had taken up the old blue door and was attempting to fashion a shelter with it. I watched him prop up the long edge with a pair of crooked sticks. Bent over, he studied the sheltered ground then went around smoothing the sand with his hands. Personally, I didn't like sleeping on the ground. What strange creatures might creep around at night in a place like this? Although, the captain seemed content to roll out his bed mat on the floor of the desert, so it was probably safe enough.

Ozzie positioned his baseball bat beside his lean-to and scooted beneath, lying on his side. He looked to me.

I owed him an apology. I'd turned a cold shoulder on him since the door fell shut on our home. He only did what was natural. It wasn't his fault.

Also, replaying the scene in my mind, I wasn't even sure the portal allowed for two-way travel. When I first looked back at the captain climbing up from the hole, I'd thought how much the rectangular pit looked like an open grave. Shouldn't I have seen the turning world below, or at least the huge, orange fuel tank of the Nautilus—which wasn't a fuel tank, but a big balloon? Wouldn't I have seen that through the open door? The problem was, I didn't know how any of this worked, and the good captain was short on answers. He expected us to take it all on faith and punished me when I didn't trust him. That wasn't fair, and another dark idea was only beginning to form.

When I first asked Captain Kid to tell us more about the girl who kidnapped the fairy, he said her name was hard to remember, and we should keep moving while he thought about it. At the time, I accepted his answer, but Marshal Rayban was with us, and surely, he knew Castatine's name. When the marshal investigated the fairy's abandoned cart, he would've asked the neighbors to tell him everything about the girl. "What's her name?" would've been his first question. After that, he'd want a description, how long she'd lived there, those types of things. The neighbors would know all of that. So, if that was true, why did the marshal keep his mouth shut when Captain Kid couldn't answer my question?

Furthermore, why didn't I, or any of my friends, think of these things? The answer that came to me was, *Because I was under the captain's spell.* We all were, maybe even the marshal, as crazy as that sounded.

Or, there could be another possibility, something I'd not yet thought of.

I felt a sharp lump in my pants pocket. Then digging with my finger, I brought out the bent cap from the Coke bottle. Such a strange little piece of home—trash, really—but it felt oddly special, almost like a memory in physical form. The cap was red and its thin metal edges crimped into sharp little teeth, like gears.

I felt the bent top with my thumb then turned onto my side.

Dawn was going through the pockets of my backpack. She unzipped a small, side pouch and took out my little Yoda action figure. She smiled and noted its presence on the inventory she was listing in her notebook. I imagined her inscription, *One toy Yoda, complete with robe and orange plastic snake*. But to me, Yoda wasn't a toy, he was my good luck charm. She stuck him back in the pouch.

It seemed there should've been a campfire to paint her face with a warm glow, but we had no fire that evening. Too hot. In that place, even in the coolest hour, I doubted it dipped much below a hundred. Instead, she made her list by the light of the moon, which was marvelously white. I considered showing her my secret relic from the world below—*One Coca-Cola bottle cap, red, complete with dent*—but that was stupid. The captain wouldn't care about bent bottle caps, so I returned it to my pocket.

Then a new thought, optimistically bright—

"An alias," I said to myself, but Dawn looked at me.

"What's up?" she asked.

"I was just thinking, maybe Marshal Rayban didn't know Castatine's name because she was using an alias at the rented house."

Dawn had no idea what I was talking about, but it didn't matter. All I wanted was a way to believe the captain wasn't lying to us. He probably wasn't because, in the control room, he told us all about her, about the garden, the well, everything.

"Are you okay?" Dawn asked.

"I guess so."

She handed me my book bag. "I like your Yoda."

"Thanks. I'm sure it'll be super useful."

"I didn't know you brought it. It's cute."

I laid back in the sand. "It's supposed to bring me luck."

"Maybe it will," she said.

Maybe, but right about then, good luck would have come as an incredible surprise.

After a night of fitful sleep, our journey continued toward Salvation Mountain. As we set off, I felt more exhausted than I had the night before. I had a headache, my lips were dry, and my body craved water like it never had in Florida. Captain Kid passed around his canteen with a warning to drink sparingly. The water was hot and tasted of plastic, but we drank anyway.

Captain Kid led us along a trail rutted by off-road vehicles long since gone. As we marched, I saw more of the scampering black and white reptiles that Ozzie identified as zebra tail lizards, and off in the dead weeds we came upon the remains of cows. They were little more than bones.

Upon finding the second carcass, the captain turned over its hornless skull with the toe of his loafer and said, "She wandered out into the desert and lost her way," which I associated directly to our present course of action. We were not lost, however, at least not in the eyes of our leader. According to him, we were right on course. I supposed we must've been because there was only one road, and it hadn't branched a single time.

A little while later, William spoke. It was a complaint about the heat, but at least that meant he was talking again.

Captain Kid directed us to cover our exposed skin with the lightest clothes in our backpacks. Dawn had a white bedsheet perfect for the task, though, I couldn't fathom what impulse drove her to pack it in the first place. The captain had something similar but made for the purpose. When he wrapped himself, he looked to me like an Arabian dune-dweller. William, Oz, and I made do with T-shirts. We pulled the neckbands down around our foreheads then cast the shirts backward, wearing them like flappy turbans with dangling short sleeves.

What an odd lot we were, even stranger looking now than when we walked along the lake with the old cowboy: Captain Kid and Dawn in their desert robes, and the rest of us looking like a group of kids playing Egyptian pharaohs in a backyard sandlot. Only, we were miles and miles from anybody's yard, much less a house.

Ozzie used his baseball bat like a walking stick, leaving egg-shaped divots in the sand beside his footprints. William had thought to bring sunglasses. I was jealous of those even more than Dawn's bedsheet. My biggest regret, however, came from my tennis shoes. They were black, fake leather. My feet got so hot I feared I might literally cook them.

Even so, the walk beneath the rising sun and the bread I snacked on for breakfast did me good. My blood was pumping again. Also, I was curious to know what manner of salvation the mountain offered, perhaps some cooler weather, or water, or maybe even a town with friendly people.

We saw the mountain at first from a distance, however, when I saw it, I doubted it was a mountain at all.

"Is that it?" Dawn asked.

"It is," the captain said.

William and I exchanged looks. *Not much of a mountain*, more like a hill set away by itself on the flat desert plain, far from the jagged peaks along the horizon. As we got closer, through the shimmering air baking up off the sand, I could make out strange colors splashed upon the hillside. *Maybe a mirage*, I guessed, but the closer we got to the place, the more real the colors looked.

The rutted trail brought us to a pair of splintered gate posts, sans the gate. Beside the left post, an antique truck with curved fenders sat sunken to its axels in the hardpan. The entire vehicle was painted, as if with a brush—not painted like a car at all—and not one solid color, either. It looked like a kid's Sunday school art project. Across the front bumper was written in bold white letters, *JOHN 3:16 GOD IS LOVE.*

On the dented hood of the truck, other such religious sayings were scrawled amidst a handful of crosses and loads of colorful adobe flowers. On the flatbed, someone had constructed a shed. That was also painted with colorful suggestions to repent of sins and turn to Jesus.

Where had the shed come from? Who put it there? Too many questions ran through my head at once. The greatest of which was not about the shed, or even the truck, but the mount itself. Leading from the gate into the strange landscape was a road of yellow paint—*Paint*—applied directly to the ground. On each side of the yellow road, more paint stretched out in a kaleidoscope of colors: reds, blues, greens, pinks, every color of the rainbow.

Between the gate posts and the base of the mountain, strange walls of stone, bricks, empty paint cans, and dismembered car doors divided the yard. The walls were only a few feet high, and like everything else, they were covered with layer upon layer of paint.

As I walked into the yard, I inspected a wall. This portion looked constructed of large, plastered bricks, but where a corner broke open, I saw hay poking out. Who would build such a wall, and why? But then I looked again to the mountain. Considering that, all the rest was perfectly reasonable.

# CHAPTER 15

# SALVATION MOUNTAIN

Salvation Mountain was no natural land formation, it was a construction of clay, paint, straw, dead trees, and every other thing found in the desert. It stood the height of a three-story apartment building—maybe a little higher—and from its peak rose a tall, skinny cross. Judging size was difficult at a distance, but I thought the cross was as tall as a telephone pole. Or, maybe it *was* a telephone pole.

Beside me, I heard Dawn's feather-soft voice reading a message painted on the mountainside. "Jesus, I'm a sinner. Please come upon my body and my heart." The message was formed in white letters, each as tall as a person and painted onto a huge, red, heart-shaped backdrop.

Confession was one of two major themes offered by the strange man-made hill. The other—the most prominent—stood out like a sculpture near the peak. It read, *GOD IS LOVE,* in bulging, red bubble letters.

Then I noticed the yellow road we were walking on continued its winding way up to the mountaintop.

At the base of the hill, Ozzie and William had ventured over to a little adobe hut. When I caught up to them, Ozzie was peering inside.

"This place is weird," he said.

William ducked his head through the doorway, and I walked over to see inside. The interior walls of the hovel were painted with messages of hope and love, also, of turning away from evil ways. There were small cubbies dug into the dome. Some held candles. One contained a journal filled with prayers. I saw in another a toy station wagon decorated in a style similar to the truck in the yard. I picked it up. The roof bore a raised heart, formed in painted clay. From the open window of the toy car sprouted a rolled-up piece of paper. I slid it out, careful not to chip the brittle paint.

"What's it say?" William asked.

I opened it and read, "Come unto me, all ye that labor and are heavy laden, and I will give you rest." I was feeling the weight of my burdens plenty at the moment, but I supposed the same could be said of everyone who found themselves in this strange place. Rotating the little station wagon in my fingers, a part of me wanted to keep the car, to make it my souvenir. That felt like stealing, so I rolled the message and stuck it back in the window for the next curious passerby. Then I returned the car to its hollowed-out garage in the wall. "Either of you guys ready to go back home?"

They looked to each other. William's eyebrows lifted, and he shrugged. He was getting close, but Ozzie grinned.

"I like it here," Ozzie said.

"Sure, but…" I didn't know how to finish.

William stepped back through the open door, into the daylight. "We're here now. We may as well see it through. It would be great to rescue the fairy, ya know."

When we got back outside, we found Captain Kid waiting for us by the yellow road. His desert robe billowed behind him in a light breeze. His chin was uplifted, his head cocked to one side like he was listening to something far away.

When I concentrated on the wind, I could hear the gentle whine of a distant engine. "What is it?" I asked.

The captain crinkled his nose. "Desert folk, I guess. People come out here sometimes." He turned to the hill, cupping a hand to his mouth. "HELLO, Man of the Mountain… Anybody home?"

After a moment, we heard a reply. "Ahoy. Up here."

I searched the hillside. Near the "V" in *GOD IS LOVE*, I spotted a thin-framed man. He had a white, short-cropped beard and wore a checkered shirt with the sleeves rolled up below his elbows. His skin was the color of a baseball glove. He waved to us with the paintbrush in his hand. "Have you come for a tour? I'm fixin' a crack. Be done in an hour or so. Else, you can show yourselves around. All who come are welcome."

Our leader lowered his hood and repositioned his white captain's cap back onto his head. "It is I, old-timer, Captain Kid. Do you have a moment to share with us knowledge of travelers going west to the Great City? We are on an important quest. Also, we'll take water if it's offered."

The man stood straighter. "It would be an honor to share a drink with one of the Seven…" He shaded his eyes. "…and your knights, if they come in peace." He stepped up between the giant letters "O" and "V" in *LOVE.*

"We mean you no harm," the captain said, "neither to you nor to your mountain." He looked to the horizon. "Although, someone else comes this way, by the sound of it."

The mountain man looked to the west. "That would be the moon folk. Kybees, I call 'em. They ride motorcycles and drive dune buggies. Come out here to go wild, they do. 'Tis all right, I'm expecting 'em."

Captain Kid squinted against the sun. His fingers were drumming at his thigh. He wore no pistols, but he was standing with the cool tension of a gunslinger in a western movie. To my right, Ozzie adjusted the grip on his baseball bat. Dawn took a step closer to William who was making fists again. And what was I doing? Nothing, just standing there.

The captain looked to the sky then relaxed, regarding Dawn. "It's okay. We're safe for now." Then to the rest of us, "Go explore. The chief and I will hold council with the Man of the Mountain. But stay within shouting distance. I don't wanna have to look for you when it's time to leave."

I walked with William and Ozzie along the trails around the mountain and into its caves and secret places. Then I followed my friends up the yellow street, past the giant, free-standing proclamation *GOD IS LOVE.* There, we found the mountain man's paint bucket and brush and the subject of his repair: a series of cracks in the plaster, some as long as our arms and wide enough to insert fingers down into the gaps. At one such fissure, the old man had stuffed the hole with a mashed-up blend of clay and straw. Other places, he was on the painting phase, his choice of color brightest yellow. Why yellow and not some other color? No reason that I could see.

Near the mountain peak, the scale of the art project amazed me, and even I was moved by the carefree playfulness of it. Yet, even looking through the hole in the giant red "O" in GOD, I felt the disappointing undercurrent of my demotion. Down in the yard, the captain and Dawn stood with the mountain painter on the shaded side of the sand-sunken flatbed truck. Dawn was taking notes in her notebook. They were deciding what course we'd take next. I should have been down there.

I meandered behind William and Ozzie, continuing up to the top of Salvation Mountain. As I stood at the base of the towering cross, wind carried the sounds of revving engines across the flatland. I looked in that direction—in the direction of another mysterious place the captain called *the Great City*. The city must've been on the other side of a mountain range because I saw no sign of it. However, in the far-off distance, I could make out a trailing dust cloud.

*The moon folk. The Kybees.*

I looked to my friends. Ozzie stared up at the white cross as reverently as possible for a kid with an orange T-shirt on his head. Next to the cross, his head covering reminded me of a nun's habit. *Ozzie the nun*: that was a funny thought. Instead of a nun, he'd have to be a priest, or maybe a monk, but, somehow, that was even more ridiculous.

I followed his gaze up to the telephone-pole cross. We had come through the desert and found in the wilderness a root that linked this world to my own, and it was an important root at that. If people here knew of religion, what else would they know of our world? Maybe someone could show us the way back?

That was one hope, a thin one. Below it ran another. The demotion had sunken me into a semi-serious depression, also, my body was exhausted, yet, despite those concerns, I still could not deny a sense of purpose to this journey. My trip into the Attic had begun with a prayer, and this flamboyant mountain was as bold of a confirmation as anyone could hope for. What purpose could such an odd construction serve, and for what audience was it made, if not for downtrodden travelers like myself?

In the clear desert sunlight, the whiteness of the cross was too bright to look at for long, so I shaded my eyes with my flapping T-shirt turban and looked away.

William crouched to peer into a hole in the mountain top. When I stood beside him, I could see the scrambled patchwork of painted tree branches and columns of plaster-coated tires supporting the inside of the monumental hill.

"You think that man built this place all by himself?" I asked.

William looked at me through his black sunglasses. The shirt on his head flapped white in the wind. "If he did, probably took twenty years. I wonder where he gets all the paint." He straightened, looking out at the yard.

Below us, the strange, old mountain-painter went up into his shed on the back of the truck. When he came out again, he was holding an armful of water bottles.

The captain whistled and waved to us. "C'mon, we're leaving."

At the gate posts, Dawn passed out the waters.

After gulping down half a bottle, I wiped my mouth and asked, "Where are we going now?" I pointed to the growing plume of kicked-up dust. "Those people are coming this way, coming fast."

The captain unscrewed a bottle cap and refilled his canteen. When the bottle was empty, he crushed it against his leg and shot a glance to the west. "We'll see them on the trail. Most likely they'll be friendly but be prepared to fight if they test us." He eyed Ozzie. "Keep that bat ready on your shoulder." Then he dropped the crushed bottle in a pile at his feet and took Dawn's notebook, flipping it open to her inventory. "Charles, says here you have an army knife." He looked at me with curious attention.

I dug in my pocket. "A *Swiss* Army knife. It isn't for battles. It's a survival tool—got a saw blade, and toothpick, and whatnot."

Uselessly, Ozzie asked, "How's a toothpick gonna help you survive?"

Captain Kid huffed, "Sounds like junk. Let me see it anyway." When I gave it over, he opened all the various tools. Before passing it back, he weighed the little red knife in his palm. "I stand corrected. It's a fine instrument, Charles Miller. You should be proud of it—"

I was.

"—but it's not made for fighting," he agreed. "The blade doesn't have a lock. In a skirmish, it could close on your fingers. Don't use it unless there's nothing else." His finger ran down the items listed in Dawn's neat cursive. Pausing, he looked up at William. "What's a...Rubik's Cube?"

William shrugged. "It's like a...square puzzle thingy. Wanna see it?"

With a straight face, Captain Kid asked, "Could you kill someone with it?"

Ozzie laughed openly, but William managed to restrain his reaction to a crooked-faced grin. "If I made 'em eat it."

That only made Ozzie laugh harder.

Stuffing my knife back in my pocket, I interrupted. "Captain, you're barking up the wrong tree. None of us brought weapons unless you count the baseball bat."

The captain offered the notebook back to Dawn. "What say you, Chief?"

—That was seriously starting to annoy me—

"Sorry," she said. "Charles is right. We weren't planning to fight anybody."

The Man of the Mountain thumbed toward his shed. "I got a pistol and a couple of sabers if you want 'em. I've no use for 'em out here."

"Then why do you have them?" Dawn asked.

The old man rubbed at his thin chest. "Took 'em in on trade. Figured I could trade 'em again if I had the need."

The captain shouldered his pack. "Thank you for the kindness, sir, but you may need your weapons if you stay here long enough. Perhaps we'll make a withdrawal from the king's armory if we go all the way to Atsuma. Besides, by the sound of those engines, I doubt we have to worry about the Kybees just yet."

The elderly man dipped his head. "You know best."

We left the tranquil grounds of the painted mountain and ventured back out into the desert sand. How far we were from the Great City, or this other place, Atsuma, I didn't know. If they were any sort of reasonable distance, I would've seen them from atop the hill. I looked to the west again. The only thing I saw above the scraggly brush was the trailing wafts of dust. *The Kybees, the moon folk,* and they were getting closer.

I felt the bulge in my pocket, the knife, a good tool, but not built for battles. Marshal Rayban should've come with us.

Captain Kid led the way, but I lingered by the gate. All the desert offered was bleak mystery and danger. The mountain, at least, spoke of Jesus and love, things I knew something about. Then I noticed by the gate a mailbox covered in the same painted adobe as the rest of Salvation Mountain. The flag was down. Maybe there were letters inside.

Dawn waited for me, her hand reaching for mine. "Come on, Charles." She was wrapped in her sheet like a desert princess.

"I guess I don't wanna go," I said.

"It wasn't your fault." She stepped closer. "Making me chief was a mistake."

"Maybe…" I looked to the others. They were giving us space. "You're a good chief," I said. "You took a better inventory than I would've."

She reached for my hand again. "We need to stay together, especially with you. You're our glue."

I puffed out a bitter laugh. "I'm trying to do the right thing, and I wanna be like a team player 'n all. But I said it before, and I'll say it again, we can't just follow this guy endlessly so far from home there's no hope of going back." I took her hand, desperately wanting someone on my side.

"What about the Patch Fairy?" she asked.

"Like Marshal Rayban said, she's outside our jurisdiction." When Dawn didn't immediately respond, I pressed the point. "You know I'm not wrong." Then, feeling so isolated I could die, I released her fingers.

She stared at me a long time, her face like an angel's enshrouded by the beaming, white sheet draped over her blonde hair. At last, she sighed then waved the group over to us.

When we were all standing in a circle, she addressed the gathering. "Charles makes a good point. Even if the Patch Fairy is kidnapped— and I'm sure she is, and that's *awful*—still, we have to have some idea of what we're committing to." She paused, standing stiffly, her lips working against her teeth. Then she looked to our leader. "How far are we going?"

The captain's voice was reserved, patient, even cautious with his answer. "That depends… It matters how far ahead of us she is and how long it takes to find her." His eyes took in our expressions, which were mixed, but everyone present was very interested to know how this exchange would turn out.

Dawn cleared her throat, glanced to me by her side, then looked to our leader. "We need something more solid than that, sir." Then she added in a low, regretful tone, "With all due respect."

The captain's right hand adjusted its grip on the shoulder strap of the rifle. As he moved it into a comfortable position, the barrel of the gun tilted in the air. "I reckon we'll aim for Doloptree. It's a tiny town, not much more than a bus stop, but they have a phone. We'll call ahead, let the king know what's going on and that Castatine's headed his way."

"Then we can go home?" I asked.

Captain Kid rolled his lips together. "We'll see, Charles. I hope so, for your sake."

"What about that other place," William said, "the one that starts with an *A*?"

The captain nodded. "Atsuma, that's where the king lives. If we're lucky, maybe we don't have to go that far, but I just don't know yet."

"And the Great City?" Ozzie asked.

Captain Kid regarded him. "Atsuma *is* the Great City." He turned to face the desert. "Chief, is the crew ready to go now?"

Dawn looked to Ozzie, and Ozzie gave a thumbs-up. When she met eyes with William, he nodded confirmation. Then to me, "What about you?" she asked.

"I'm with you guys," I said and made myself smile.

I was with them, for better or worse, so I would make the best of it. If Dawn would be the chief—and that wasn't likely to change any time soon—I supposed I should try to embrace my newfound title of electro-technical officer. At least, I should embrace it until we got to Doloptree. Wherever that might be. Only problem was, since crossing into the Attic of the World, I saw nothing with working electricity.

The captain started into the wilderness, and when he was a dozen paces ahead, he turned, beckoning us to follow. "C'mon if you're coming. We have a long way to go."

I put on a brave face and stepped lively. "Captain, I have one recommendation."

"Oh," he said, whimsically, "what's that?"

"If you think the Kybees mean to harm us, we should come at them with the sun to our backs. I saw that in a movie once."

Captain Kid looked to the sky. "In your world that wouldn't be possible this late in the day—not with us walking west. Here, the situation's reversed." He looked to the others in our party. Their faces all tilted upward, studying the sunshine.

The captain put his hands on William's shoulders and moved him sideways off the road. "When we meet the moon folk, step off the trail to the right. That should put the sun where we want it." Then to me, "Anything else?"

When I shook my head, he called out, "Then what are we waiting for." He turned on his heels. "The wilderness awaits, and beyond lies the bus stop in Doloptree. Between here and there—closer to here,

I imagine—we will find the Kybees and see what their mood is like."
Then he was walking.

Funny how the captain could so quickly lift my spirits. I looked
back one last time at the red hearts and flowers, white crosses, and
the colorful messages of repentance and love. What a sight, so full of
hope, like a beacon of life in a land of dry bones. Then, with one
hand taking Dawn's and the other on the knife in my pocket, I
stepped again into the unpainted sand toward whatever new mysteries lay ahead.

# CHAPTER 16

# WEST ALONG THE DESERT ROAD

The captain halted our progress at the crest of a low hill. The Kybees were close now, the sounds of their revving engines growling and barking across the desert basin. Into the sky west of us, a drifting dust cloud marked their approach.

Captain Kid took off his backpack, unslung his rifle, and inspected his ragtag subordinates. Then walking over to Ozzie, who was practicing his swing with the baseball bat, our leader waved for him to stop. "You won't be hitting baseballs. Let's see you swing that thing like you're tryin' to crack a skull."

Ozzie considered the morbid critique then went about clubbing dry bushes like he was a caveman surrounded by saber-tooth cats.

*Will that be necessary?* I wondered.

My grip tightened on the Swiss Army knife. I imagined thrusting the small blade into someone's neck and blood spurting out like ketchup from a squeeze-bottle. I looked at the knife in my hand. The blade was folded closed, and I was glad. I was a kid from suburbia. Kids like me didn't fight with knives. Why would we? The thought of a turf war in my neighborhood was ridiculous. If any boy tried to start something like that where I lived, his father would be the one who finished it, likely with a belt across the trouble-maker's backside.

The captain examined Ozzie's violence with the concentration of a wildlife biologist trying to detect patterns in the random movements of a squirrel. "Much better," he said. He pulled his desert robe off over his head and stuffed it into his pack.

As he straightened his vest, I thought how his many patches were like a peacock's feathers. Or, perhaps, they were more akin to a WWII pilot marking his aircraft with the number of planes he'd shot out of the sky. And another possibility: the vest with all the patches, and the captain's crisp plaid shirt and khaki trousers—also his cap, can't forget that—were his uniform. He was about to engage in formal greetings with strange people; to be out of uniform would be unprofessional.

I pulled the T-shirt-turban off my head, rolled it up, and hung it from my back pocket. William and Ozzie followed my lead.

Captain Kid turned his bright, amber eyes on me. "You ready, Charles?"

"I am," I said, glad he hadn't called me by the clunky title *Electro-Technical Officer.*

Beyond the flat-bottomed basin—perhaps two football fields from our side to the raised lip on the other—I saw the first movements of the moon folk, *the Kybees* as the Man of the Mountain called them. There were two figures riding dirt bikes with motors that sounded like whining chainsaws. The riders stopped at the edge of the slope. From such a distance, their thin bodies and bulbous helmets made them look like giant insects.

William shifted his feet. "Should we move off the trail?"

The captain glanced behind him into the sky. "I suppose we better, but spread out, okay?"

As we got into position, one of the distant motorcycle riders looked back over his shoulder and waved for the rest of his party to advance. Then, with hands on the grips of his motorcycle, he revved his engine, leaned forward, and took the bike down the sloped trail into the sand below. The other rider followed, and then came the rest of the Kybees.

There were thirteen vehicles by my count: the two motorcycles and the rest a mix of dune buggies and modified cars. One vehicle looked like a fenderless VW Beetle on knobby balloon tires. All the machines were the color of dirt and rust, fading in and out of dust plumes. Some of the buggies flew triangular flags on tall, thin poles that waved back and forth in the air.

My stomach turned. I had to be ready to fight. But who were these people, and why would they want to hurt us? Were they pirates?

Outlaws? Desert drifters who roamed in violent packs like wolves, searching for water, or oil, or fresh meat?

Captain Kid stepped forward, his rifle held in clean hands. He looked so much like a child. Even though he had a gun, what grown-up would listen to him? And yet, the shadow he cast down the rutted path was long. He reached up with his left hand and tugged the black brim of his hat, angling it downward with a confidence that bordered on menacing. As his hand drifted to support the wooden rifle stock, I thought again how he carried himself like a hero cowboy before a shootout.

William stood beside one of the giant cacti. He had no weapon. That was all right. If it came to fighting, he'd use his fists. He nodded to me, his eyes hidden behind sunglasses.

I nodded in return.

Ozzie rested his baseball bat over his shoulder, his Jose Canseco jersey, white with green and gold trim, unbuttoned and flopping open at the collar. He bit at his chapped lips. If he was scared or getting nervous, it didn't show.

Then I realized I wasn't nervous, either, nor was I scared. The Kybees had us outnumbered, and they had vehicles, probably weapons, too, but that didn't seem to matter. *Why not?* Maybe it was Captain Kid's stone-like coolness, or because the Man of the Mountain had called us knights—we were on a quest, after all—or maybe it was just that I was with my friends.

Dawn stood near, between me and the captain. She'd taken off the white sheet, and her hair was a mess of glowing strands. She held her notebook in front of her, her thumb securing a blue Bic pen to the folder's laminated cover. Her backpack was red, the same color as her dad's Corvette. Was she a knight, also? Could girls even be knights? I didn't think so, but what did I know about knights, or quests, or other worlds?

The approaching motorcycles came to a stop a dozen yards in front of the captain. The helmeted figures regarded one another then shut off their engines, looking less like insects now that they were close. Besides their dusty helmets, they wore ragged scarves, tight-fitting long-sleeve shirts, and slim pants. Their feet were clad in tall, lace-up boots. One had a leather armband studded with rusty skull-shaped cleats. On his belt was a holstered revolver. The other man had crisscrossed machetes on his back.

When they took off their helmets, it surprised me to see they were Asian teenagers, maybe only thirteen or fourteen years old. The one on the right had straight, shoulder-length hair. The other was shaved bald. Something was wrong with that one's face; it looked abnormally long in the chin.

"AHOY," the captain called out.

The long-faced biker grunted and sniffed the air. He said something, but I couldn't hear over the approaching buggies.

The others in the eastbound convoy rolled to a stop, their knobby tires dragging at gravel. The cars and buggies formed a long line behind the two leading motorcyclists. I wondered why they even used the trail. Their vehicles were made for off-roading, so why not spread out? Then, I thought of *Star Wars*, how the Sand People walked in single-file lines to hide their numbers.

I leaned over and whisper to Dawn, "Did you and Cap talk to the mountain man about these guys?"

She spared me a glance out the corner of her eye. "Not really."

"What'd you talk about?" I asked.

Dawn motioned with her chin to the line of Kybees. "I'll tell you later."

To look away from her windblown hair took effort, but when I did, I saw the desert strangers climbing off their bikes and out of their carts.

One of the motorcycle teenagers went to the passenger side of the dune buggy Beetle, opening the door for a heavyset woman. The woman carried a white purse with a picture of Minnie Mouse on the flap. She lifted a pair of goggles onto her forehead and pulled the layers of scarves down off her face to reveal... *Not a woman. She's a girl.* The girl was a little older than the motorcycle scout, but not by much. Also, she wasn't Asian but black with smooth, rounded cheeks and large, threatening eyes.

Wisps of hair swirled about her face and she wiped them away. Then, after exchanging words with the motorcyclist, she slipped the revolver from the boy's holster, turning her dangerous eyes on us.

*As coolly as I could, I worked to open the longer of the two blades on my knife. The stretched-faced motorcycle scout, the one with the machetes, was watching this with interest. Could I kill that kid with a Swiss Army knife? Stupid to think I could. And yet, I had no thought of running away. The captain bolted his rifle, and that was good enough for me.*

# CHAPTER 17

# THE MOON FOLK

The Kybee leader approached the front of the line, holding the scout's revolver. As she walked, she held the gun loosely, swinging it around her hips. That casual swing could become a draw with positively no warning.

Captain Kid, his head tilted to the right, regarded the armed girl. "Howdy, madam. Have you come from the Great City?" Then I noticed he was wearing boots like the marshal's. Before, I'd only seen him barefoot or in a pair of worn-out loafers, so where had these come from?

The Kybee girl grinned, her cheeks gathering into mounds beneath her eyes. She spoke with a ringing, southern sway. "Atsuma?" she half-laughed. "Ohhh, you know we did. Left two weeks ago." She gestured to the captain with her pistol. "Now, toss away your rifle before someone gets their feelings hurt."

Behind her, another figure emerged from the off-roader Volkswagen. This time, it was a boy my age. He was stocky, like the Kybee leader, with the same walnut complexion, but instead of a Minnie Mouse purse, he was wearing a Mickey Mouse hat with ears. He came up beside the girl. Maybe she was his big sister. They had similar features, although, his were erupting with warts and sores.

The Kybee girl put an arm around his shoulder. Then looking to the captain, "Go on, now. Be a good'n and toss your gun away 'fore someone gets hurt."

"No, ma'am," Captain Kid said, his pitch perfectly sensible. "I mean you no harm, but we are strangers in the desert. My companions and I will keep our weapons."

The Kybee girl rolled her neck and shot an annoyed scowl at the machete scout. "Willie, take that boy's gun, and if he gives ya trouble, cut his head off."

As the scout reached over his shoulder, Captain Kid dropped the barrel of his rifle to hip-level and fired. The bullet struck the ground between the scout's dusty biker boots, spraying his pant legs with gravel.

His hand froze in its over-the-shoulder reach. He snarled, his long, animal-like jaw working up and down.

The captain's tone changed not a single note but was as smooth as ice cream on a summer day. "Don't move, or the next one will be in your eyeball."

The Kybee girl released her brother's shoulder, her right hand still holding the pistol. Then she twirled the revolver on her finger—flip, catch, flip, catch—and flipped it again, but this time when she caught the ivory grip, the barrel pointed at Captain Kid. She smiled cruelly. "You best lay down your weapon or shoot, but I'm here to tell you, son, I been shot before, and it only made me angry."

The captain brought the butt of his gun up to his shoulder. He stared down the long sights at the girl. "We came here on the shuttle, through the blue door in the sand, and I brought bullets made special by a U.S. Marshal. If you and your henchies don't tell us what we need to know—and afterward, let us pass in peace—I'll kill you all and leave your bodies for the birds and lizards."

I'd never heard a real person speak that way. It chilled my blood.

The Kybee girl's half-moon smile flattened into a line. "You're a *world hopper*—like the other one—that girl!"

Captain Kid took one step forward. "When did you see her?"

"I don't know—maybe a week ago." Her fingers quivered on the pistol grip.

The two motorcycle scouts moved, the long-faced boy reaching for the machetes on his back, the other one crouching down on all fours like an animal ready to attack. Behind them, the rest of the Kybees, all savage-looking kids or ragged teenagers, prepared for mortal combat. I saw one boy, no older than seven, take up a splintered board, the narrow end wrapped with tape and the other hammered through with a dozen bent nails. An older girl had a bow and arrow. Some of the others swung chains or held up wooden stakes as if they were spears.

The Kybee leader looked around at her tribe of juvenile warriors then waved for them to stand down. Some gnashed their teeth in protest, others looked relieved, but all obeyed. When they lowered their weapons, the leader stuck the borrowed gun in her belt and turned again to the captain. "Look, mister, we've no quarrel with such as you. We come out here to go wild."

Captain Kid glared at her. "I know you do." He shot a glance to the flag above her buggy, on it printed a happy-face moon against a field of deep blue sky. He looked to her again. "Lady, we're in a hurry, and I've no patience for your kind. Do you understand me?"

She nodded, looking guilty of some shameful crime. "What do you want from us? Tell us and be on your way."

Dawn stepped beside her captain. "You saw a girl, where was she headed?"

The Kybee leader spoke in a hurry now, the false southern drawl gone from her voice. "Westerly, of course." She shoved the boy next to her with her hip. "I thought Billy Boy would run away with her on account of the blue in her hair. He never did have sense with girls."

Captain Kid slung his rifle over his shoulder. "Any word from Atsuma?"

The Mickey Mouse kid, the one the leader called *Billy Boy*, was winking with a watery eye. "You're the boy captain, ain'tcha, Captain Kid?" When he spoke, the cracked skin of his cheeks wept fluid. Then I noticed he was sprouting a beard.

"I am," the captain said.

The boy's tone deepened into reverence. "You killed the Molly Snatcher."

By the older girl's growing eyes, I could tell she also knew our captain, only she hadn't recognized him. The other Kybees seemed to know of him, too. The girl with the bow and arrows crossed herself and kissed her fingers, lifting them to the sky.

Captain Kid said, "I didn't kill it, only fought it."

"To save the mermaid, Lady Osiris," the Kybee leader said.

"Yes, ma'am." The captain stepped off the road, looking down the line of desert vehicles. "I'll pay you for one of your carts, any that can carry the five of us."

The leader spat between her feet. "No need to pay. Consider it an offering to the Seven." Then looking back across her trail of followers, she waved at a little kid no older than my brother. "Glover, unload your sand rail."

"Yes'am." The boy curtsied then went to his work.

With her little brother at her heals, the Kybee leader approached the captain and Dawn. "My name is Patricia Trease. I'm the leader of this outfit, and this is my brother."

"Billy Boy," Captain Kid said. "Got it."

Dawn addressed the Kybees, speaking with an authority that startled me. "I am Dawn of the world below." Then she introduced each of us. As she spoke our names, we stepped forward and bowed. After each name, she added, "of the world below."

When the greetings finished, Patricia eyed the captain. "The king will want to see you, boy." She stepped closer, her hand still on the revolver tucked into her belt. "And these others, too. They your knights?"

"We are, so beware," Dawn warned. Her threat was hollow as a balloon—she was unarmed—but somehow it felt real.

The Kybee leader paused, nodded her understanding, and dropped her hand off the gun. Then she approached with caution, leaning forward to sniff at Dawn's hair. She spoke with genuine wonder. "The world below is stranger than I thought." She lifted a hand to Dawn's face, touching her rosy cheek. Then the Kybee bowed and stepped away.

"Wait," Dawn whispered.

She took her house keys from her pocket and worked them off the ring. I thought she'd give the Kybee a key, but she gave the ring instead. Then I understood; dangling from the ring, encased in plastic, was a picture from *The Little Mermaid*. Ariel and the prince sat smiling at each other, and behind, the octopus-witch loomed.

The Kybee turned it over in her hand. "This is from Disney."

"It is," Dawn said.

Hesitantly, the strange girl ventured, "Do you know the Mickey Mouse? Or Minnie? Have you seen her?"

Unlike Ozzie, Dawn managed a straight face. "I'm afraid not."

The desert girl nodded, only a touch disappointed, then showed the keyring to her little brother who was anxious to see it. "I will add this to my collection," she said and gave it to the boy to show the others.

I thought of giving them another small treasure, my secret relic from the world below, a genuine Coca-Cola bottle cap—*complete with dent*—but when I felt in my pocket, the cap was gone. Maybe I'd dropped it pulling out my Swiss Army knife. In any case, now it was missing, and that gave me an unreasonably nervous feeling deep inside my gut. Why should I care if I lost a bottle cap, it was garbage anyway? But I did care. Something about the cap was important, the way it felt in my fingers, or maybe it was the color: bright red.

*So what?*

I didn't know why, but I remembered the way it seemed like a memory more than a physical object. Now, I'd lost it.

Patricia requested that we break bread with her and her friends before leaving. To this invitation, much to my surprise, the captain agreed.

As the Kybee leader retrieved a picnic basket from her VW, her tribe set up a canopy. When they finished, Patricia invited me and my companions to sit in a shaded circle along with Billy Boy in his Mickey Mouse hat and one of the motorcycle scouts.

The offer of bread-breaking was only figurative because what we ate was meat. Patricia offered us jerky strips, some of it beef, some dried turkey, but most of it was venison. The venison was spicy, herbs seasoned the beef, and the turkey had almost no flavor. *Covering all the bases.*

I sat between William and the Kybee scout. The scout sat hunched, his long hair blocking most of his face. I could tell he was strong by the way he fed himself, gripping the jerky with his teeth and tearing it with quick pulls. The rusted skull-studs on his armbands grinned at me as he ate. Then I noticed the bullets tucked into loops on his gun belt, and his empty hip holster dragging C-shapes into the sand. His revolver was still with Patricia.

He looked at me only once with narrow, brownish-orange eyes. I'd never seen eyes like his before. Altogether, he looked more normal than he acted, and he smelled like a dog.

During the picnic, the Kybee leader seemed content to lay back on her side, propping herself on an elbow as little Billy Boy told very unusual stories. As for Billy, he was nice to us, but his rash of warts and sores caused me to question the meat we were eating.

I sniffed the food. The chunk of dark-red beef in my hand smelled smoky and sweet. I'd already eaten a handful, and it tasted delicious, so I ate again, allowing myself to get lost in the boy's strange stories.

# CHAPTER 18

# BILLY BOY'S STORIES

The first story the Kybee boy told was a joke. It was his warmup act. The story was about a fellow named One-Eyed Joe. He was a horse thief who went on mischievous adventures and escaped many times from various jails.

About halfway through the tale, One-Eyed Joe was escaping on the roof of his prison. The sheriff raced out into the street with a rifle. "And you know he was serious," Billy Boy said, "because he shot ol' Joe in the head!"

At that, Ozzie erupted into laughter.

Billy Boy was laughing, too, his left eye watering so fiercely he was crying. "BANG! Shot his eye right out! That's why they call him 'One-Eyed Joe'—get it?"

But the joke wasn't over. The story went on another several minutes and ended with someone looking for Joe's brain in a jar.

At the end of the story, the boy claimed the tale was based on a real person and events from my layer of the Reality Deck. I didn't know if that was true. Neither did my friends. We'd never heard of One-Eyed Joe. I doubted the captain knew, either, but he said nothing one way or another.

The next story was about an unnamed boy who was turned into a murderous, gigantic elephant by an evil witch. Nothing good happened in that story, and it was thankfully short.

Finally, the Kybee boy recounted a tale that seemed, at least in some ways, relevant to our own adventure in search of the Patch Fairy.

Once there lived a knight named Sir Ronald who served Queen Ayanna in the land of Hayadon. Their kingdom was across the desert many miles, over hills, mountains, and plains, through jungles, beyond rivers, oceans, and more. Perhaps, even beyond reality itself. Which was to say, the story might've been made up.

At the queen's royal palace, which stood on the edge of a towering cliff, Queen Ayanna called her knights, all ten thousand of them, to assemble in ranks in the fields outside the castle walls. Then, climbing down from her chariot, she summoned Sir Ronald. He was her general, a fearsome warrior, long experienced in leadership and bravery on the battlefield. Also, in the queen's opinion, he was very handsome.

She brought him into the palace, her servants offering him wine, grapes, and juicy chunks of pineapple as they walked.

"Care to tell me what this is about, Your Majesty?" the knight asked, sampling the fruit.

Queen Ayanna only looked at him, her dark eyes sharp, penetrating, and her face shrouded behind a colorful silk sheet. She motioned for her armor-bearer to remove the knight's gauntlets. When Sir Ronald's gloves were off, the queen placed her hand into his. This was forbidden according to their customs, an offense worthy of whipping if she were anyone other than the queen.

However, the knight, Sir Ronald, forgave her transgression and repaid it with his own dangerous display of admiration. He raised her hand to his mouth and kissed it, then arched an eyebrow, grinning crookedly.

As he did so, he heard a voice shout, "Off with his head!"

But the protest was only his imagination.

The queen enjoyed the kiss, so it seemed, and her guards, stone-faced and implacable, were not reaching for the hilts of their scimitars. Also, all her servants, both male and female, stood with eyes downcast, looking at their shoes.

Queen Ayanna led Sir Ronald to her salon, and taking him into her confidence, she entrusted him with many secret things, not least of which was the existence of a hidden realm.

According to her, powerful magic called *Quizcally* spread across the land. In her slow, bewitching, musical voice, she whispered into his ear, "The magic is like a shroud that covers a woman's beauty." Then she unbuttoned the corner of her veil, revealing her face to him for the first time.

He was astonished, both by her audacity and by her loveliness.

"Quizcally," she said, "conceals a world that is—in a way not entirely describable by words—colored by a deep and permanent crimson stain." After kissing the knight on his cheek, she told him that a door to the secret red world was hidden just behind the mirror in her bedroom. "Over there," she said.

Sir Ronald looked, seeing nothing unusual but his own reflection, impassioned and enthralled, in the company of his queen. They sat together, so close their hands touched on the cushions of her sofa. "Are you serious, my queen?" he asked.

"If only you were brave enough to look." Then she lowered her face, once more concealing her modesty behind the sheet of silk. When her head raised, it was only her eyes looking up at him. That was enough.

He stroked the chin of his beard into a point, stood, then went to the mirror. Being a curious man, he put some of that inquisitive nature to work. The mirror hung on a wall between the entrance of Queen Ayanna's bathing den and her bedchamber. The mirror was quite tall and rather wide, and he had to admit, it looked somewhat out of place. He had taken Queen Ayanna's story as a test—a game, perhaps, for him to play his part—but as he approached his reflection, he grew suspicious.

Intrigued, he scrutinized the shadows around the gilded frame. However, when he saw his queen watching in the reflection, he cut to the chase and tried to lift the mirror from its mount. It would not lift.

*So, how to get the mirror off the wall?* he wondered.

He felt its edges and tested its weight in his hands. As he pulled, he heard a *click* and felt the frame pivot on hinges.

"A door, indeed," he said with fascinated slyness. As the mirror swung to the side, in the space behind, he saw an empty corridor no wider than his shoulders. The passage was dark and the air that flowed out cooled his face. He sniffed, smelling ancient dust. "Is this one of the secret tunnels King Azullah built before the Valormen invaded?"

Queen Ayanna turned her back to him. "I already told you, this door is magic and leads to the Red Realm."

Sir Ronald felt the walls, cold and made of stones as smooth as a crypt vault. "Red, you say?" He had never heard of a Red Realm, although, many strange things were in the world, including magic, but into the narrow shaft he saw nothing red, only pitch black.

The queen went to him, wrapped her delicate hand around the muscles of his upper arm, and together they looked into the dark.

She squeezed his bicep. "I have an errand for you, Sir Ronald."

Then he noticed she was holding something in her other hand: a box, no larger than a cantaloupe, but secured with a sturdy lock.

"What is this?" he asked.

Her eyes narrowed. "It is my plan for you."

With the dead air of the corridor cooling them, she said the box was to be delivered in secret to a king in the hidden world. She was serious, and to prove it, she gave him two gifts of incredible worth besides the treasure hidden in her lockbox. One was her royal sword, which previously belonged to her father, and the second was a *machine*, which belonged to her father's wizard.

The sword was immeasurably sharp and displayed a wide, curved blade. Its pommel and guard were ornamented with gems and inlaid golden serpents. The machine was less impressive to behold, its gray steel scuffed and its grip made of simple wood and brass. But it carried in its wheel six deadly projectiles the wizard named "bullets." These bullets could kill from far away and made an awful discordant racket when the machine fired.

Queen Ayanna promised that if Sir Ronald succeeded, she would award him whatever prize he required, including her own hand in marriage. Then she sealed her oath with blue wax pressed with her signet ring onto the heart of his breastplate.

He was to select twelve knights to accompany him, whomever he wished from the entire gathered army. Another knight, the thirteenth, would be decided by a priest, as was their tradition. Also, she said they were to leave at sunset.

When the knights assembled in the salon, Queen Ayanna offered gold coins in leather bags, small provisions of herbs and dry meat, and whatever weapons they wanted, including poison arrows. Then she gave them torches to light their way. Last, she hung her father's royal sword from the left side of Sir Ronald's belt and holstered the wizard's machine at his right hip.

As the sun set, she bowed to the knights, ushered them into the secret corridor, and sealed them away in the dark behind her mirror.

"Imagine it." Billy Boy, sitting cross-legged in the dirt, felt in front of him with groping fingers. "The knights go into the cave, the rock walls so close on either side they scrape their shoulders." Billy's voice lifted. "Their torches consume the air, heating their hands and faces. The only light is fire. A rat scurries over Ronald's foot!"

The boy flinched away from the imagined rodent. We all did, all but the captain and Patricia. The captain sat on his bottom, leaning back against his rucksack, his legs outstretched and Marshal Rayban's rifle across his lap. He was quiet, only eating the jerky, sipping from his canteen, and occasionally looking up to watch our reactions to the Kybee boy. Patricia reclined onto her side, propped up on one elbow and twisting weed stems into braids. She only watched; she'd heard all this before.

Billy Boy scanned his audience then went on in a quieter, prodding tone of voice. "As the knights go into the dark, the walls widen away from them. Deepening layers of accumulated dust cover the stone floor until there is no more floor, only ground. And no more walls, but a wide-open field of flat gray dirt. Then, one of them notices, no more ceiling, either. Instead, they stare up at a late-evening sky that looks blue…but feels…*red*."

"What do you mean, it *feels red?*" Ozzie had already interrupted several times but went unacknowledged until now.

Billy Boy touched his chin. "You know how our sky is blue? Well, often it's not blue. Sometimes it's gray or white or all different colors when the sun sets. Sometimes it's even red. I'm sure you know what I mean. At night it can go all the way down to total black. But all the time, even then and always, forever the sky is blue." He said this with conviction.

Ozzie shook his head. "No, it isn't. You said it yourself, sometimes it's all sorts'o colors."

The Kybee boy leaned out past the flapping canopy to sun his face in a sky as bright-blue and cloudless as ever could be. I could see his chin hairs illuminated into glowing patches of rose gold by the afternoon sun. "Looks blue," he said, "some of the time—like now—but *feels* blue *all* the time." Smiling, he let the desert sunlight fall on his upturned face. Then he lowered his eyes to my questioning friend. "In the Red, the sun does not feel like this."

"Like it's slow-cooking us into human jerky," I said.

The Kybee leader laughed and tossed her grass braid into my lap. "You got that right. Human jerky—that's 'bout the size of it." She squinted at her brother. "Go on. I like this story."

Billy Boy scratched the patch of orange hair beneath his chin. "Where were we?"

"The sky," I said.

"Oh yeah." He nodded, sitting forward again out of the sun. Then gathering his thoughts, he tossed a glance over his left shoulder. When he faced forward, he was looking at Ozzie. "When Sir Ronald turns around, what do ya think he sees?"

"A monster," Ozzie guessed instantly.

I was thinking along those same lines, but the Kybee shook his head, the Mickey Mouse ears on his hat turning like satellite dishes searching for a signal. "Nope. No monsters. No *anything*. Just his knights spread out, and behind them only dark. The passageway to the queen's mirror is gone. All the knights do the same thing—they draw their weapons, swords, axes, and spears. Sir Ronald draws both the sword and the machine given to him by the queen. *The gun.* They're ready for battle."

"What's Sir Ronald do with the box," William asked, "if both his hands are full?" His tone was flat, and his black sunglasses only added to his unreadable expression.

The Kybee boy shrugged, but then the answer came from another member of our circle, from Captain Kid. "He had the box bound up in his walking pack."

Billy Boy eyed his sister, wiped his nose, then kept talking, but much of his showmanship was used up. "The knights continue across the flatland, leaving impressions of booted feet behind them in the gray dirt, like breadcrumbs left by children in a story."

*Breadcrumbs. Children in a story.* Even told deadpan, those were themes that resonated. Also, the dirt beneath the knights' feet had more meaning than it should. I considered my desert surroundings. Dirt everywhere.

"Footprints," Dawn said, "so they might find their way back."

Billy Boy lifted one finger into the air. "Yes, but did they look to see if their trail remained, or was it erased…as if by magic?" The boy patted his chest. "Me, I think they forgot. And I can tell you now, none of them would ever see their queen again."

Captain Kid eyed the young storyteller. "If you mean to finish this, best get to it. I've got better things to do than listen to you go on and on."

Billy Boy looked for a signal from his big sister.

With some effort, she made herself sit upright. "You heard the captain. Wrap it up."

"Okay then." Billy Boy sounded disappointed. He brushed his hands together. "I'll give you the short version—the Red King killed them all."

"That's it?" Ozzie asked.

"No, but that's how it ends."

Ozzie looked at me. "So, what was in the box? I bet it was somethin' real bad."

Again, it was our captain who answered. "It was the heart of Queen Ayanna's father. She cut it out so the Red King could use it in a spell."

Dawn sat bolt upright. "Oh my God!" She covered her mouth with her hands. "I thought the queen was good—I mean, not totally, but—"

"Why did you think that?" Captain Kid asked, shaking his head.

Dawn shrugged. "I don't know. I guess because she gave Sir Ronald her sword and the gun. Those were special things, I thought."

"They were very special." Captain Kid took a bite of jerky and chewed, then got to his feet. "And maybe she was good. She just had to get rid of the Red King no matter what."

Who knew *no-matter-what* included killing her own father? Unless Queen Ayanna's dad was dead already, she'd murdered him, but maybe she cut the heart out of his corpse. That was a possibility left open by the incomplete story, albeit a remote one.

Now, I had a real question. "The Red King is the unicorn, isn't he, even though the unicorn is actually black?"

The captain brushed sand off his backside. "Very good, Charles. Nightmare is king everywhere in the Red Realm."

It still didn't make sense. "So, how'd the queen get rid of him?"

The captain hung the rifle strap over one shoulder and crouched to pick up his traveling bag. He paused there. "With blood that's royal blue, he can do big magic, dark, evil tricks like making forbidden doors that face the upper realms."

Then I remembered what he said about Reality Gravity, *harder to go up than down*, and it was fresh in my mind how difficult the shuttle was to operate. How could anybody do that on their own, especially a horse? "You're saying he used the blood of a king from the Blue Deck to open an Upward Facing Door in the Red Deck?"

"Precisely."

"Well…" I stood with my backpack in my hands. "How'd Castatine go up? There's no way she flew that shuttle all by herself."

"Yeah," Ozzie said. "I was wondering about that. Please tell me she didn't have some poor king's heart in a box."

"I don't think so." Captain Kid looked grim.

I had an idea why. Castatine didn't have a king's heart, but she had a princess folded up in her pocket. And not just any princess, but one from all the way up on the Roof Top of the World, the very highest part of the Reality Deck. Surely that made a difference when it came to evil spells. And hopefully, it meant Castatine could get by with only pricking the fairy's finger or slicing her palm instead of carving out her beating heart.

The captain looked to the west. "I know what you're thinking, Charles. It's not as bad as that. At least not yet. The shuttle changes with its passengers. Castatine could fly it by herself if she were brave enough."

"Then I guess she was," Dawn said.

"I guess so." Captain Kid offered a hand to the Kybee leader. When Patricia took it, he said, "Thanks for the jerky and the sand buggy. It will help greatly." Next, he shook hands with the storyteller. "And thank you for your tales of woe, even if I didn't want to hear them." Then he looked to his crew. "Better be off."

Patricia tucked *The Little Mermaid* keychain into her purse and waved for us to follow her. As we walked behind her to the sand rail, she asked, "You know how to get to Doloptree?"

"Follow your back trail," the captain said.

The Kybee leader pulled her goggles down over her face. "God be with you on your journey." Then she trudged to her own dune buggy Beetle.

Billy Boy saluted William and trumpeted, "I'll say a prayer for you at the foot of Salvation Mountain."

"And at the top," William added.

I looked to him, surprised he had spoken, but glad.

The Kybee boy beamed. "Good idea. At the top. Yes, brave knight, at the end of the yellow road."

Then the Kybee troop let us walk through their midst, patting us on the backs and shaking our hands like we were heroes going off to war. Everyone shook our hands, including the scout motorcycle rider with the long jaw and machetes on his back. He grunted at me, but the sound was friendly enough. What a peculiar change from our original confrontation. There was even hugging, and some of the younger gypsy girls chanced kissing us on our blushing cheeks as we passed them by.

After the farewells, we came to the sand rail. The buggy was skinny at the nose with a bumper that looked robbed off an old pickup truck. Where the license plate should have been, a crooked bumper sticker read, *Life is short and so am I*. True enough. The driver, Glover, was a ten-year-old.

William felt at the skinny front tires. The rubber looked in good shape up front, but the bulging rear, off-road tires were worn down to slicks. Maybe that wouldn't matter.

We climbed aboard the battered sand rail, William taking the wheel. I stepped into the open cabin, supporting myself with one hand on the roll bar and another on the waving flagpole. Then looking up, I saw flying above me the kybees' triangle banner, a weathered dark blue background and, in the middle, the circular face of a cartoon moon.

*The Moon Folk. The Kybees.* We'd tested their mood and found them…threatening, sure, but also generous.

I sat in the rear seat behind my best friend. There were no seatbelts, only a padded bench. Ozzie and Dawn squeezed in beside me, Dawn in the middle. The captain took the front passenger seat. Behind us, I noted three gas cans bungee-strapped to the roll bars.

Glover explained the controls, then at the order of our captain, we set off to the west, following the Kybee's back trail.

Later that evening, when we stopped to stretch our legs—and take care of private business hidden behind bushes—I found an opportunity to speak to Captain Kid alone. He was standing off by himself, his hands on his hips, looking out at the mountains in the distance.

"Captain," I said. When he looked at me, I asked, "Why don't you like those people, the Kybees? I mean, they're rough around the edges and a little strange, for sure. I think maybe radiation or something like the plague was turning Billy Boy's face into road-pizza. But that wouldn't make you dislike them, so level with me."

Captain Kid lifted off his hat and raked fingers through his sandy hair. What he said next, I would never forget. "They're werewolves."

I stepped back, remembering the round face on the flag flying above our borrowed buggy, a cartoonish, smiling full moon. "The moon folk." I looked to the mountains. The captain was not looking at those old, jagged peaks as I had first assumed, but at the even older orb glowing above. At the moon.

His warning came back to me then. *Monsters live in the Attic of the World.*

Floating across the night air drifted distant howls. How long had that been going on? I didn't know. I wouldn't have heard it over the whining dune buggy engine.

The captain looked out across the plain in the direction of the howls. "They would've told us stories and fed us till nightfall. Then it would be too late. Little Billy Boy was starting his mutation already. It wasn't radiation. Not disease, either. Which means he's a very powerful lycanthrope if he transforms in daylight."

I watched Captain Kid's face. "They were trying to trap us?"

His brow crinkled. "Maybe not. They went out to the desert, so they don't want to kill people when they change. I guess they make those arrangements when they're thinking straight. After they're wolves, the urge to kill is uncontrollable. But hunting humans is always a temptation for their kind. Finding us in such a desolate place..." The captain shrugged. "An encounter like that could be considered fate. Just bad luck for us. They didn't exactly run us off, did they?"

"No, they didn't," I had to admit. "Are we in danger now?"

He repositioned his cap, looking down the road toward the howling. "I don't think so, but we should press on until the gas runs out. Kybees have long legs when they're wolves. They run fast." He didn't have to mention that they knew which way we were headed. Also, our go-cart screamed like the world's angriest leaf blower. They'd be able to hear that from miles and miles away.

He playfully shoved my shoulder. "Don't look so grim. It's a beautiful night and you're out with friends."

All true. My friends and I were on a quest—on an adventure in another world—and the night air was much cooler than the evening before. Perhaps that was due to the rising elevation, but a homesick swell was rising in my chest. "None of this is happening like I thought."

The captain took out his flashlight. When he flipped the switch, nothing happened. "You're doing a good job, you know."

I stopped short. "That's not what you thought yesterday."

"Well, I just had to find the right fit for you. Dawn is a better chief than you are. No offense." He handed me his flashlight. "It doesn't work. Can you fix it?"

I tested the switch then twisted the barrel. "It's probably just a dead battery. I have some in my pack."

"There you go," he smiled. "If you can make it work, it's yours."

"Thanks," I muttered, stuffing the light in my pocket. "If I can change a battery, that makes me a good electro-technical officer? Is that how it works?"

The captain brushed past me. "I'm trying to encourage you, Charles. You could be a great chief—maybe one day—but now you stink at it. You want to look out for your friends, *fine*, but a time is coming when we will need to stand together."

"Or what?" I demanded.

He didn't answer. He didn't have to. I was right. He *was* putting us in danger. He knew that but didn't want to admit it.

In the distance to the east, the wolves were howling. To the north and south, the desert disappeared into darkness. And in the west, the silvery moon cast its reflected light onto the jagged, black mountain peaks. Would we climb those mountains? Not in a dune buggy. But we were only taking the buggy until it ran out of gas. After that, I guessed we'd continue on foot.

Ozzie climbed onto the back of the sandrail to dump the last of our gas into the tank. William helped. When they finished, Ozzie flung the empty can as far as he could into the weeds. Littering was apparently a nonissue in the Attic of the World because this was the third time he did it without reproach.

As we squeezed back into the cart, William cranked it to life, but when he pulled the switch to turn on the headlamps, nothing happened. Like the flashlight, they were dead.

Captain Kid turned in his seat to look at me.

I glared at him. "You want me to fix it?" I was in no mood for that. But I was the electro-technical officer. It was my job.

"You can do it," Dawn encouraged.

Begrudgingly, I climbed out of my seat. When I looked beneath the dash, I found a wire had come off its prong on the back of the switch. After reconnecting it—with the aid of my new flashlight equipped with brand-new batteries—the lights came on just fine.

"See," Dawn said, "I knew you could fix it."

The captain, on the other hand, kept his thoughts to himself.

# CHAPTER 19

# THE DOLOPTREE SHOPKEEPERS

The sand buggy ran out of gas in the middle of the night. Where it sputtered out, we camped, and in the morning, we left it where it sat. Perhaps the moon folk would find it on their return trip to the city after they'd turned back into humans.

We'd almost made it to our destination. An hour's walk brought us to a real road—the first paved road we'd seen in the Attic of the World—and an hour after that, we found the place we were looking for.

As Captain Kid had said, Doloptree was hardly a town. The only prominent place of business was a combination gas station, convenience store, restaurant, and post office. As we approached, I saw a dozen empty gas pumps waiting for their next nonexistent customer. A sign on the side of the building said diesel was available around back. From what I'd already seen, that area was oddly setup.

The diesel side laid out in one long line that reminded me of an off-ramp to a roadside rest area. We'd come upon the outermost pumps half-a-mile before reaching the store. The pumps were at intervals forty or fifty feet apart. Each pump had one huge, green-nozzled fuel dispensary. I supposed busses or semis would fill up parked in an extended, single-file line down the ramp, but that seemed like a very inefficient arrangement. Travelers in the back would have to hoof it several minutes just to eat at the restaurant or use bathrooms. Most people wouldn't be willing to do that. *Think of all the lost customers.*

We kept walking, the heat of the blacktop baking the soles of my feet.

William pointed to a dusty, blackened shape on the other side of the street. "Check it out, the Doloptree Motel."

In the lot opposite the truck stop, only the ruined, burned bones of the motel remained. It had been a sizable structure once upon a time. Now it was only a mess of rubble with an empty swimming pool out front. Any other town would've cleaned up the mess. The fact that the people of Doloptree hadn't bothered said something unpleasant about the desert settlement.

A shop neighboring the burned down motel claimed to sell land, though, that place looked long closed to me. Aside from the few businesses, there were a handful of trailer homes scattered like children's toys in the weedy plots behind the main road. They were not parked with any kind of geometry that made sense, but unlike the motel and real estate office, they appeared inhabited by something besides ghosts.

No one was outside, however, and the only transportation I saw was a generic, square-bodied pickup truck and a collection of rusty bicycles in front of one of the trailers.

"What kind of people live here?" I asked, but no one answered.

As we approached the store's blue double-doors, Captain Kid paused at a message board to study the bus schedule. Then he checked his watch. "We're in luck. The bus only stops here twice a week, but the next one's coming in three hours."

"I thought you just wanted to use the phone," I said.

Ozzie raised his hand. "Can we get something from the restaurant? I'm starving."

The captain straightened his cap. "Phone first, restaurant second." He felt his stomach with his hands. "I could eat, and this place makes great pancakes and sausage. I bet you guys like milkshakes."

We all nodded.

Captain Kid smiled and waved theatrically to the door. "Right this way and mind your manners. You represent more than just yourselves now."

By that, I took it to mean our actions were a reflection on him. He eyed me as I walked past. What a strange leader we had, so young and innocent-looking, but so sure of himself. Even so, lurking beneath his cool demeanor, I suspected trouble.

I offered him an ironic salute, which he accepted graciously.

We walked in through the gas station. Where the convenience store ended and the restaurant began, the floor changed from gray squares of laminate to long rectangles of fake wood. There was also a greeter's stand, but no one manning the unnecessary post.

When we walked into the restaurant, a boy turned on a barstool. He reminded me of a kid I knew in the third grade, thin, red-headed, with freckles, but this version had a full mustache. His diner-worker uniform looked like a costume. For that matter, so did his facial hair; it looked glued to his upper lip.

He slid down off his stool and grabbed a pile of menus. "Sit anywhere you like."

I advanced a step. "First we need to use your phone."

"Ah, yeah...well." The kid waiter looked abashed. "Sorry, but the phone's outta order."

My heart sank. "You gotta be kidding me?"

"Sorry, sir, not kidding at all. Might be fixed next week."

I eyed the captain, wanting to strangle him.

He nodded to the doors. "What about the gas station. They have a working telephone?"

"No, sir," the waiter said. "All the phones are out...in the whole town. The line was cut."

Dawn stepped forward, offering a fake smile to the restaurant worker. "We'll sit over there." She pointed to a corner booth.

We began to move in that direction until Ozzie intercepted the red-headed waiter. Ozzie studied the boy's name tag, then asked, "So, *Limpkin*—Is that how you say it? You work here?"

The uniformed boy nodded eagerly. "You said it right, and yes, sir. I can take your drink orders now, or...wanna sit first and look at the menus? We mix a fine Cherry Sprite. It's kinda our specialty."

Ozzie took a closer look at the kid's mustache. "I think we're having milkshakes, but hold on a sec. Is that thing real?"

The boy smirked, thumbing the bright red-orange patch of hair. "Sure is. Makes me look older, don't cha think?"

Captain Kid slid into the corner booth. "That's enough, Ozzie Ernesto. You're being discourteous."

William disagreed because he lifted the sunglasses onto his forehead to meet Limpkin's eyes. "Older than what?"

The waiter's face contorted into a curiously confused look. "What do you mean?"

William pressed in. "I mean, how old *are* you?"

Then I heard myself ask, "And where are all the grownups?"

The waiter was handing out the menus. Now he stopped, looking each of us over. He eyed our backpacks and the captain's rifle. Captain Kid had set the gun on the lip of wood between the seatback and the window.

The waiter's good humor vanished. "No grownups 'round here. Not no more, 'cept at Salvation Mountain, and the Blue Skulls, and the king. But lookie here, if you come about that girl, it wasn't my fault. Besides, she's gone already."

"Left a week ago," Captain Kid said. "Took the bus to Atsuma— We know."

"Why aren't there grownups?" I asked again.

The boy licked the corner of his red mustache. "You're not from around here. Mister, out here, monsters dwell."

William nodded in a direction that might've been east. "Like the Kybees."

"Werewolves," the waiter said. "Also, zombie, vampire, the weird horse-people who live out on the Hojo Flats."

"Lots of things," Captain Kid agreed, "but most have moved on, isn't that so?"

"Most," the mustached boy said, "but far from all. I seen a giant out walking in the mist, must've been a hundred feet tall. He had a tail with bone plates all down his back. Some say he breathes fire."

"Like a dragon," Dawn said.

"Like that." The waiter nodded. "They call him the *All-Be-Gone*, say he's looking for his family, but they died long ago. He doesn't know that, just wanders around like a lost pup."

The mood began to relax.

Dawn sat in the booth beside our leader. Then taking a menu from the waiter, she eyed the uniformed boy with serious intent. "What's not your fault?"

He looked confused, then scared. His eyes moved to our captain, then to the rifle resting beneath the window. He took a step back, bumping into Ozzie, then tossed our menus on an empty table and ran from the restaurant.

Captain Kid turned to the window, watching as the boy darted across the deserted parking lot. Then he snatched up his rifle. "So much for our pancakes." Practically shoving Dawn out of the booth, he stood, glaring at William. "Maybe next time you'll use your manners."

But it wasn't William's questions, or even mine, that made the boy runaway. It was Dawn's. *What's not your fault?* Something about Castatine. And with our overlapping questions, he hadn't told us where all the grownups went.

Two pallid teenagers manned the attached convenience store. The older boy behind the counter had long, wavy hair pulled back into a ponytail, the hair held in place by the kind of ribbon Benjamin Franklin might've worn. According to him, the young red-headed waiter had agreed to let Castatine stay at his house while she waited for the bus.

With the pretentious voice of a butler, the gas station clerk said, "Ordinarily, she would've stayed at the motel, but that burned down a year ago." This he explained while petting the lapel of his blue velvet suit coat as if it were a housecat.

Why was he dressed so nice to work the register of a crappy gas station, I wondered. Maybe he was going somewhere special when he got off work, but where? Doloptree was the deadest town I'd ever seen.

Then remembering the Kybees, *if they were werewolves, this guy might be a vampire*. Only, daylight streamed in through the windows, so that wasn't right.

The teenager gripped the lapel of his coat. "The last day, the girl told him that if he emptied the money box into her purse, she would use a potion to turn him into a radar man. Can you believe it?"

The captain tapped a silver coin on the counter beside the register. "How much was in the money box?"

"A hundred-and-some," the clerk moaned.

Captain Kid tossed him the coin.

The clerk caught it in one hand then held it to the light, pinched between two long fingers. "A lot of money, mister." After a moment's hesitation, with a meaningful look to his coworker who was half-sweeping, half-listening, he tossed the coin back. "Limpkin will make recompense out of his paycheck. Your money would lessen the blow, but silver is no good around here. Bad for business."

Captain Kid returned the coin to his vest pocket. "What'd she do with the money?"

"Made a phone call." The pale teenager fluttered fingers at a payphone by the restrooms. "Don't know who she called, so don't ask."

"I thought the phones didn't work," I blurted.

The clerk breathed heavily. "They didn't...when she finished with them."

William twitched his brow, and the sunglasses perched on his forehead dropped over his eyes. "Hundred bucks is a lot for a phone call."

"Not when it's long-distance, and everywhere is long-distance from here, young man." The clerk's fingers returned to his lapels. He had lengthy, old-woman fingernails, milky-white and thin.

"What's a radar man?" the captain asked.

The other gas-station worker walked over with her broom in hand. She was dressed with old-fashioned formality equal to her snooty coworker. Her outfit was a morbid, maroon dress with black lace trimmings. "Someone who hears music in the air without a radio," she said.

That made me think of Captain Kid and Castatine at the well in the Gossamer Gardens, how they'd sit, listening to music drift up from other worlds. Was that what the Limpkin boy was trying to do?

The female clerk turned the broomstick in her hands, looking ever so much like a witch. "She gave him a potion, but it only made him fall into deepest sleep for the rest of the day."

"Lucky it wasn't poison," Ozzie said. He looked back toward the dinner. "Can either of you work the kitchen, maybe make some of the pancakes we heard so much about?"

They refused. Making pancakes wasn't their business. Limpkin's replacement would be along in several hours. Too late, in other words. The bus we were waiting for would come and go by then.

When Dawn asked if they could send for someone else to work the diner, sooner rather than later, again they answered with stiff courtesy, calling us *sirs* and *madam,* but declining to help in any way.

So, feeling even hungrier than before, we gave up on a cooked meal and shopped from the convenience store instead. The food we paid for in trade, handing over William's Rubik's Cube rather than the captain's silver. William thought he'd gotten the short end of the stick. A Rubik's Cube had to be worth more than a jar of pickles, some peanut butter, a loaf of white bread, and a round of fountain sodas. But we had little else to bargain with, and before he showed the cube was solvable, the station clerks weren't ready to give him anything for it.

Before we left the store, I checked the payphone for a dial tone. There wasn't one. After that, we ate in the shade of an outdoor bus shelter. As we snacked, I stared out across the horizon, my eyes focusing on nothing in particular. An idea floated across my free-drifting thoughts; maybe I'd spy that fire-breathing giant somewhere off in the distance. The monster sounded like Godzilla. Seeing it from a distance would be a thrill.

No such luck, however. I saw no movements other than the clouds which rolled like huge, slow-motion beach balls in sand and birds soaring on breezes that blew too high in the atmosphere for us ground-dwellers to feel.

Unprompted, the captain said, "People here can stay kids forever...like in..." He'd taken out Joseph, holding the little aquarium in his lap. When he gave the tank a swish, the tiny red crab twirled up off the rocks. "Like in Neverland."

When we first sat down on the sheltered bench, Dawn had started on an old paperback. Now she closed the book, returning it to her backpack. With her hands folded over her crossed legs, she asked straight out, "Are you Peter Pan?"

The captain snickered, "Golly, no. I'm Captain Kid, and Neverland is make-believe, so I've been told."

"Then what happened to the grownups? Or, are you saying there are no grownups?" She waited for his answer.

The captain didn't look at her, just went on watching the red-shelled crab swish about its tank. "I've not spent much time here—terribly hard to get here, as you know—but the marshal told me a plague of worms descended on this place. Little buggers got into everything, including the food."

The half-eaten sandwich in my hands was losing what little appeal it already had.

Captain Kid gestured to my lunch. "That was decades ago. Your sandwich should be safe." Then eyeing his crustacean friend, he continued in a conversational tone. "The worms carried evil spirits, or dark magic, or something like that. They were poison, and nearly everybody died. Afterward, the kids who lived stayed young. Some thought the worms were a weapon sent from the Red Realm. Who knows? Nowadays, if people want to grow up, they have to cross the gate in the Wall of Broken Hearts that leads to the red side of the Reality Deck."

"And the monsters?" Dawn asked.

Captain Kid sighed, "If the people come back from the Red, they can grow up, but some of them turn to monsters. No one knows why...least, I don't."

I took another bite of my sandwich, why not, I'd already eaten half of it. It went down dryly, so I wet my throat with a splash of Cherry Sprite. "The Kybees weren't grownups," I said.

The captain tugged a rubber plug from the top of Joseph's tank. "Not yet, but they're aging. You can tell."

"What about the king and the skull-guys?" William asked. "Are they monsters, too?"

"Not them." Captain Kid pulled the straw from his soda and dipped it into the miniature aquarium. Then he blew a torrent of bubbles into the water. The little red crab danced in a storm of churning pebbles.

William looked at me and shrugged. What was there to say?

Dawn began to pack away the remains of our picnic. Either the bread would fit in her backpack or the peanut butter but not both. Deciding to keep the bread, she turned to the captain. "Who do you think Castatine called on the payphone?"

The straw drifted away from his lips. He took the straw from the water, wiped it on his leg, and stuck it back in his soda. "Very likely, some representative of the Red…*unfortunately*."

He tossed back the flap on his military pack, shark teeth swinging from the leather cords, and returned Joseph into the darkness of the satchel. Then he got up and strolled away from us down the cracked and dust-caked blacktop.

Ozzie and William continued discussing the worm plague, exchanging baseless theories about why some of the kids who went into the Red came back as monsters. Dawn returned to her book. My mind went back to its aimless wandering. Funny how natural it seemed to think so little of our *unnatural* circumstances.

I was too out of sorts, too tired from my second night without a bed to think about mysteries. Also, I was generally in a bad mood—and for good reason, but I hated feeling that way. I always despised useless complaints, but I found myself ready to go on a tirade over just about anything. I didn't even like my sandwich—peanut butter. Pickles weren't much better. I liked ham sandwiches and chips. Or, if it had to be peanut butter, at least have a little jelly with it. I'd already been demoted for saying I didn't trust the good ol' Cap one hundred percent. What would he do if I complained about a free lunch?

So, I ate my food along with the others and kept quiet. Before long the bus would come and take us to the city, which was even farther away from our home than we already were. Once we got there, I could only hope things would make more sense.

Regardless of what we found in Atsuma, that was the end of the line for me. After that, I was going home, and I would take my friends with me.

# CHAPTER 20

# THE BUS TO ATSUMA

I was confident the bus to Atsuma was the longest road-going vehicle ever to roll. At first, when we saw it pulling in behind the Doloptree way station, we took it for a convoy of busses, but that was wrong. It was one bus, as long as a train, with flexible accordion-joints between the sections. Each section had a number. When the thing stopped, the portion in front of us had a placard that read *Car 64*.

A whistle sounded and boys in mechanic uniforms stepped out at intervals up and down the preposterous length of the vehicle. These people went about the refueling operation. That explained the truck stop's extremely long, one-lane diesel setup. When the second whistle tooted, passengers rushed out in a well-ordered mob, but a mob all the same. One moment there was only the five of us on the sidewalk, the next there were hundreds. And no adults anywhere. It was like the world's biggest field trip. Also, there were hardly any white people, which amplified my feeling of being a stranger in a foreign land.

Captain Kid arranged for our passage, and we boarded the giant bus in section 64. In all, the bus spent only fifteen minutes in Doloptree. That was quicker than normal due to the restaurant being closed. We heard many passing complaints about that.

Shortly after finding our seats, the bus-train departed.

While the captain used his downtime to take a nap, my friends and I wanted to explore. Most cars we found were nothing but row after row of seats, like any other bus. The only difference was the doors to the flexible hallways where the driver seats and windshields would have been. That, and the absence of grownups. The ages of the westbound travelers ranged from high schoolers all the way down to preschool-age. Where were the parents? Gone, into the Red Deck, or changed to monsters, else they were here, living in the bodies of young people.

Despite the many ethnicities represented by the travelers, nearly everyone spoke English, although, with accents that were not American.

As we passed through one of the passenger cars, Dawn asked a row of travelers where they'd come from. A boy, looking like an escapee from a child labor camp, said in a quiet voice, "Bonneville, over the Western Drop, near the Castle of Shields."

"How far is that?" Ozzie asked.

The row's designated talker narrowed his eyes and answered with a distance that seemed impossibly far: "Nine thousand miles, as the crow flies." The implication was clear; it was even farther by road.

"And you've come all that way by bus?" Ozzie looked up and down the aisle. "I mean, a train-thingy?"

The traveler shrugged. "How else?"

Other passengers offered equally perplexing answers to our queries. They were from unfamiliar places like Truckney, United North Overland, the Nation, and a dominion by the spooky name of Dead Canyon. How far were these places? A thousand miles was the closest.

Other cars had more than just seats. Some were "sleepers," which meant passengers with money to spend could lie down rather than pass their nights sitting upright. I saw one girl offering to sell her bed for seventy-five dollars a night.

There were also dedicated cars for the kitchens and dining rooms, and another where men in red chairs sat smoking cigars and drinking from crystal glasses.

We saw the men through the window of a door marked *Smokers' Cabin*.

"Grownups, after all," I whispered when we saw them.

William put his face to the window. "What're they up to?"

We crowded together, obviously spying, but hoping not to be noticed. There were three of them, all dressed in mobster-boss suits with pinstripes. Two of the men sat across a chessboard at a window with the curtains drawn. In our section of the bus, the windows had no curtains.

The chess player with his back to us was thin and tall with slicked-back hair. His opponent was fatter, in his late forties, and wore the long sideburns that look terrible on everyone but Wolverine. The fat one appeared to be more than half asleep but, rolling the butt of his stogie into the corner of his mouth, he pushed a black knight in an L-shape across the field of battle. He said something I couldn't hear, probably, *Check.* The thinner man leaned in close, his cigar left burning in the ashtray and ice melting in his drink.

The third man sat alone, legs crossed and eyes looking in a direction out the window that didn't follow the passing landscape. Using only his right hand, he shuffled a deck of playing cards, sliding the deck apart with quick, slicing movements of his fingers, then fanning the halves together again. That was the kind of one-handed maneuver only a magician could manage, and he was doing it with such speed and confidence like he wasn't even thinking about it. I looked from his hands to his face. A magician he might've been judging by the showman's mustache, thin, waxed and curled in the corners.

Ozzie whispered in my ear, "Do they own the train, or have they come to rob it?"

"Beats me." I sniffed, smelling the cigar smoke through cracks in the door. It smelled good in a way.

As we watched from the little window, a woman strolled in through the front of the car. She was the only woman I saw on the train, and what a beauty. She wore a dazzling silver-white dress that sparkled as she moved. Below the hem of her gown, tips of red high heels punctuated her steps.

Then she reached up to slip a sheet of blonde hair back over her shoulder. Dawn was pretty, no doubt about it, but this woman—I'd seen nothing like her in all my short life.

She flicked a glance in our direction, immediately looking away to the fellow with the playing cards. After a brief exchange, the man uncrossed his legs, rising from his seat with an air of theatric grace that made me think once more of a magician.

The deck of cards did its shuffling dance in his fingers, but when he lifted his hands to curl his mustache, the cards were gone. *Vanished.* His first magic trick. Next, he would make us disappear.

He picked up a pair of gloves from the lampstand and pulled them snugly over his lean, magician's hands. Then walking to the rear of the cabin past the inattentive chess players, he grasped the door in front of us and slid open the entry.

His voice strained, choked practically, in the most villainous way imaginable. "May I help you?" His calculating eyes settled on me.

"N-no, sir," I sputtered. "We were just...."

"Good. You're bothering the lady. That means you're bothering me. Move along."

I felt Dawn's hand on my arm. She pulled me back. I let her. So did William, but Ozzie was not so easily deterred.

As we drew back, he stepped closer to the man. "Well, you're bothering my buddy, Chucky, so that means you're bothering me."

I gaped.

The magician's dry lips bent upwards in the corners beneath the curled horns of his mustache. He opened his coat to reveal a dagger sheathed to his belt. The handle was corded leather, the guard dull brass, and the scabbard a wicked spike of black steel stamped with the face of a roaring lion.

Something crazy was happening. I knew—*knew*—if Ozzie had his baseball bat, he would've brained the man. Across the back of Ozzie's jersey, I saw the blocky number *33*, and above that the name of his favorite slugger, *Canseco*, but Ozzie wasn't some hulking athlete who hammered balls into the upper deck. He was a kid, same as me.

The chess players looked up from their game, deciding something more interesting was happening at the rear of the cabin. The thinner player rose from his chair. When his arms came to rest at his sides, the right hand was holding an open straight razor.

The overweight Wolverine impersonator eyed the lady in silver, received a nonverbal cue, then reluctantly scooched to the edge of his seat and stood with the aid of a cane. The cane handle was brass, in the shape of a duck's head. When he gripped the duck and twisted, out from the shaft came a slim, double-edged blade.

The magician's gloved hand rested nonchalantly on the corded handle of his weapon. In direct contrast to his sly body language, his constricted voice strained. "It seems we're at an impasse."

"It seems we are," Ozzie agreed.

Then from the front of the car, the woman in silver cackled.

# CHAPTER 21

# THE SMOKERS' CABIN

The woman in silver slid in behind the magician, her red high heels twinkling like Dorothy's magic slippers. But she was no Dorothy, more like a bombshell version of the Wicked Witch of the West.

She purred, running her hands down the length of the magician's arms. Her hands were soft as rose petals—I could tell just by looking at them—and her fingernails reflected light with a silvery sheen.

When her pink lips parted, I was surprised to hear her speak in a lazy accent that might've been part Irish. "He's a feisty one." She eyed Ozzie with new interest. "Would you care for a cigarette, laddie, or perhaps a cigar?" When she asked this, a heavy breath of grey smoke flowed from her mouth.

Ozzie jeered, "Gave 'em up when I was ten."

"Right." She sounded suddenly bored. "Come in and let us have a look a'cha." She turned on her red heels, certain of our obedience.

We did what she asked with almost no hesitation because we were used to listening to adults who spoke with authority. As we lined up in front of the strangers, the fat man slipped his saber back into his walking stick, and the fellow with the razor folded his blade away.

The lady in silver lowered her face to mine and sniffed. "Where've you come from?"

I smelled her as well. She didn't smell like flowery perfume, which was what I expected, nor of the cigar's rich incense, or even the cheap, acrid stink of cigarette smoke. Instead, her breath was like the charred remains of a campfire. She traced thin fingers over my paltry biceps. Her touch was even softer than I imagined. I didn't understand why, but her fingers made me think of ashes.

"We come from the Nation," Dawn blurted. This was a place we'd heard from other travelers.

It was a good attempt, but the woman laughed in that shrill Irish tambour, "I think not, my dear."

"Do so," William protested.

"You most certainly do *not*." The woman drew this out so *not* sounded like *naught*. "The people of the Nation have skins as dark as Lord Nightmare. Yours is lily-white, as cute as baby cherubs." She took William by the shoulders, turning him around, peering into his ears, and pinching his bottom. "We saw you get on at Doloptree, but you don't come from there, either." When William was facing forward again, blushing with an embarrassment that bordered on furious, she swatted him on the chest. "So tell me, boyo, where're you really from?"

William pressed his lips together.

A dark tension fell across the woman's features—a tightness in her hazel eyes, an inward curl of her full lips. Breathing in, she gathered her patience and stepped to the left. Now she stood in front of Dawn, not our captain but our chief.

Dawn stood tall, but the woman seemed to gain a few inches of unaccounted for stature like she'd willed herself into becoming a taller person. She reached over Dawn's shoulder, gathered a bundle of golden hair, and pulled it forward over the strap of her red backpack.

Fondling the locks, the woman whispered, "Tell me the truth, dear heart. Where're ya from? Speak truthfully, or I'll have Barnabas cut off all this lovely hair with his straight razor—" Then with a hateful ferocity, "—Cut it right down to the bone!"

Stunned, I stared at the woman.

She snarled at me, "You have something to add to this?"

"Jacksonville," I said. "For goodness sake, we live in Jacksonville."

Her demeanor changed instantly. "Florida," she gleamed in her vaguely Irish accent. "How int'restin. You must've come through that door in the sand. I've wondered what lies beneath. But I reckon it's no place for an ol' smoker like me." With hips swaying, she strode to the magician with the dagger. Using his shoulder to steady herself, she pried off her heels. "Was that other girl one of yours?"

I looked across my line of friends.

Dawn answered. "No, she wasn't."

The smoker woman turned on the bare pads of her feet. "I find it odd that two crossings come up in as many weeks." Her narrowing eyes flicked to the fat man with the cane. "What say you, Henry?"

"Passin' odd," the man puffed.

The woman tossed one of her shoes into an unoccupied chair, but the other she gripped like a weapon, testing the spiked heel against her open palm. When tension raised the muscles in her arms, she looked remarkably strong. "Tell me, children, whacha come up here for? Not on vacation, I know dat. Tell me now, and let no more lies tumble out of your reckless mouths, or the men will tie you screaming to these chairs, and I'll climb up on ya like prancin' ponies and stab your eyes out with the heel of my shoe—*Now tell!*"

To the left of the woman, the magician grinned wildly, one hand pawing at the hilt of his knife, the other curling his mustache into demonic fishhooks. His face was pale, and not pale like William's, who was the whitest in our little gang, but pale like death. Where William's cheeks and nose were flush, this man's were gray. Again, like *ash*, like he'd stuck a paintbrush into the ruins of a fire—not the burnt black stuff, but the lighter powder the color of skies in black and white movies—and used it to paint around his eyes and beneath the hard, angular bones of his skull.

Why had Ozzie picked a fight with a man so obviously dangerous? And now this woman was even worse. She glared into Ozzie's defiant eyes. He wasn't so quick with his tongue now, and that was a good thing, but too late.

Dawn should've been the one to tell the crazy woman why we were here, Dawn being our temporary leader in the absence of Captain Kid—who had taken a nap at exactly the wrong time—but she waited on me to speak. All I knew was that if we didn't play our cards right, by the time Captain Kid woke up, he'd preside over a crew of knights with their eyes gouged out.

But we were knights, chosen for a reason, even if I couldn't name it with a thousand guesses. And I felt some vague sense of knowing what to do. *Somehow*, this encounter was attempting to access recollections deposited into the basement of my memory banks.

The woman moved across our ranks, her bewitching eyes scrutinizing William. She said something—more threats, I'm sure—but I couldn't focus on her words, not now, any more than I could see the blimp-station in the sight glass of Captain Kid's telescope. The smell of cigar smoke lingering in the room and the gentle bump of the bus-train over the road, the noise of engines and wind, the flying reflected shapes on the window glass; all of it together was lulling me into a strange trance.

In a basement-level vault inside my brain, a thought, not entirely random, was being processed up to the control room at the forefront of my mind: when we asked Captain Kid if he knew the girl who kidnapped the Patch Fairy, he'd said, *I think I must...* Did that mean something to us here?

Two more ideas—coming to me like supersensory movies—arose and clung to the roof of my mind like the feet of hanging bats: there was the ashy quality of the smoker-witch's skin, that was one, and the second had to do with the layers of reality stacked like decks of playing cards. We were in a layer—*a card*—right up near the top of the deck.

I mouthed to myself, "The Attic of the World is no place for grownups."

The woman turned her hateful, hazel-flecked eyes on me. She was still beautiful, but something was wrong with her—something in the same neighborhood as whatever malady gave the magician his ashy look. The shape of her head was there, but the depth of it was not. The swell of her bosom was there, but the heart beating beneath was not. It was as if seeing her at the wrong angle might reveal her to be nothing more than an illusion, like a ghost in a magic show.

She passed Dawn, stomping toward me, because I was no longer paying complete attention to her. Her free hand drew back and whipped forward, slapping my face. I felt like a tree struck by lightning.

Then pressing in, she shoved the spike of her blood-red high heel to my face. "You have something to say to me, boy?"

My vision rippled. The magician's gloved hand seized my right arm, his grip like a band of iron. Dawn caught me by the elbow on the other side. Regardless, I felt I might topple over, or pass out.

Out the corner of my frayed vision, I could see Dawn watching me with an emotional blend of terror and motherly worry.

Still, I couldn't focus on the seriousness of the situation. All I could think about were ashes and decks of cards. They were less like ideas and more like memories brought on by the smells, and sounds, and the odd floaty movements of the train. The man with the dagger had been sitting by the window, shuffling a deck of cards one-handed, like a magician. When he got up, the cards were gone.

I looked away from the spiked heel threatening my face to the man glaring at me, black, pinprick eyes above a mustache waxed and twirled, yellow-white teeth clenching together. On his gloved magician's fist, the leather knuckles were scuffed, like they were once smooth, nice looking to match his striped suit, but that was before he used them to demolish someone's face. Then finally, to the gray under his cheekbones, beneath his nose, and in the sunken cavities below his eyebrows; it should've been shadow there, but it wasn't. *Not a trick of the light, but still a trick.*

The other men were the same. The fat one—a bloated cross between Wolverine and a bad-guy lieutenant in any daytime crime drama—when my eyes left him, all but his clothes seemed to vanish. His duck-head cane was like something right out of a movie. He was real, but not one hundred percent real.

And the other guy, the creep with the straight razor folded in his pocket, *Barnabas* the woman called him, he looked like your standard gangster in any generic mob movie: stringy hair combed to one side; his nose broken a few times and fixed on a budget. His suit might've come from a film studio's costume department, gray with dark pinstripes, wide lapels, four buttons down the front, and cuffed and pleated pants. Even his weapon, the straight razor, rang of movie villainy.

My vision cleared, focusing on the woman in silver, *the Silver Witch*, with her high-heeled Dorothy Gale knockoffs. My words growled past gritted teeth. "I think you're not what you appear to be. You're no more a woman than I am."

No more laughter. She slapped me again, harder than before. My cheek felt like a burning forest, my right ear rang with a tinny whine, and here came one of those basement-level messages again. This time it was marked, *URGENT!*

# CHAPTER 22

# URGENT

The idea springing into my head—a memory, if I could call it that—felt like a wartime communiqué smuggled across enemy lines. It felt dangerous, overwhelming in its importance, and costly. Though, what was the price and who paid the bill, I had no way of knowing.

Before that Silver Witch slapped me the first time, I'd thought of ashes, cards, and the captain's soft voice saying, "I think I must." Just below that stirred an unarticulated comparison of the woman and a living campfire, or a *dead* campfire, but that made no sense even to me. Then her open hand connecting with my face for the second time shook something loose inside my mind.

I remembered first seeing the men through the window in the door. They were smoking. Then, in walked that stunning woman, her silver-white dress shimmering over the curves of her body. When the magician-man got up and opened the door in front of us, Ozzie spouted off to him. Why did he do that?

Inside the Smokers' Cabin, we lined up for inspection.

The woman wanted information.

She slapped me.

*Yes, yes,* all that made sense . . . except it didn't.

Because I'd been on this ride before.

I'd stood in front of these people, smelling their smoke and feeling that sting on my cheek. *Yes,* and last time—so hard to remember, but I was trying—*What happened?*

I could feel mental fingers tearing open a package to get at the memory. I looked across my line of friends, all staring back at me. Then I had it.

The last time I was here—if this déjà vu fantasy could be believed—I'd come with my friends, Dawn, Ozzie, and William, just as it was now, only the boy I saw standing between Dawn and Ozzie was not the William I knew. Not exactly. He was a little thick for William and maybe a little taller, too, but looking so much the same as my best friend they must've been brothers. William didn't have a brother.

It was a lie. A trick. Somehow these movie gangsters and their Irish mistress were putting thoughts in my head. I'd never been in this place before, much less in this situation.

The dagger-toting magician with his fancy one-handed shuffle had made the cards disappear because he did a magic trick. Now he was using telepathy; he had to be.

His iron grip clamping down on my forearm shook me out of my trance. When he let go without warning, I fell against Dawn's shoulder.

"*Fine*," the witch sang. She turned on the bare pads of her feet. "Grab the girl!"

Barnabas seized Dawn, one hand in her hair, the other tugging at her wrist.

She screamed, and William was already moving—the *real* William this time, not the imaginary lookalike.

I moved in that direction, but the magician tripped my legs, caught me with an arm around my neck, and wedged his dagger beneath my chin.

Just then, William's fist smashed into Barnabas's nose, breaking it for the second time, at least. Instead of blood squirting from the wound, the man's nostrils blew out a cloud of smoke. *Smoke.* Before any of us had time to process this unexpected development, the full weight of a flying Ozzie Ernesto smashed into the man's lower back. Both boy and man crashed to the floor in an erupting shower of ashes.

Ozzie seemed okay—aside from his wild screams—but the man was, *on fire?* I saw no flame, but he'd become a living cremation. As he writhed on the floor, his face crumbled right off his skull, and then the skull was going, too, shedding apart and spilling down his shirt in wispy, smoky flakes.

The witch in silver spun, shouting orders at the fat man.

He'd withdrawn into a corner but, at her wailing, found his courage and whipped the slender saber from his cane. The point of the weapon collided with a swaying chandelier. He slashed anyway, narrowly missing William's ducking head.

The magician dragged me backward, the cold steel of his dagger stinging my throat. I was cut. My right hand fought for the Swiss Army knife in my pocket, but with my body twisted, I couldn't pry it free.

The Irish woman whipped her shoe at Dawn, missing. Dawn snatched up the forgotten chessboard, then with an amazing two-handed swing, flung it at the witch's face. The woman drew back, but the corner of the board crashed against her temple, black and white bishops, pawns, and royalty scattering to the four corners.

Grabbing her head, the woman recoiled. Between her fingers, smoke roiled as if from a chimney. All the hair on that side of her head fell out. If she were pretty before, now she was a sunken-eyed nightmare.

The magician yelled, flinging me aside, his dagger raking my neck. The instant before, I'd thoughtlessly pried my left hand under the blade, else I'd be dead. I tumbled backward across an armchair, crashing into the side table.

Forgetting my knife—no good for battles anyway—I yanked up the table, a reading lamp, whiskey glass, and ashtray spilling against the wall. Then screaming and wide-eyed, I sent the table sailing for the back of the magician's head. I missed, finding his hip instead. When the table struck him, two things happened: the section of impacted fabric collapsed in on itself as if filled with nothing but air, and from the front pocket of his jacket spilled a handful of playing cards. The falling cards seemed too familiar by far.

He stutter-stepped, then turned to face me. Where his face looked thin before, now it was little more than a mustached skeleton wreathed in smog.

Behind him, Dawn engaged the witch, the woman's bald head now churning black smoke from a hole—*yes, a hole*—where the chessboard cracked her temple. Ozzie, covered head to toe in soot, rolled onto his feet, looking dazed. Where was Barnabas? Gone. He'd burned up, leaving nothing behind but ash in an empty suit.

William dashed away from the fat man's madly swinging slashes.

Just then, a thunderous *BANG* came from the rear of the cabin, followed by a shrill, metallic crack. The fat man looked dully at his hand. His blade had disintegrated above the brass duck-head handle.

Captain Kid stood at the open rear door, his rifle to his shoulder. Behind him, two uniformed train attendants covered their ears with their hands.

"Surrender!" the captain ordered.

The smoker woman shambled hairless toward him, the hole in her head filling the air with smoke. "You are cursed," she moaned. "The Red King will run you through with his horn."

The captain shot her outstretched hand, and the entire arm exploded in a gray plume.

She leaped into the air. Rather than crashing down again, she floated. "He'll eat your flesh and trample your dead bones." She hung there, a one-armed demonic apparition.

In my rush to get away, I crashed into the fat man, but like me, he only wanted to escape.

As the woman turned in the air, ash and smoldering chips of what might've been bone rained to the floor. Dawn, *God bless her*, snatched up the broken chessboard and hurled it at the demon woman for a second time. The board collided with her face, but this time her whole head became a cloud, sucked in the board, shredded it, and spit it out the bottom of her dress in a thousand splintered pieces.

Lights flickered in the coach, the bus filled with a sound like thunder, and just like that, the witch blew herself out. The storm ended with her silver dress dropping lifeless onto the pile of ashes and wood chips on the floor. Like Barnabas, she was gone.

The fat man pushed toward the door, but Captain Kid shot him point-blank, his melon-head popping like a smoke-filled balloon. If shooting him was the right thing to do, or even legal, I didn't know, but it seemed like a good idea.

Only one smoker remained, the skeletal magician. He stood at the front of the cabin, twirling his dagger between his fingers. He eyed me, perhaps thinking to take me prisoner again, but he was outnumbered, and the blow from the side table had screwed up his hip.

When he dropped the dagger into the sheath on his belt, ash drifted from the untucked tails of his shirt. "One piece of advice," smoke rose from his lips, "turn back. You will not save the fairy."

The captain shot him, but it didn't matter, he was already falling in a mound of ash and smoking clothes.

Drawing by Connor Poovey

# CHAPTER 23

# THE KNIGHT & THE DAGGER

When it was clear the magician wouldn't rise out of the ashes, the train attendants—both lovely, teenaged Asian girls—came in to thank us for getting rid of the terrible smokers. The girls bowed profusely and offered us candies from the pockets of their skirts. One of them opened a window to let out the smoke, then they went around cleaning up the mess.

Dawn joined them, William also, even Ozzie who was never one for chores, but I couldn't bring myself to help. I stepped on one of the scattered chess pieces, cursed under my breath, and kicked it into a corner. Then I noticed a fallen playing card on the floor, the same King of Hearts I'd seen falling from the magician's pocket.

*Ashes, cards*...the subjects of my vision, and now here they were, scattered across the carpet and dusting the overturned chairs. That part of my premonition had come true, but what of that last bit, the part about William; what was that about? I picked up the King, his glum face drawn with thin blue lines. What was he so sad about? And then I compared the face to William. I had to admit, there was a similarity if ignoring the king's shoulder-length hair and curled Amish-style beard.

*A coincidence, I'm sure...*

The drawing on the card made it look like the king's sword plunged into the back of his head. Was that also meaningless? The King of Hearts was always like that. That's why people called him the suicide king.

I let the card fall to the floor. *Let the maids pick it up.*

Dawn carried Barnabas's straight razor, holding it away from her in two fingers like the body of a dead mouse. She dropped it onto the man's clothes, and up puffed a wisp of smoke. Then she gathered the ash-caked laundry, stepped into a chair, and shoved the bundle through the open window.

Liking this idea, Ozzie took up the fat man's tattered suit and out it went. Then he used the opportunity to poke his own ash-dusted head outside. When he ducked back in, his black hair stood up at a crazy angle, but most of the soot was gone.

I rubbed my eyes. The open windows had filled the cabin with moist air from the tunnel—we were beneath the mountains now—but the sting of smoke lingered and so did the campfire smell.

Captain Kid collected the brooms from the train workers. "That's good enough, I think. Will you excuse us? Maybe finish later with help from the janitorial staff. For now, I want to meet with my knights."

"Oh, I see, I see," they said repeatedly. More bowing, then the girls backed out of the room, every subservient gesture made and obsessive courtesy shown.

The captain closed the door, propping the brooms against the wall beside his rifle. "Shut the windows and gather round." He scooped up the Silver Witch's torn and tattered dress, balled it, and tossed it out before Ozzie could seal us in with it.

As the dress billowed into the air and tumbled against the walls of the tunnel, through one of its tattered silver tears, I could see a thin loop of red. It was the witch's underwear. *Red to match her shoes.* That idea made my skin crawl.

We followed Captain Kid to the front of the car where he knelt next to the magician's empty suit.

Ozzie dusted off his hands on his pants. "What were those things?"

The captain flipped open the magician's coat with the point of his bone-handled knife. "What do you think they were?"

"Ghosts?" Ozzie guessed.

Captain Kid looked to me.

My dazed attention drifted to the closed windows. Beyond the glass, rocky walls sped past illuminated by yellow lights. We were in a mountain, deep underground like dwarves, but the figures who'd turned to smoke and disappeared were something very different.

Then a painful swell arose in my hand. I looked at the cut. Beneath my left thumb, a section of skin the size of a quarter peeled back, revealing the wet meat below. That part looked the worst, but the pain was throbbing out of a darker, narrow line at the base of the fiery red oval. That was where the magician's dagger sliced deepest. In all the excitement, and with adrenaline coursing through my veins, I'd all but forgotten about my injury.

Wet blood leaked down my fingers, and streaks of red stained the front of my shirt. During the skirmish, I'd thought of the woman as a witch, but I doubted that was right. Finally, I asked, "Were they vampires?"

The captain shook his head and sheathed his knife. He eyed William.

William was ready with an answer. "The molly-things. Like the Kybee boy said?"

The captain pulled the belt from the loops in the magician's striped pants. "The Molly Snatcher." Then discarding the belt, he took up the man's dagger. "The Molly Snatcher lives in water, but thanks for playing. They're phantoms."

I glanced at Ozzie, then to our leader. "Aren't phantoms the same as ghosts?"

"In your world, maybe, but usually ghosts are spirits of the dead. Phantoms are living illusions."

Ozzie huffed, "How can illusions have real clothes?"

"They're puppet masters." Captain Kid rubbed the lion face stamped into the black, metal scabbard. "The clothes are enchanted. So are the ashes."

"And the knife?" Ozzie reached for it. "Can I have it?"

Feeling my pocket, I considered my own feeble blade.

The captain closed his eyes, breathing deeply. When he opened them again, he said to Ozzie, "You can have it, but the phantoms aren't dead, ya know? The knife may draw them to you. The decision is yours."

Ozzie took the dagger. While the scabbard and guard were tarnished, the blade itself had a mirror finish. "Nah," he decided. "I got my bat with my stuff—should've had it with me, I guess." He offered the knife to William.

William shook his head, a vehement rejection, so Ozzie extended the knife to Dawn. Like William, she quickly turned it down.

Captain Kid took back the blade and stuck it in his pocket, the handle jutting out awkwardly. "For knights, you shy away from weapons. I hope that won't always be the case."

Ozzie stomped at the pile of clothes. "How did we beat them? I mean—like what made them go all ashy and burn out?"

The captain ruffled the vanished man's suit. "Phantoms make better assassins than street-fighters. Disrupt their puppetry and they use too much energy. They fall apart."

"Can they be killed?" I asked.

"Killed for a while." The captain stood up. Then putting his arms around Ozzie and Dawn, he smiled. "I've arranged beds in a sleeper car. We'll arrive in Atsuma in twelve hours. Let's rest while we can."

Just then, the speeding bus-train emerged from beneath the west side of the mountain range, washing the cabin in light too bright for my tired eyes. I blinked and rubbed my face then tried to focus on the dagger handle poking from the captain's pocket. He had to know I noticed when it wasn't offered to me.

Then a rebellious thought: *Why not take it?*

He was keeping it, so if it led the phantoms to us, what did it matter if the knife was with me instead of him? I fished the Swiss Army from my pants and tossed it to William.

Then, without asking, I pulled the dagger from Captain Kid's pocket. "I'll take it."

He offered me a subtle, thin-eyed nod that seemed to say, *I see, so that's how it'll be*, but if that was approval or disappointment, I couldn't tell.

I showed him the dagger, defiantly. "If I'm gonna be a knight, I'll have a proper knife—something made for fighting not just survival. You should've taken the mountain man's sabers when he offered them." I felt so angry, boiling over. The phantoms could've killed us. It wasn't fair to make us knights, to send us off into wild creation to face real monsters.

Ozzie looked at me with a quivering grin.

"What's so funny?" I demanded.

"Nothing," he sputtered. "It's just...it's just." He shook his head. "They were monsters, ya know. Remember, don't you wanna know how many heads they have?" He looked to William. "They only had one head each. I just thought about that. That's not so bad."

Then he tried to take the dagger from me. I wouldn't give it.

"That's enough!" Dawn commanded. She eyed the knife mistrustfully, proving she hadn't lost her wits like the boys in her company. Standing a little straighter, she said, "The captain's right, we should sleep." She turned to our leader, playing her role as first mate to perfection. "Sir, the crew is ready to lie down. Where are the beds?"

When the captain kept watching the dagger in my hand, I felt like it was heating up. We were playing hot-potato with a knife, and I was the sucker stuck holding it. But, no, I *chose* the knife, I wasn't *stuck* with it.

*Stuck with it, no. Sliced with it, yes.*

With that thought still in my mind, a troubling throb radiated from my palm. I unclasped my belt buckle, pulling free enough slack to slide the belt in through the opening on the back of the scabbard. When I finished, the weapon hung at the front of my hip much like the captain's own bone-handled blade. Only, mine was streaked with blood.

"Looks good on you," Captain Kid said. "Just remember the phantoms—to beat them, you must—"

"Disrupt their puppetry," I said. "I got it."

He nodded. "And we should do something about that cut. It looks bad. I have a first aid kit in my pack." He eyed the chief then turned toward the rear door that led to the jointed hall between the cars.

Would I be able to sleep knowing that phantoms could come calling anytime? The answer to that question was a resounding *yes*. In fact, the smoky apparitions were welcomed to show themselves again. I was a knight, a knight with a dagger. What did I have to fear from them? Then again, in my heart of hearts—at that moment, at least—I thought we'd live forever.

# CHAPTER 24

# WEST OF THE MOUNTAINS

I awoke in an upper bunk of our sleeper car. The shades were drawn, but daylight glowed in around the edges. I'd slept long and hard, but still, I wasn't ready to get up.

Rolling over, I slid open the sunshade to see the passing landscape had changed from barren desert to hills of luscious green grass with trees down in the meadows. In less than a minute, I'd spotted hundreds of cows, a few dozen roaming horses, and a flock of sheep. These were beautiful animals to behold, a welcomed change from the desert with hardly any life at all. I lay there for quite a while, not moving, just looking out the window and trying not to think of home.

Occasionally, we'd pass large houses set away by themselves on scenic hilltops. The houses looked modern, squared off with loads of windows, the kind my mother liked to look at in magazines.

We came to a town next, pausing at their absurdly long bus stop. Two people got on. No one got off. Then we were moving again. There wasn't much to the community, just a square in the middle of town, but parked at a corner store, I spotted a van like Mom's Dodge. It was even the same color, white with tinted windows. A little while later, I saw a truck like Grampa's Ford. That was interesting, and farther along in front of a home that looked half-a-castle, there was a miniaturized Corvette. It was a convertible painted beautiful metallic bronze with chrome bumpers. Grownups would not fit in a car that size.

*The owner must be a kid.* That was a strange idea to have about such an automobile, not to mention the house.

Leaving the town behind, I rolled away from the window.

Dawn was awake in the bunk below me. I heard her moving. When I leaned down to check on her, she pointed to something outside. "Look."

I slid off my bed and ducked to see what she was talking about. A sign at the side of the road read, *Atsuma 218 km.*

"How far is that in miles?" she asked.

I slipped in beside her. She had her backpack open and a sketch pad out. "I don't know," I said. "Less than two hundred. Maybe one-seventy, but that's a guess." I looked at her paper.

She'd drawn a cartoon girl jumping over a snake. The girl wore shorts and a vest covered with patches. She had a red backpack. The girl was holding a magic sword—*magic* because of the green light rays shooting off it.

"It's good," I said, smiling.

Across the aisle, William and Ozzie were still passed out in their bunks.

"Where's the captain?" I asked.

Dawn shrugged. "Dunno. He left a while ago." Her pencil moved across the page, stopped, then spun in her fingers to make use of the eraser. After brushing eraser shavings onto her bed covers, she closed the sketchbook and looked me in the eyes. "I took a walk a while ago and saw a girl...*checking under her pillow.* She was looking for a patch. She had a jacket with patches sewn on the sleeves. I saw lots of kids with patches."

Now that she'd mentioned it, I had, too. Only, with everything else that was happening, it hadn't registered. "Guess they haven't heard the fairy's kidnapped. That's a depressing thought."

Dawn took her spiral notebook from her backpack. "You wanted to know about the meeting with the painter?"

"The Man of the Mountain—sure I do. Can you tell me?" I'd asked her in the desert, but that wasn't the time or place.

She looked down the hallway to check the door. No Captain Kid. "I think so," she said. "It wasn't much. The man didn't know about the kidnapping, either."

I scooted closer to her. "Did he see Castatine?"

Dawn nodded slowly. "He said she looked dog-tired. She spent two nights in the little prayer dome—I think you guys went in there. When he asked her about the crossing, she clammed up. That was the last they spoke until she left. Then he only said, 'goodbye.'"

"Anything else?" I asked.

She flipped open her notebook. "Some stuff about Atsuma. He said it was seven hundred miles away. The king lives there. He's called...*Katsuro*." She pronounced the name carefully, a hard *K* and a little roll of her tongue in the middle.

The title *King* filled my head with heroic imagery.

Her finger tapped a pair of words written in all caps beside the king's name. "He's called, *THE DESTROYER*."

"Katsuro *the Destroyer?*" I asked.

She grimaced. "That's who we're going to see."

I sat back against the wall. "Fantastic. First werewolves, then phantoms, now this."

She sighed. "I know. Bad, right? And get this, I spoke with Captain Kid this morning. He's worried about the phantoms. He said if they're looking for us, this whole thing's worse than he thought."

To that unwelcomed news, all I could do was groan.

Without thinking, I picked at the bandage on my left hand. Dawn had helped wrap it after the skirmish with the phantoms. Now her eyes kept returning to her work, checking to make sure I wasn't bleeding again. Thankfully, I wasn't.

However, my bandage wasn't the only thing she was checking. "I was surprised you wanted that thing." She was referring to the dagger leaning across my lap.

I rolled my eyes. "I should've chucked it out the window."

"Why don't you?"

I felt the corded handle. "I don't know. Maybe I will." I hesitated. "Can I ask you a question, a weird one?"

"Sure."

I lowered my voice and nodded to William sleeping in the bunk across from us. "Notice anything...*odd* about him?"

Her eyes narrowed, an expression that meant, *What's this about?* After considering our friend, she looked to me again and shook her head. "No. Why?"

"Man, this is so weird." I scratched the back of my neck. "When we were in the Smokers' Cabin, I had a...I don't know what—like a vision or something. Did you have that?"

"No," she said emphatically. "But you were acting strange."

"I know." I pulled my knees against my chest. "It was almost like I'd been there before, but it was different...*William* was different."

"How?" A subtle sternness came into her voice. She sounded like my chief officer rather than my friend.

The truth was, it felt like I was going crazy, or like someone was trying to break into my mind, but I didn't want to tell that to the chief. She'd think me unfit for duty. Reluctantly, I admitted, "He looked a little different is all. You didn't see that?"

"No, I didn't, but I'll tell the captain."

"I don't think so—I just needed a good night's sleep." As evidence, I rubbed my eyes and yawned.

As if on cue, William turned over, rolling his pillow onto the floor.

When he looked up, Dawn reached a leg across the aisle and shoved his arm with her foot. "Wakey-wakey eggs and bakey."

William eyed the bottom of her foot, his nose crinkling. "Your sock's filthy."

She pulled it across her lap to look at the sole, then showed it to me. He was right, it was black with grime. But she hadn't bathed in three days, other than the little bit of washing we'd done at the bathroom sinks before packing it in for the night.

William pulled open his sunshade to inspect our new environment. We were in wide-open ranch land again. He kicked the bunk over him. "Wake up, fart stain. We're here."

Ozzie's head jerked up, narrowly missing the ceiling. He wiped his nose with his whole arm and glared one-eyed across the aisle out my top-bunk window. His own shade was still drawn. "Thisss-is-Atsuma?" he slurred.

I thumbed over my shoulder. "Yeah, the middle of the country. I think the king is that cow over there."

Ozzie's one open eye blinked. "Shut up. I'm going back to sleep."

William booted the upper bunk again. "I'm hungry. Let's see what they got to eat around here." That was William, always thinking with his stomach.

It was really him, and whatever strange ideas I'd had around the phantoms, those could not be trusted. The phantoms were magicians—one of them, anyway. My vision had been a trick of the light. Of course, it was. Perfectly logical, the only problem was I couldn't quite believe it.

Way down deep, I heard a murmured suggestion, a disturbing whisper, coming up from the basement in my head. *Was that the first time I saw William change like that? Be honest.*

No, I didn't think it was…

*Nonsense.* The phantoms were screwing with my head again. This was their secret warfare, my price for taking their stupid knife. William was my best friend, so they were trying to shake my trust in him. Surely, that was all.

After learning our upgraded tickets included full-service meals in the dining car, we happily ate as much as our shrinking bellies would hold. The food served wasn't as fancy as the white linen tablecloths suggested, but that was fine with us.

Having slept through breakfast, Ozzie and I ordered fried chicken, William a roast beef sandwich, and Dawn a bowl of wedding soup with french-fries. When our first courses were finished, we started on seconds. Only then, at a lull in the conversation, was I brave enough to broach the delicate matter of our departure from this world.

"Soooooo," I began, dragging the word out until I had the attention of my friends. "I've been thinking about this a lot, guys. I know you're not gonna like it, but if we don't find the fairy when we get to Atsuma, we need to go home."

"You homesick?" William asked.

"I am, but that has nothing to do with it. It's not like we're out camping. We've run away." I looked to Dawn.

She raked a fry through a puddle of ketchup, making swirl patterns on her plate. "I know. I bet my parents are flipping out."

I sat straight. "All of our parents. You know they called the police. Bet you anything there's a big investigation."

William turned an unused fork in his fingers. "What will we tell them when we get back?"

"I don't know," I confessed. "They'd never believe the truth."

Surprisingly, Ozzie didn't immediately protest the very notion of going home. Instead, he sniffled, almost like he might cry. "My mom, ah-man. You know she watches all those crime shows." His face became a mask of torment, his voice taking on the sound of a desperate, elderly woman. "Ozzie Ernesto was such a good boy. Why'd somebody have to take him away?" He shook his head. "She probably thinks we're chained up in some freakshow's basement about to get ax-murdered." He looked to Dawn, nodding with importance. "Except you."

"Why not me?" Dawn asked.

Ozzie blushed, pressing his lips into a squirmy line.

William answered for him. "Cause you're a girl. Girls get worse than killed."

"Oh, crap." Dawn's hand shot to her mouth like she wanted to put the words back in.

I turned to her. "You haven't thought about that?"

"NO!" She swatted my arm. "Why would I? Men are so *gross!*"

I sat forward. It was now or never. "What do you say, guys? We need to stick together."

William prodded his second half-eaten sandwich with the fork. "How would we even find our way without Captain Kid? You know we can't go back through that door in the desert."

I leaned in closer and waited for them to mimic my posture. "I thought of that." After checking over my shoulder, I continued. "If he doesn't let us go, we have to get his compass."

Dawn frowned. "You mean we have to *steal* it?"

"I hope not, but if he means to strand us here, we have to do something."

"*Ugh.*" She sounded sick. "I wanted to help the Patch Fairy."

"Me, too." Then putting a hand to my heart, "I did. I still do, but maybe we did enough just helping Captain Kid get here. You didn't think about that, either, did you? How was he gonna fly that shuttle all by himself?"

"He wasn't," William admitted.

Dawn tucked hair behind her ears then peered at me with concentration. "If you're leaving, I'll go, too, but I don't like it."

Ozzie shook his head. "Sorry, folks, me and Captain Kid got a date with destiny. When we find Castatine, I'm gonna clock her with my Louisville Slugger."

William slapped the back of Ozzie's head. "You actually think that'll happen? Charles is right. She's gone. She can go to other worlds, and you heard what the phantom said—Nightmare will run us through with his horn." Then sounding even more surly, he slumped in his chair. "He probably knows we're coming."

Ozzie gave him an evil scowl. "Then I'll clock him, too."

Dawn reached for Ozzie's hand, but he pulled away. "Sorry, Oz," she said. "They're right. We're just kids."

Ozzie leaned his chair back on two legs, extending his hands to his sides. "Have you seen this place—they're all kids." He let his chair crash down then took off his hat, scrubbing his greasy hair into a rat's nest. "I don't know. This place is so awesome. I finally feel like I'm doing something good." He stared at us. "You don't feel that?"

The problem was, we did.

Ozzie looked each of us in the eyes then poked the table with a finger. "I'll agree under one condition. We're not gonna ditch Captain Kid. He's the coolest guy I ever met. If we're going home, you have to tell him." His eyes narrowed, waiting for my response.

"Fine," I said.

After that, there was little to say. We sat in silence for another ten minutes, picking at our food. Our waitress came to check our progress, not rushing us, but went around clearing the empty plates. She looked no older than twelve. For a uniform, she wore a modest gray and white dress with a name tag that read, *LaMeg*. Dawn commented that the two of them had the same color hair, and the girl seemed to appreciate that.

When the waitress left, finally Captain Kid appeared. He strolled casually into the dining car, plucked a chair away from an unoccupied table, and scooted in between William and Ozzie. "Good morning?" The way he said it sounded like a question.

Cleaning beneath his fingernails with my Swiss Army knife, William eyed our leader. "Where've you been?"

Captain Kid nodded toward the front of the bus. "The railing out by the middle engine. That thing's a monster. There's a diagram that shows how it works, drive shafts going in both directions, forward and aft." He snagged a piece of untouched fried chicken off Ozzie's plate. "Six engines in all. Cool, huh?" He took a bite. "We should start seeing more towns now."

Nursing the watery remains of her lemonade, Dawn said, "We saw one a little while ago. It wasn't much."

"Trail Head Ranch." Captain Kid tugged a sliver of meat from the chicken bone, his amber eyes studying our faces. When his inspection finished, he raised an eyebrow at the chief officer. "What spoiled your moods?"

Dawn glanced to me, but I had the feeling her eye movement was involuntary.

I coughed for no reason, deciding to expose our mutiny in a roundabout way. "So, Captain, what's the plan when we get to Atsuma?"

"We'll go see King Katsuro." He worked the side of his jaw like he had a piece of meat stuck between his teeth.

"Then what?" I asked.

He wasn't quick to answer. "I don't know, Charles. Why do you ask?"

I was becoming defensive again. I could feel it, and beneath that ran a hot current of anger, an emotion that was becoming all too familiar. "Oh, no reason," I said. "But the king will have people to help you find the Patch Fairy, right? The police will help, or—*heck*, I don't know, the army or something. Somebody besides us."

Captain Kid tossed the chicken bone onto Ozzie's plate and wiped his hands on a napkin. "I get the feeling our electro-technical officer isn't much for adventures."

Leaning forward, my hands braced the table. "I'm not much for running away from home to find a psycho, kidnapping girl." I scanned my friends' faces. "If we don't find the fairy in Atsuma—by tomorrow—we're going home. All of us." I stared into the captain's eyes, but his expression was unflustered.

He leaned back in his chair, hanging an arm over the seatback. "So, you've talked about this without me? Fascinating. Charles, I'd be tempted to call you 'chicken', but you just want what's best for our crew. I admire that... Also, I'd say you were right, if not for one thing."

Feeling blood heat my face, "And what's that?" I asked.

"Magic," he said. "We're dealing with magic." Now he was talking not just to me but to the whole crew. "I can't expect the four of you to recognize that, having never lived with magic in your whole lives—not magic you understood."

His eyes drifted skyward. "Remember I said the shuttle was built by a wizard? It changes to challenge those who dare ride it. All of you faced fears." His face brightened. "For me, my test was getting this crew together and trusting you to do your jobs. Other than that, my part was easy." He smiled, his voice quieting. "Notice there was no seat for Marshal Rayban? That's because he wasn't going with us."

"And the bracket on the wall!" Dawn exclaimed. "It fit Joseph's aquarium perfectly."

The captain made a checkmark in the air with his finger. "Quite right."

I could feel my argument unraveling.

The captain's eyes moved in my direction. "As to your suggestion about going home, I submit to you a possibility, that perhaps you're not *meant* to go home. In fact, you're supposed to be just where you are, with me and your friends...whom you care so much about."

I sensed he would offer me his hand, to shake on it, and if that happened, my line of questioning would be cut off. I wasn't ready for that. "We're not going to find the fairy in Atsuma, are we?"

"I doubt it," Captain Kid said. "The problem is two-fold. First, she has at least a seven-day head start. Second, the phantoms."

"What about the phantoms?" William asked, looking from the Swiss Army knife in his hand to the boy he was speaking to.

"Powers are at work," the captain said. "Big ones. Dark powers, maybe even the black unicorn himself."

William's voice was dead calm, his expression flat. "In the Red."

Dawn reached across the table, touching the captain's arm. "But we're not going there, are we?"

With a new, disheartened inflection in his voice, Captain Kid looked to her. "I'm not planning on it."

Clearly, the idea of facing the unicorn bothered him, but there was something else, too. When I said we would leave him tomorrow, none of my friends disputed me. Our quest was coming to an end. The young captain would have to do the hard part without us. For that, I felt sorry for him.

When our waitress came around again, the captain ordered us another round of drinks. We weren't thirsty, but we weren't in a hurry, either. The Great City was still a ways off and the dining car chairs more comfortable than the regular bus seats.

Like most large cities, Atsuma had outlying towns, some large enough to be cities unto themselves. The first sizable community we came to was Big Baby Lake, after that LaDingo. As the bus-train passed through these places, we watched out the windows for billboards promoting products and TV shows we'd never heard of.

There was one show called *Yosioto* that seemed to be about a barbarian warrior and his dragon—right up my alley—and another called *Waygate 9*. That last show looked like a rip-off of *Quantum Leap*. The star of *Waygate 9* even looked like a Japanese version of Scott Bakula, tall with the same haircut and even wore a brown leather flight jacket.

Most of the signs, however, were not for shows, but advertisements for colas, cigarettes, and real estate developments. A sign for a new-construction housing community boasted a total lack of ghosts, a real selling feature. The Attic's monsters were also catered to. There was a Coke lookalike called Howl and a blood drink that came in a jug, the packaging and logo baring eerie resemblance to a V8 tomato juice bottle. To lighten the mood, William and Ozzie ordered those.

The waitress popped the top off the Howl, which came in a glass bottle, and set the drink on the tablecloth in front of William. He raised the beverage to his nose, sniffed, then put it to his lips. He sipped, cautiously, then took a longer drink.

When he lowered the bottle again, he said, "Tastes like Dr. Pepper. Not what I was expecting, but it's good."

The waitress bowed, smiling, and offered Ozzie the blood drink.

He twisted off the cap, "Here goes," and put the open mouth of the bottle to his nose. He recoiled, thrusting the juice away. "No-can-do. Uh-uh. No way I'm tryin' that."

The waitress apologized and offered to replace it with a Sprite, but Ozzie said that wasn't necessary. Instead, he passed the bottle around to his curious and amused crewmates.

I had a different curiosity. Before the waitress excused herself, I asked for the cap from the bottle of Howl. She placed it in my hand, showing me respect I was not used to. When she bowed to me, I nodded to her, and she backed away. Then my attention turned to the circle of metal in my hand. The cap was red and bent in the middle across the white, cursive Howl logo. As a matter of fact, it was a perfect Attic-of-the-World echo of the Coka-Cola bottle cap I'd lost out of my pocket.

The blood drink made its way around to me, and I smelled it with a reaction much like Ozzie's. "I think it's actual blood," I said, passing it to Dawn.

She wanted to read the ingredients label, but that was written in Japanese or Mandarin—some language that used slashing, box characters instead of an alphabet.

"Look at that." Ozzie nodded to the window.

Outside, a sign read, *Come see the Wizard in Olly Land's new Black Castle.* The text was in blue wavy letters, the word *Wizard* standing out, bordered in white sparkles. Below the message, the image of a jagged hilltop fortress cast its dark reflection onto a shimmering lake.

"Olly Land's an amusement park," Captain Kid explained.

"So, it isn't real—not a real wizard?" Ozzie asked.

A robotically feminine voice came over the bus speakers. "Thank you for choosing C. C. Road Masters for your migratory needs. We hope you have enjoyed the trip. Please, be seated as we enter Atsuma, the Great City, as the bus may experience unanticipated stops. We expect to arrive at Atsuma Super Terminal in ten minutes. Again, thank you, and we look forward to serving you in the future." Then the message repeated in other languages.

# CHAPTER 25

# THE GREAT CITY

Stepping off the bus at the terminal station, we pressed past the moving throng of disembarking passengers. When we gathered out of the stream of bodies, Captain Kid checked us over—no one forgot their backpack, glasses, or baseball bat, nothing silly like that.

Satisfied, "This way," he said and led us to a promenade where travelers could stretch their legs in the open air.

It was good to be outside. The air was pleasantly warm, not hot, and seasoned with peppery spice and the smell of frying fish from food truck vendors parked along the walkway. One truck was a Mercedes of the same vintage and spec as the one summoned to our neighborhood by Captain Kid. The workers at this one, however, were a boy and girl, rather than grown men. They sold three things by the look of it: cheese wedges, bottled milk, and colorful crocheted hats.

"That's cute." Dawn leaned against me, pointing to a little girl with a stocking cap so large it swallowed half her head.

Cute, sure, but my attention was drifting toward the first real view of the city. Behind us, the hustle of the terminal faded; along the left side of the walkway, the food vendors and makeshift shops-on-wheels welcomed us to Atsuma with pleasing smells and inviting wares; but ahead, a panorama of skyscrapers emerged as the narrow promenade widened into a lakeside park.

Back home, Jacksonville was a decent-sized city. I lived in the suburbs, but we went downtown often enough that the sight of a cityscape no longer provoked a sense of wonder. Even so, Jacksonville was nothing like Atsuma.

The building closest to us, built at the far bank of the water, rose squarely from the ground then tapered with sloping angles to its pinnacle. The shape of it, and the way light reflected from its silver-tinted glass, made the whole thing look carved from a giant chunk of crystal. Next to it, a building was all black. That one split near the top into two spires, one higher than the other. Some of the buildings were flat-topped. One had red glass, another had blue, more were gold and copper-colored. Other buildings were brick with regular clear windows like on houses. On one such, brightly colored flags lined the rooftop. All in all, it was a cheerful, hopeful sight.

Near the waterside, travelers set down their bags and suitcases to have their pictures taken. They had arrived in the Great City and wanted to share this moment with their friends and to preserve the memory for future generations.

"Look at that," William said.

A policeman strode across the grass, his hands on his belt, his eyes scrutinizing the faces and postures of people passing by. Nothing unusual about that, except he had a sword on his back. *A sword.*

I looked again to the groups of picture-takers—either tourists or immigrants—then to the figures moving away from the bus terminal in slow droves. The police swordsman was a grownup, and there was a lady in her sixties talking on a payphone, but all the other thousand faces were kids or, at most, teenagers.

*Not a place for grownups.* I knew that, but so many kids unattended took some getting used to. Why was it not total chaos? Why hadn't the city descended into a tribal gangland? The structures were not rundown, the park not overgrown. In my world, any city left to the upkeep of kids would return to the earth in a mountain of vines or runaway fires would burn it to ashes. The answer must've been that many of the people who looked so young were grownups, in age if not in body. Some force kept them children, like Neverland, the captain said. It had something to do with the worm plague, but was it genetic? Magic? Anything was possible. For all I knew, happy-gas lingering in the air stunted the people's growth.

I sniffed. No gas that I could detect, but somewhere nearby, someone was frying an egg. I touched the captain's arm and nodded to the old woman at the phone.

He looked that way. "A grownup, I know. I saw her."

"That's not what I'm talking about." When I had his attention, I continued. "She's talking on a payphone. Shouldn't you call the king?"

"We're here now, may as well go see him in person." He shrugged. "Plus, it'll take hours to get through to him on the phone. Best to go to the palace and knock on the gate."

Dawn found her camera in her backpack, a little yellow and black Kodak disposable. "We should take our picture," she said.

Captain Kid looked from her to the policeman. "Okay, but let's hurry."

We piled our backpacks on a bench, and Dawn handed off her camera to a girl tourist who knew just what to do with it. As the girl raised the Kodak to her face, I saw the shirt beneath her paisley vest was lined with merit badges.

"Say cheese," the girl said. The way she said *cheese*, it rhymed with *geese—Say cheese*. The camera flashed. "Have fun in *Atsuma*." She spoke the name of the city in an accent even more pronounced than Dawn's interpretation. The *tsu*-sound blew past her tongue like a dart from a blowgun.

Dawn bowed to her, which seemed to be the custom. The girl bowed in return, a pair of smiley-face earrings dangling at the sides of her face. Dawn took back the camera, and the girl turned away, her cheeks rosy as she met eyes with William.

Dawn lifted the camera and snapped a quick picture of my best friend, probably because he looked too cute blushing at the girl. Then she lowered the camera, winding the crank with her thumb. The little gears inside made a plasticy ratcheting sound. I wished she had taken more pictures, some of the Nautilus space shuttle and Salvation Mountain, but I guessed she'd forgotten about her camera until now.

She looked to me next, then to Ozzie. I guess Ozzie and I weren't picture worthy because she moved on to the captain. "Smile," she said.

Captain Kid offered the warmest, most innocent smile ever seen on the face of a boy. His eyebrows lifted, his mouth bending with awkward playfulness. Sunlight illuminated his eyes, and his cheeks were as red and merry as Santa's.

Dawn took the picture. Her camera clicked, and just like that—*poof*—the boyish lights in the captain's eyes blinked out and he was our leader again, in charge, and turning to speak with the police officer.

The policeman stopped in front of us, a serious look on his angular face. He pointed with the arrow of black whiskers on his chin. "You Captain Kid?" The hilt of his sword stood over his shoulder. Like on a ninja sword, broad laces wrapped the handle. Yet, even in cartoons, I'd never seen a ninja in a police uniform, much less one who wore glasses.

Captain Kid adjusted the rifle resting on his shoulder. *The rifle.* He'd been carrying it around so long I scarcely even noticed it anymore. What was he doing? Reaching for a gun was how people got shot in dealings with police.

But the policeman wasn't bothered, and Captain Kid's hand continued to rise until his finger touched the brim of his hat. He tipped it forward. "It is I, Captain Kid, at your service."

Around us, the passerby travelers took notice. One tourist turned the long lens of his camera our way and started snapping pictures.

The policeman began again in his clipped accent, "Sir Kid, you are wanted in the palace of King Katsuro." Then he looked to the rest of us. "Where is Marshal Rayban?"

"He couldn't come," Dawn answered.

The uniformed man glared at her doubtfully. "No?" He eyed our leader.

The captain's lips tightened. "The chief answered you. Why do you look at me?"

The officer huffed, "Enough talk. You must come with me."

Captain Kid stepped closer to the man. "First, tell me how you knew we were coming?"

The officer considered his answer. He breathed deep. Something about this exchange had ruffled his feathers. At last, when he spoke, it was in a menacing whisper. "The cyclops saw you coming. Come now. We do not want to keep them waiting."

# CHAPTER 26

# THE BLUE SKULLS

As we followed the ninja-policeman to the street, two more officers came over to flank us. One wore a sword on his hip instead of his back. The other's hat was red. Perhaps that signified his rank. We rounded a café to find a line of squad cars parked by the curb, their engines left running, just like the cop cars in Jacksonville. But ahead of them was a sight quite different from any municipal procession I was used to.

A classic, gloss-black Lincoln convertible led the convoy of police cruisers. Riding in it, half-a-dozen caped warriors carried assault rifles. These men had black Samurai helmets with blue, skull-faced masks.

*The Blue Skulls.* The boy in the Doloptree diner had mentioned these in his short list of grownups. But if they were here to escort us to the palace or kill us before we got there, I wasn't entirely sure.

An all-black, full-size van rolled past the police cars and pulled in behind the convertible. As we approached, the side door slid open, and our escort hurried us aboard. Captain Kid took the front passenger seat beside a blue-skulled driver. Dawn and Ozzie sat behind him. William and I took the next row. In the far back, two more Blue Skulls occupied the rear bench seat. One of those was a woman.

The driver put a radio handset to the mouth of his skeleton mask and said something that might've been Japanese. Then he turned to our leader.

To my surprise, when he wasn't speaking the foreign language, he sounded like one of the islanders from the food truck. "Aye, Captain, good to see you, sir. It's been a long time since you's come round to the Attic of da World."

"Indeed, it has," Captain Kid said, "I wish the circumstances were different. How's this new king of yours?"

We pulled out into the street behind the Lincoln full of warriors in flying capes. Police cars were filing in alongside us and behind in a line of flashing blue lights.

Our driver checked his mirrors, both hands on the wheel. Between the front seats, a short-barreled pump shotgun stood in a mount. "Katsuro da Destroyer is wise."

Ozzie, always willing to say whatever crossed his mind, asked, "He done much *destroying* lately?" He was leaning on his baseball bat, the slugging end down between his feet.

Captain Kid raised a disapproving eyebrow at his assistant engineer—maybe not disapproving, maybe just interested to hear Ozzie interact with the grownup warrior.

The driver laughed behind his blue-skull face but didn't answer.

I chanced a backward glance to have a better look at the masked woman. When I met her eyes, she looked away, back out the windows to the passing cars, storefronts, and all the many people turning to watch our procession. The blue cheekbones of her mask were painted with golden stars and hearts. Across her lap, her gloved hands closed on a blue-painted Uzi, the snub-nosed barrel brightest gold, so was the folding stock. Who was this woman?

The man next to her was no less accessorized. From the eyes of his mask flowed painted silver tears—*for all the people he killed*—and his samurai helmet had white enamel-coated horns. He wore necklaces dangling with crosses, bracelets with skulls, and his cape had a clasp made of gold shaped like a man and woman kissing. For his weapons, he had chromed-out handguns strapped to his thighs and a compact assault rifle in his hands, all polished to a mirror finish. They looked like the kind of assassins Cobra Commander would hire to hunt down the G.I. Joes.

Fortunately, for all the theatrics of our escorts, our transit was undramatic. No shots fired from alleyways or black-clad ninjas leaping down off rooftops. No monsters, either. Not even bad traffic. The lanes of cars ahead of us divided, and we sped past without so much as slowing down. I watched out the windows for threats and saw none. Only the strangeness of the city made me uncomfortable but in a curious way.

There were kid-sized mannequins in shop windows and hundreds of boys and girls on bicycles in the streets and driving strange, miniature cars. When our convoy left the shopping district, we came to a part of the city where every building looked at least a hundred years old. There were three-tiered Japanese dojos with sloped tile roofs that curved out to long, pointed corners, and there were colonial mansions, and trendy-looking coffee shops and bars.

*Bars*. Why, in a world populated by children, would there be bars?

Maybe they only served soda and milkshakes.

As we passed beneath a cluster of old-growth trees, Dawn claimed to see a monkey hiding in the branches. Why not in a world like this? Next, we might see a load of kids riding a yellow elephant home from school.

Shortly after the second monkey sighting, we arrived at the palace gate, tall and black, made of iron, and framed in an arch of gigantic golden roses. There were guards to either side of the gate. Like our driver, they wore skeletal masks of blue. Through the bars of the gate, in stark contrast to the deadly presence of the skull-faces, I saw girls on the green lawn in gold dresses, a hundred of them, easily. They moved in unison between practiced poses, either Yoga, or Tai Chi, or some other discipline I didn't understand.

As the huge iron gate began to open, William sang, "Off to see the king."

Ozzie chimed, "The wonderful king of Atsuma."

Then Dawn, "because, because, because, because, becauuuuuuuse …" She looked to me to complete their improvised jingle.

I tried to smile. "Because of the wonderful things he *destroys*."

An irrefutable energy buzzed in the atmosphere, like something super important was about to happen. Yet, I felt that familiar hole in my stomach deepening into a pit. This could be the part of the story where the runaway children got eaten alive, or turned into zombies, or entered a gladiator-style deathmatch.

Dawn rolled her eyes.

"Sorry, Chief," I said, "but with a handle like Katsuro the Destroyer, what do you expect?"

"He's only a man," the captain said from the front seat, "but an important one. You will show him respect."

As the gate swung out from beneath the arch of roses, I saw for the first time the blue-tiled roof and snow-white stonework of the palace.

The captain waved a hand before our eyes, returning our attention to his face. "Once inside, follow my lead. Do what I do. If I bow, you bow. If I call someone *sir*, you do the same. If I say *Your Majesty* and take a knee, that's what you'll do. Understand?"

We all nodded.

Ozzie asked, "You think this king will help find a fairy from another world?"

"I hope so." Captain Kid looked to the palace. "If you were staying, I'd ask him to help you, too, but...not if you're leaving tomorrow."

Even though the remark was spoken to Ozzie, I was its true target.

"What could he do for me?" Ozzie asked.

The captain took out his compass and tossed it to him. "He could fix your busted compass."

Here was our chance, to have the compass without stealing it, but he'd given it to Ozzie who was the shakiest member of our conspiracy.

"*My* compass?" Ozzie stared at the instrument.

"Sure." The captain faced forward again. "And he could arm you for battle."

Ozzie turned in his seat, scowling at me, his spoil-sport friend.

I mouthed the words, *No way*.

The up and down motions of his head firmly disagreed.

We looked to William, who refused to give a signal either way, then turned to Dawn to be the tiebreaker.

Scooting to the edge of her seat, she snubbed her responsibility to settle the dispute and leaned toward the captain instead. "When we're inside, can we ask questions?"

The van stopped, and Captain Kid opened his door. "Questions are welcome. So are comments." He looked to his boy knights. "As long as they're not silly ones."

Ozzie grinned idiotically.

"Get that out of your system, First Assistant Engineer."

Dawn pulled open the sliding door and stepped out. Ozzie followed.

I climbed out onto the pavement, watching the girls in gold dresses continue their smooth, meditative poses. Then looking to the palace, I saw a pathway of white marble dividing a yard as green as any ballpark. At the end of the white lane, gleaming steps led to a pair of king-sized blue doors set into the white walls of the palace. Great pillars beset the doors and standing between them was the strangest monster I'd yet seen in my visit to this wondrous new world. It was a cyclops.

*Oh yes*, and he was holding a massive war-hammer in his leathery fists.

# CHAPTER 27

# THE CYCLOPS

As we approached the palace, Dawn groaned at the sight of the hideous monster. Then she gripped my arm as if I could protect her from the colossus with my measly dagger.

Standing at the top of the steps, the creature waited for us. His head was the size of a watermelon, grisly, bald, and topped by a single stunted horn. Above his flaring nostrils, he looked out at the world through one great eye, red as a stop sign and white in the center. The gigantic cyclops wore shaggy animal fur around his waist, but nothing else besides silver bracelets and sandals with straps that wrapped his lower legs. We had faced monsters already, but the phantoms and Kybees could pass as human. Not so with this one.

As the captain drew near, the giant lifted the hammer, which must have weighed two hundred pounds, and let the shaft of the handle come down into his open left hand. *Thwap.*

Did he intend to smash us into boney puddles or drive us into the ground like tent stakes? The captain had a gun but using it might only make the cyclops angry.

When the monster spoke, his words crashed down on us like falling boulders. "Captain Kid, I knew you were coming. I saw you in Doloptree waiting for the bus."

"Oh?" the captain replied, as cool as ever. "You should've sent a car for us."

The monster's broad, frowning mouth spread into a smile. "The bus is faster. Come. I will show you to Katsuro." His lumbering body rotated toward the blue double-doors. I imagined him smashing the entrance open with a haphazard swing from that terrible black hammer, but he grasped the door handle instead, turning it with care.

He was on our side, or so it seemed, but he was still a monster. I didn't like him.

As we entered the palace, Ozzie looked up at the one-eyed creature and asked, "If you were in Doloptree, why didn't we see you? No offense, but a giant cyclops is hard to miss."

When the monster answered, I could see his sharpened rows of teeth. "No, boy, I was not in that Podunk-snot-clop. I *saw* you." With a massive finger, he pointed to the misshapen white iris at the center of his singular red eye, as if that explained all. The giant faced the gallery, directing us forward with the head of his hammer.

We entered a room that was several stories tall. Along the walls, narrow windows let warm daylight cast in upon the marble floor. Between windows, life-like paintings decorated the gallery walls, some of battles while others were portraits of kings and queens. In one such picture, a man sat in a straight-backed chair, his eyes shaded beneath a lacey, wide-brimmed hat.

I went to the picture.

The painted figure had a violet and gold checkered shirt and tight-fitting striped pants. His clothes were ridiculous, but the katana resting across his lap was beautiful. The curved scabbard was a brilliant turquoise, the handguard and other metal fitments bright silver.

A placard mounted below the frame labeled the man, King Andabo the Destroyer who reigned from 1646 to 1670.

"Another Destroyer," I said. "What's up with that?"

William came to me and glanced at the painting through his sunglasses. "Don't know, but we're about to find out." He nodded to the others waiting for us in the center of the room.

They stood near a cluster of chairs arranged so palace visitors could sit while admiring the artwork. I imagined women in fancy dresses and men in tuxedoes milling about and laughing at mean-spirited jokes. Someone would play music on the room's grand piano, Castatine, perhaps. She was a piano player.

This felt like a trap.

I looked to Dawn and Ozzie, then to the captain with his monstrous companion; I didn't want to go with them. The king was probably a tyrant on a throne of gold. I had no interest in meeting someone like that. Also, I wasn't ready to follow the hammer-toting cyclops. He was a *for-real* monster and my friends had accepted him as readily as any new kid in class. Not I.

The cyclops had sharp, pointed teeth. There was only one reason to have teeth like that: he was a predator.

I pointed to the painting. "Why's he called *the Destroyer?*"

Captain Kid tilted his head, annoyance showing through those amber crystal eyes.

I threw up my hands. "Why are you looking at me like that?" I marched to the next portrait on the wall. "See him? He's a Destroyer, too. Don't act like I'm the only one who thinks this is odd."

The cyclops rumbled, "They are all Destroyers, kings or queens, but the sword itself is the ruler of Atsuma."

"The Destroyer Blade," Captain Kid offered. *So generous of him,* but like everything else he said, it meant nothing to me. I looked down the wall, noticing the same sword in every portrait. Whether king or queen, the sword was the same, a long katana in a turquoise-blue scabbard, the handguard and hilt decorated with silver.

The cyclops looked to the far corner of the room, then back to me with his red eye. *Red like blood. Red like Dawn's backpack. Red like Darth Vader's lightsaber.* I wanted to yell at them all.

The monster held out his hand. "Come with me. The king is on his throne. I will show you to the Presence Chamber."

Captain Kid had that miniaturized gunslinger look again, his eyebrows rolling into a slanted squint.

"How can a sword rule a kingdom?" I pleaded.

The way the cyclops and captain looked at each other, I feared I would be demoted all the way down to senior butt-wiper and left in the gallery.

William, who had stopped between me and the others, took a step back. In *my* direction. He lifted his glasses onto his forehead, looking at one of the painting placards more closely. His lips moved without sound.

*Go on,* I mentally begged him. *Take your time but work it through. I know I'm not crazy.*

At last, he found his voice. "He's right. It's weird." He looked to the captain. "Tell us how it works. How can a sword be the king?"

Then Dawn added, "And tell us why it's called the Destroyer Blade."

The captain let his backpack fall to the floor. "I guess this is happening now. You know we're kinda in a hurry?"

Dawn nodded. "It's important. Important to the crew, sir."

After waving William and me over, Captain Kid sighed and said to the cyclops, "Sorry, Jack, the king has to wait. You can go tell him if you want, but I'll try to make this fast."

The monster looked again to the corner of the room. Was he looking through the walls? I guessed he was. "He can wait," the cyclops rumbled. "I want to hear what you tell them."

Captain Kid sat in one of the chairs left out for art lovers. "Where to begin?" He took off his hat, tapping the black brim against his leg. "The sword is magic. That's the main thing." He turned the hat in his fingers then hung it on the armrest. "It was made by a wizard— not Doctor Alkatan who made the shuttle, but a different one. A dark one. He killed himself with the blade, but it was part of a spell."

"Why would he do that?" I asked.

"Stop interrupting me, Charles. Let me think. It's hard, ya know?" He didn't give me time to respond. "I don't know why he did it. Maybe it was so he could live forever. Maybe it was a mistake."

The cyclops added, "Maybe it was a trick to ruin time."

The captain shrugged. "Maybe. It feels like that sometimes." He twirled his hat back onto his head like the world's saddest clown. "Anyway, he did it, and now the sword can totally destroy whoever it cuts. As in, *forever and always*. It cuts them right out of time. Even their past, like they never existed."

"Even their past?" William repeated.

The captain looked at him wearily. "Yes, like they were never even born."

After the concept had time to sink in, William's brow furrowed. "How do you know... I mean..." He struggled to form his thoughts into speech. "If they never existed, how would anybody know if someone got cut? Does that make sense? Like if it cut me, would you—would *anyone*—even remember me, anything about me, much less that I died?"

"That's true," I said, excitement growing in my chest. "Does anyone *remember* someone being cut? They wouldn't because every time the sword was used, people would forget about the dead guy—That can't be right."

At first, Dawn looked puzzled—I felt some satisfaction at that—but then her eyes widened. "RIGHT! If the victims never existed, no one would remember them, so how does anybody know if the sword works? The magic might just be a story. You know, like a legend."

Hope arose in my heart. Maybe the sword was a fraud, just a regular blade. That wasn't so scary. The cyclops chuckled, but our questions seemed to suck the life out of Captain Kid.

The captain pressed his thumbs into his temples. "You guys are smart. Most people never think of that. Whenever someone's cut, the person is gone. King Katsuro can't even remember them. When a person's entire life disappears, that changes things. Changes time. The whole situation might be different one time to the next, but the blood still appears on the blade as a warning to anyone who sees it. The victims are forgotten, but not their blood. And hear me very well, not everyone forgets the lives of the destroyed. Not me. Not the black unicorn." He looked up. "Not the cyclops. Speaking for myself, it can be a sad and confusing state to remember the lives of people cut right out of time, especially when not even their closest friends know to miss them."

Dawn knelt beside him, one hand on his shoulder, the other on his knee. "Is that why it's hard to remember some things, because time gets mixed up in your head?"

Captain Kid shrugged.

The cyclops rumbled, "We are nearing the end of a split in the river of time. I have seen it." He touched the mound of spotted cheek beside his great red eye. *Red like a Radio Flyer wagon. Red like a Corvette.* "Pray it isn't split again."

The white in the middle of his eye changed shape, moved, little white splotches dividing and coming back together. He looked to me, and I wondered what he saw. My future? My past? All my secrets?

When I looked away, the cyclops spoke again. "Captain, tell them of the touch, the one who lives."

Captain Kid rolled his neck. My mother did that same thing when she was getting a headache. "Only one person can touch the blade and live, the one the sword chooses. That person is king of Atsuma in the Attic of the World." He looked to Dawn. "Or queen, if she's a woman. The only higher royalty are the Blues who live above."

I remembered Captain Kid folding the decks together in the cabin beneath his homemade raft. He was in his element talking about the Reality Decks. Even with this conversation taking its toll on him, I saw some of that same spark now. He stood up. "Charles, are you satisfied?"

"I am, Captain."

He smiled. "Then what are we waiting for?"

The cyclops lowered the hammer off his shoulder, extending it toward the door on the far side of the gallery.

*Off to see the king,* I thought.

Then, behind me in a very small rumble, I heard the giant answer. "The wonderful king of Atsuma."

# CHAPTER 28

# KATSURO THE DESTROYER

The cyclops led us deeper into the palace. With his voice rumbling like the engine of a gravel truck, he gave abbreviated descriptions of rooms as we passed by them: "Grand Room," "Queen's Audience Chamber," "Kitchen and staff quarters."

I was too caught up in my head to fully pay attention, my ears buzzing I was so nervous.

"This way," the cyclops said.

We exited through a library, coming out onto a paved, open-air courtyard. In the corners, flowering bushes grew from gigantic masonry pots, and in the middle of the court was a pool with a fountain shaped like a humungous koi. The fish's splotches were golden, and the white patches were carved marble.

Ozzie had the captain's compass open in a hand, the needle bouncing between three points. As William looked on, Ozzie dug a fingernail into the slot where the selector switch broke off.

The cyclops gestured to the right. "The queen's nursery."

*Nursery?* Did he mean for plants or babies? The door was a framework of thin wood and stretched canvas. The canvas was patterned with colorful birds. I couldn't be sure, but I thought it opened by sliding to the side. Also, the frame of the door was red. It seemed to be the only door in the palace not painted blue.

Ozzie looked from the nursery to the compass, shook his head, and folded closed the lid.

Cyclops waited for him to tuck the compass away then continued across the courtyard to the entrance of the Presence Chamber. Again, the doors there maintained the blue theme, and these were guarded by men with skull faces.

The sentries had the fancier masks painted with silver and gold symbols, but unlike those in the van, these didn't wear samurai helmets, rather, had cloth hoods pulled up over their heads. They also had ornamental swords and handguns in embroidered holsters. There was something cowboy-like about their stances, the way they stood with shoulders back, their weight shifted onto one leg, and in the leaning angles of their gun belts.

One of the guards stepped aside as another opened the door with a hand encased in a golden gauntlet. The guard holding the door looked down at us with eyes shaded behind a blue and gold skeleton mask. His face was grinning, like skulls always do, and on his chin was painted a fiery red heart.

"The king awaits," he said in a deathly rasped and crackling voice.

This man stood out even among the more ornamented royal guards, his eye sockets wreathed in golden thorns, the golden gauntlet on his left hand, and that heart painted on his chin, looking so much like fresh blood.

Standing at the open door of the Presence Chamber, it struck me how underdressed we were. Everyone at the palace, with exception of the cyclops, wore uniforms of one kind or another. The guards had the black cloaks and elaborate Blue Skull masks. The girls in the yard wore golden dresses. While traversing the palace, we'd passed other people whom I'd taken as servants; they were in blue livery with white hats and yellow gloves.

Now, looking into the Presence Chamber, I saw men in matching green pea coats and gray scarves kneeling on mats. They all held fedoras to their chests. *No hats in the king's presence, just like the dinner table.* Along the wall, women were dressed much like the men, but in skirts instead of pants. Unlike the men, the ladies were standing. All these people were grownups.

Of our little group, not only were we kids and two of us wearing hats—Ozzie and the captain—but our disheveled clothes were casual at best and more likely falling into the category my mother described as "play clothes." We'd changed after sleeping on the bustrain but hadn't showered. William's white T-shirt had a dingy smudge on the collar from rubbing against his unwashed neck.

Ozzie's left shoe had come untied, and he was carrying a baseball bat. Dawn looked better than the rest of us, but even her hair was out of sorts. Captain Kid, on the other hand, looked perfectly tidy.

The captain gave each of us a once-over. "Charles, tuck your shirt in. Ozzie, tie your shoe. William, take off your glasses." He reached out and fixed a flyaway strand of Dawn's blonde hair. "You guys ready?"

Dawn answered for us. "I think we are, sir."

The captain turned his attention to the giant standing behind us. "What of you, Mr. Cyclops of the Seven, are you ready to see the king of Atsuma?"

There it was again, *the Seven*. The captain was also one of these.

The barrel-chested monster huffed, "The Destroyer doesn't frighten me. His power is his prison, and he knows it." From atop his head, the stunted horn cast a triangular shadow that pointed to the eye in the center of his face.

"That's one way to look at it." Captain Kid turned to the open door and stepped through.

Dawn and I followed him into the room, William and Oz behind us, then the enormous cyclops coming after. When we were all inside, the guard with the golden gauntlet joined us in the chamber, closing the door.

The room was dark, lit only by thin slashes of sunlight coming in through cracks in shuttered windows. Incense burned, smelling of campfires and cinnamon. That made me think of Castatine. According to Marshal Rayban, the girl smelled of *candy and smoke*. I looked to Dawn, and she reached over to take my hand.

We were standing on a carpet, probably fancy silk spun by hand and worth a fortune, but to me, it looked dreary and old. The carpeted aisle continued between the rows of kneeling men, straight down the middle of the room to the king's throne, which wasn't gold but blue, like the roof tiles and doors.

On the throne sat a man with black, shoulder-length hair. I guessed him to be a little older than my dad, which made him one of the three oldest people I'd seen in that world. The only people older were the peculiar painter at Salvation Mountain and the gray-haired woman talking on the payphone at the park.

The Destroyer Blade—same as the sword in the paintings—was enshrined in a mount built into the top of the king's throne. It was by far the prettiest weapon I had ever seen.

The king motioned for us, and we started forward again. When we gathered at the foot of the steps leading up to the throne, Captain Kid gestured for us to file in alongside. Dawn and I moved to the right. William and Ozzie went left. The cyclops, able to see over us, stayed a few steps back.

Again, I was confronted by a growing conviction that we were not the right kids to stand before a king. Although Ozzie had slipped off his ballcap to show respect, he now presented the world's most incurable case of hat-hair. The captain—even though he was more-or-less neat and clean—dressed like a boy scout who'd raided his father's war-time footlocker. Also, he had the marshal's rifle slung over his shoulder.

Every man in the place was kneeling on mats, the women standing along the wall, well away from the king on his throne, and here we were, standing up, not even at attention.

The booming voice of the cyclops broke our awed solemnity. "Majesty, Katsuro the Destroyer, I present to you Captain Kid and his knights of the world below."

To my left, the captain bowed. Dawn and I did likewise. I could only hope William and Ozzie were doing the same.

When I looked up, the king inclined his head, recognition enough for the likes of us. As he moved, a delicate, silvery band encircling his head caught the light. *His crown.* He lifted his hand from the armrest, and that same colorless flicker shimmered around the navy-blue serpents and panthers embroidered into his robe.

He spoke English, but with a deep, gruff accent influenced by his heritage. To me, he looked and sounded Japanese. "You have come seeking the one they call Patch Fairy, either the fairy or the one who carries her in her pocket."

"That's right," Captain Kid said. "And I'm curious to know how you discovered that. Do you have spies in other worlds?"

The king's hand drew attention to the giant standing behind us. "Other worlds, no, but Cyclops sees much."

"Ahh," the captain sighed. "Of course. What else has his great eye seen?"

The king grinned slyly. "Only that the captor comes from a terrible place and returns to the same. You know the place I speak of."

The captain bit his lip. I had the eeriest feeling he was trying to hide how scared he'd become. He rubbed his chin, and when his hand lowered, he asked as smoothly as he was able, "You mean the Red Attic?"

King Katsuro spoke with methodical, deliberate leisure. "I mean, into the stables of the Red King."

Captain Kid drew in a tight breath, his head cocking sideways to lay eyes on the far-seeing cyclops without turning his back on the king. Whatever he saw in that strange one-eyed face caused him to look away. He addressed the king again. "You know who the Patch Fairy actually is?"

"Certainly," the king announced. "She is the daughter of the Blue King and Queen, their Blue Princess." He growled with contempt, "Castatine—your friend—has kidnapped the fairy for one purpose, to deliver her to the black unicorn. He will use her to open the red door into the Rooftop of the World. There, he will re-establish his dominance over the Red Realm."

Captain Kid's face reddened with fury. "Where's Castatine now?"

"In Salicore by the gate. She will cross into the Red before night-fall."

The captain stepped forward, his fists clenched. "Tell me she didn't come this way—Only she must've. Why didn't you stop her?"

The king dismissed the accusation with an impatient flick of his hand. "It is not my custom to interfere with the plots of those from the upper realm."

"You're a coward!" Captain Kid stepped forward again, but the cyclops restrained him with a massive hand.

King Katsuro rose from his throne. "You will not provoke me, boy. You would drag the people of Atsuma to war with the Red. I will not help you."

The captain jerked his shoulder free from the cyclops's grip. "Forget about me. King Katsuro, if you will not help the Blue Princess, you are unfit to be the Destroyer." He unslung his rifle—I thought he would threaten to shoot the king, but he handed me the gun instead. Then turning to the people in the room, he called out, "What do you say to this? Will you not come to aid the fairy princess? Help us on our quest. As you can see, we are worse for wear and not well-equipped to battle the darkness in the Red Realm."

One of the kneeling men stood up. "King Katsuro was chosen. He cut his hand on the blade and lived."

The captain turned to the king. "Then cut it again!"

Katsuro's eyes widened. "Who are you to challenge me?" He snatched up his weapon, yanking the sword from the turquoise scabbard. He laid the scabbard across the arms of his throne, then turning, he sliced the air in front of him. He held the weapon two-handed, twirled it, and the blade whistled through the air. When he moved down the steps, I heard gasps from the gathered witnesses, and out of the corner of my eye, I saw the cyclops take a cautious step backward.

King Katsuro smiled cruelly. He raised the sword, its metal so beautifully curved, a perfect bend of silver light in the darkened chamber hall. "Tell me, captain, do your '*knights*' know the power of my blade, how it cuts men from the very fabric of time?"

The captain's voice was calmer than it had been since entering the chamber. "They do." His voice lifted. "But what good would it do you to cut them? If you cut one, I would be here with another."

"Yes," the king purred, "but you would remember." He moved across our ranks, extended the sword toward Ozzie, and paused with the shimmering razor tip mere inches from my friend's cheek. The king's words were but a whisper in the quiet chamber. "Would you let me touch you with the blade, brave knight?"

For his answer, Ozzie swatted the sword away with his bat. As the bat completed its arc, the aluminum barrel flew off, clanging onto the floor, and rolled against the feet of a woman by the wall. The woman recoiled as if the severed cylinder were a bloody limb.

That only made the king laugh. "Very good," he said, smirking at the captain. "One of your babies has spirit." He turned on his heels, robes swishing, and moved again in front of us.

Captain Kid's hand drifted toward his rifle; I was still holding it in my throbbing left hand. But Katsuro swiped with his sword, the blade passing so close to the captain's face his hair moved.

The mad king passed the cursed katana—deadliest of all swords—from one hand to the other. "Oh, little captain, I would never kill *you* with the Destroyer Blade—" He spun, snatching the rifle away from me. I watched helplessly as the gun barrel tilted to point at my leader's chest. "—but shoot you with your own gun... *Yes*. I could do that." His eyes swelled in their sockets.

To my right, I felt Dawn's hand leaving mine. Then, I heard her quick voice, "I will touch the sword." The meaning of her words rung me like a bell. Already, she was reaching for the blade. I tried to pull her back, but my arms resisted movement like fingers too long out in the cold. Even Captain Kid's incredible, quick-witted reflexes were not swift enough to stop her.

# CHAPTER 29

# THE DESTROYER

King Katsuro spun away, his robes a flying blur of blue and silver fabric, his sword a flashing arc of white light. Whether he meant to strike at Dawn or keep the blade from her, I couldn't tell. Captain Kid had crashed into her like an NFL linebacker. It happened so fast, all I saw was her golden-blonde hair fanning out as they fell.

All around us, men in green coats were rushing forward. Busting through their ranks, the hooded, blue-skull guards drew bright swords and polished guns, ready to slice down or shoot anyone who made a threatening move. Ozzie took a swing at someone, forgetting his bat was cut in two. That only earned him a kick in the stomach. I was knocked aside like a bowling pin. Where was William? I think the cyclops scooped him up.

King Katsuro tossed the captain's rifle to the guard with the gilded gauntlet. "Arrest them!" he yelled.

Someone grabbed me from behind, hoisting me by my twisted arms.

Captain Kid jerked up from Dawn's collapsed body, his bone-handled knife held like an icepick in his fist. "You're a fool," he shouted, "unfit to carry that weapon!" He thrust with his finger, pointing at the Destroyer Blade. "LOOK!"

There on the blade, a gruesome smear of blood stained the mirror finish. Katsuro recoiled. "That is impossible." His eyes darted to the men around him.

They saw the blood, too, surprise blossoming on their frantic faces.

The blue-skull man handed off the captain's gun to a green coat and reached with his golden hand for the king's arm. He grasped the king's wrist and twisted it to see the broadside of the Destroyer

Blade. The blood was undeniable. Katsuro's face burned with wrath but the masked man's dead skull-eyes didn't waver.

Then the cloaked figure's blue, nightmare-face turned to Dawn, his open eye sockets rimmed in thorny vines, all his teeth gold, and on the boney tip of his chin that happy red heart. *Red. Red like a fire engine.* His bare right hand reached out from the blackened folds of his cloak to point at my friend lying crumpled on the carpet. Dawn lay on her stomach, watching the terrible, blue-faced grim reaper, her eyes brimming with tears.

Was she hurt? Surely, she was, but she was alive.

The Blue Reaper spoke with a voice that crackled with the heat of a smoke-filled forest fire. "Did you touch the Destroyer Blade?"

She must've. Blood streamed down the razor edge. But then I remembered the other possibility: if King Katsuro cut someone else— someone besides her—that person would be gone, and yet their *blood* would remain. I scanned the Presence Chamber. No one missing, not that I could see—

But that wasn't how it worked, was it? The Destroyer's victim would disappear from my memory as well as the room, their whole lifetime vanished.

Dawn lifted herself onto one elbow.

*Gone from my memory.* This thought wasn't a blaring alarm bell like in the Smokers' Cabin. It didn't feel like the same kind of dizzying mental intrusion as the fixation on cards and ashes, but it lived on the same street, maybe even in the same building. Or, in the same basement.

As Dawn wiped tears away, the king roared again, "She did not touch the sword. It's impossible. There was someone else. Look at the blood!"

The blood—what about it? If she touched the sharp edge of the sword, there absolutely would be blood.

*Yes, but so much of it?* She'd only touched it with her hand, if she touched it at all.

The guard released the king's wrist and stepped closer to Dawn, opening his shining gauntlet. To get to her, he would have to go through Captain Kid. "Step away," the guard warned. "I only wish to examine her wound…if she has one."

"It's all right," Dawn said. "Help me up."

Captain Kid hesitated but took her by the forearm, pulling her to her feet. When she let go of him, a smeared streak of red marked where her left hand touched his sleeve. She straightened then lifted her hand, fingers spread wide. Slowly she turned, showing her palm to all in the room. Blood wept from a line of open skin, beginning at the base of her pointer finger and extending at an angle midway across her palm.

"I am cut but still here. Still alive." Her voice shook. "I'll touch it again if I must." She gave her hand to the man with the golden glove.

His hollow eyes studied the injury.

Then she asked, "Sir, do you serve me now?"

I could see the guard's chest rising and falling and could hear his breath puffing against the inside of his reaper's mask. At last, he nodded. Then, thinking better of it, he offered Dawn an abbreviated bow. "I am at your service, Lady Destroyer."

Dawn pulled her wounded hand away and redirected the Blue Reaper's attention to King Katsuro. "I require my sword."

Katsuro backed away, waving the sword in front of him and snarling like a cornered animal.

The man with the golden gauntlet drew his sidearm—a revolver as flashy as the chrome on a Cadillac—and fired. The bang was enormous. It rang the ears and startled the mind. When I looked to the king, I saw him gripping his bloodied chest. With eyes bulging and lips puckered, he fell backward. The sword, which had given him his power, toppled from his hands, caught in the blanketed layers of his kingly robe.

Just like that, Katsuro died on the floor of the Presence Chamber. It happened so fast, it felt almost unbelievable.

The guardsman holstered his pistol and strode to the king's body, his black cape swaying behind him as he walked. For a moment, I imagined Katsuro crumbling to ash like the phantoms on the train. But, no, his lifeless form remained inside his clothes. I wished it

191 . BLROW EHT FO CITTA EHT OTNI

didn't, that he would poof out of existence so I wouldn't have to look at him.

The guard reached down with his golden hand and picked up the unsheathed sword. Another of the cloaked guards recovered the scabbard and offered it to him. The Blue Reaper took it but hesitated before sealing away the deadly blade. His skull-face grinned with admiration at the perfect instrument of death. I wondered if he would steal it. If he did, who would stop him? Maybe the cyclops, but more likely no one.

The guard pinched the blade between two folds of his cloak and cleaned away the blood. Then he angled the tip of the sword into the narrow, silver-lined slot at the top of the scabbard and slid the weapon home.

His voice crackled behind his mask, "If it pleases Her Majesty, we will entomb King Katsuro's body in the Hall of the Destroyers."

When Dawn stepped forward, he presented her the sword.

"It pleases me," she said, taking the Destroyer Blade with her uninjured right hand.

One of the green-coat men called out, "But first, will you tell us your name, Lady Destroyer?"

A woman by the wall agreed, "Yes, tell us the name of our new Destroyer queen!"

Dawn answered them with a tone both lily soft and razor-sharp. "I am Dawn, of the world below, Dawn McFarland." She was blushing, pride and pain, innocence and guilty wonder all rolled into one.

"Dawn," the woman repeated, "like the rising sun."

Dawn raised her voice. "Good people of Atsuma, as you have heard, my friends and I have followed Captain Kid here on an important quest. We need your help."

The captain stood beside her. "We need proper weapons for proper knights." He looked to Ozzie. "You mind giving up that baseball bat?"

To answer, Ozzie tossed the decapitated handle over his shoulder, lucky it didn't hit anybody. But what I felt was trapped. If this was a chess match, in less than a minute, I'd lost both my queen and one of my castles. No way Dawn would go home now. These fools just made her their ruler. And Ozzie wasn't going, either, not when weapons, glory, and adventure were offered.

"Very well." Captain Kid looked to the audience. "Who is the keeper of the armory?" When one of the cloaked figures presented himself, the captain said, "We will need guns and blades, maybe even a grenade or two. Can you handle that?"

The man snapped into a stiff bow.

"Good." The captain looked to the rest of the gathering. "Who can provide us with a helicopter, the fastest one you've got that can be ready in two hours?"

A woman stepped forward. "I can."

"All right then." Captain Kid looked to his *chief officer*. But was that still the case? I didn't think so now that Dawn was the queen of an entire realm. The captain said, "You had me worried there."

William slipped down off the cyclops's back, my little Swiss Army knife—*his knife*—open in his hand. The blade looked comically small in the presence of swords. He folded it closed against his leg and stuffed it into a pocket then went to Dawn, a girl he'd known his whole life. He was looking at her like she'd shape-shifted into a different person. Maybe she had.

The skin between William's thin, brown eyebrows creased as he studied her. "How did you know you could touch the sword?"

"I don't know," she admitted. "I just did."

The cyclops rumbled, "It spoke to her."

When I looked up at him, his red eye turned to me and blinked. Or, was that a wink?

Ozzie snapped his fingers and tugged the broken compass from his pocket. "Oh yeah, we need someone to fix this thing. Don't forget about that." He propped a hand on his hip, so proud of himself.

I wanted to punch him. The compass was our way home. It's needled bobbed between three points, but one of those directions led to our world. We could find it by the process of elimination if necessary, but if he handed it over to get fixed, who knew when we'd get it back, or if we'd get it back at all. If people from Atsuma fixed it, they'd give it to Captain Kid or Dawn before handing it to one of us.

I scanned the room, feeling dizzy, so unsure of myself I might throw up.

With Dawn becoming the new queen—*I had to let that settle in, she was QUEEN*—the people of Atsuma, or at least the people in the Presence Chamber, were ready to give us anything we needed. Even a helicopter. That changed everything. Maybe this mission to save the Patch Fairy wasn't as foolhardy as it seemed. Maybe we were cut out for this. We'd heard the captain's call, found him in his raft, and flew that insane space shuttle to the Upwards Facing Door. We'd met werewolves, even if I didn't know it at the time, and we'd challenged the phantoms. And before all of that, what about my prayer? Didn't that matter?

Our quest could be off to the races. I could almost—*almost*—get excited about that. Especially since staying with Captain Kid might lead to doing something great. Yet, nagging at the back of my mind was a sense that things had not gone as well as they seemed.

William put a hand on my shoulder. "What is it?"

I blinked.

*Something about the blood.*

Yes. There was too much of it.

The truth was so close to the surface of my mind, but I wasn't ready to look directly at it. Instead, I nodded to William, "I'm fine," then focused on another more practical problem: the warning from Katsuro that our quest could start a war.

*A war with the Red Realm.*

*Red like a can of Coca-Cola.*

How many more of those spontaneous color comparisons would my subconscious belch up before they ran out? I hoped not many.

The blue doors at the back of the Presence Chamber burst open. I heard screaming, and in rushed a woman all in gold. Her dress was like the girls we'd seen in the yard, but the glittering garment looked thrown on and her hair was wet, like she'd just run out of the shower.

The cyclops leaned down to whisper in my ear. "Katsuro was her husband."

The woman fell onto the body of the king. Leaning over him, she wailed. She lifted his head with delicate, trembling hands, covering his face with teary kisses. She was smearing his blood all over herself and didn't seem to know it.

*What will come of this?* I wondered.

The cyclops answered my unasked question. By coincidence, or was he reading my mind? "She will be taken to the city, to her family. Unless your friend has her put to death." He smiled. "I don't think she will do that."

"Probably not," I muttered, "but in this crazy place, anything's possible."

As evidence, I was speaking to a one-eyed monster out of a story. Even more strangely, given enough time, I thought the two of us might become friends.

# CHAPTER 30

# THE ARMORY

William, Ozzie, and I followed a blue-skulled guard to an armory in the palace basement. Captain Kid, the cyclops, and Dawn went elsewhere. They already had real weapons, the captain with his rifle, the cyclops with his hammer, and now Dawn with her terrifying sword. Also, I guessed Dawn would have some important queenly business to attend to, possibly even an inauguration ceremony, like an incoming president.

In a narrow hallway, the guard showed us to a bench outside the armory door. The door was tall, blue, and elaborately carved. In the center, a dragon-head knocker clasped a ring in its teeth. As we sat, our guide clacked the knocker then went into the room without speaking.

I felt I was in a dream. We were swimming in strangeness—not *swimming* but *swallowed* by it. Dawn had risked her life to become a queen, and moments ago, we'd seen a man shot dead right in front of us. The significance of our quest was crashing down on me. The others felt it, too, even Ozzie. I could tell by his silence.

So much for being a leader; all my plans had come to nothing. Our conspiracy was broken, and I was adrift. I sat staring at my fisted hands for a long time. Bandages wrapped my left hand. The cut, given to me by the same knife I wore on my belt, still ached. Then my eyes went blurry and refused to focus on anything. I was dazed, half-asleep, and when I regained my senses long enough to look up, William was no longer sitting beside me. I didn't even notice him get up. The Blue Skull had called him into the armory, I guessed, but he might've been carried away by angry ghosts, or eaten by the seat cushion, or any other unimaginable scenario.

Then I heard voices coming from the open armory door and a sound like someone trying on clothes. I would have looked into the room, but that would involve getting up, and at the moment, my butt felt nailed to the seat. I was so tired. So weary. I felt like a stranger living in someone else's body. Even Ozzie, who was so quick to make jokes, was coming down off his high like a kid after too much candy and not enough real food.

It seemed like we should talk, Ozzie and I. If ever in our lives we had things worthy of discussion, this was it, but somehow neither of us found the ability to start. I wanted to say something, but all I came up with was a line about the Oakland A's, if Canseco and McGuire were sticking it to the Red Sox, the same stuff we always talked about. Under the circumstances, that sounded lame.

I opened my wounded left hand. As my fingers straightened, I saw the cap from William's bottle of Howl soda resting in the center of my palm. In my muddled state, I must have dug it out of my pocket. *Tastes like Dr. Pepper*, William had said, but the white-on-red script reminded me of the Coca-Cola logo, like the bottle cap he'd given me up on the Nautilus launch tower.

Why had I kept this dented trinket? Because it reminded me of home.

I passed the cap to my right hand, rolling it over, and when the topside presented itself again, part of me expected to see *Coke* instead of *Howl* written in swirling cursive.

Obviously, that didn't happen. Why would it?

I recalled my prayer to find the Patch Fairy, whispered into my fist then left under my pillow for God to find it there. Why had I done that? I closed my fingers over the cap, concentrating on the way it felt: the sharp teeth of the crimped edge digging into my palm, my middle and ring fingers feeling the rolled dent. *Bent where the waitress pried it off the bottle. No. Not the waitress, it was William. He popped it off using the edge of the launch tower decking.*

I focused my mind.

*Red. Red like a Coca-Cola bottle cap.*

I opened my fingers. Red, yes, but no Coke, just Howl like before. Why did that matter? It mattered because it was red.

I set the cap on the bench next to me then picked at the itchy bandage on my left hand. Ozzie eyed it but said nothing.

In a little while, William stepped back into the hallway. "Whacha think?"

He was dressed like one of the Three Musketeers. He wore the musketeer version of a poncho. *A tunic.* The garment hung loosely over his body, open on the sides, and cinched in the middle with a red leather belt. Emblazoned across the chest was a fanciful white and silver pegasus. He bent over, tugging self-consciously at the knees of his pants, snug as dancer's tights. I never in a million years thought I'd see him wear something like that. *Any dude in tights—unless he's a superhero—looks like a pansy*; that's what William would've said.

Below the knees, his leggings were tucked into a pair of leather boots. From the red belt hung a long, thin sword—a rapier—with a shielded handguard and polished golden lion head at the blunt end of the hilt.

He stood straight. "Well?"

Ozzie and I joined him on our feet. Ozzie said, "I dunno, man. If you were goin' for old-timey, why not have a suit of armor? You know, like a knight or something? The captain always calls us knights."

William shrugged. "They have one if you want it, but it's real heavy."

"I think you look fine," I said. "Awesome, actually." And that was true. It was a surprise; that was all.

William adjusted his sword. "I think they're waiting for whoever's next."

I nodded to Ozzie and he bounded into the room.

When William and I were alone, the time passed much as it had before. We sat quietly, lost in our thoughts. But William, after fiddling with his sword, leaned closer to me and asked, "I'm wondering about the Seven. What's that about? I think we need to know, don't you?"

"It seems important," I agreed. Leaning back on the bench, I rested my head against the wall.

"I guess we're not going home," he said. "For the record, I thought your plan was a good idea."

"Can I tell you a secret?" I asked.

William looked at me with his chin cupped in his hand.

I took a long breath. "I don't even care about the fairy."

"You care about your pals," William said. "That's why you came with us." He picked up the Howl bottle cap. I'd left it on the bench between us. "What's this?"

"Oh…I took it." Admitting that made me feel guilty, but it wasn't like I stole the stupid thing. "Hope you don't mind. It reminds me of the Cokes you gave us."

He set the cap back on the bench. "When was that?"

"At the shuttle."

He shrugged.

I lifted my head, watching him more intently. "You don't remember the Cokes?"

He looked with questions forming in his eyes. "I remember the Howl from the train, but not Cokes. It's been weeks since I had a Coke."

I gaped at him, perplexed. "On the launch tower—You carried 'em all the way up the ladder. You brought three, one for me, one for you, one for Cap'n Kid."

His amused confusion became apprehension. "You got me mixed up with someone else, bro." Then he looked back down at the lion head on the pommel of his rapier.

My scalp tingled. I felt cold and nervous. "Did you look through the telescope? That was you—I know it was."

"Sure," he said. "But I didn't bring you guys Cokes."

"You got 'em from the breakroom," I insisted.

His head tilted, and his brow furrowed. It was a look that said I'd lost my wits. "Sorry, Chuck the Duck, maybe you should see a quack." He grinned. "Dawn or Ozzie might've had sodas, but not me. All I had was my lousy water bottle."

That couldn't be. Yet, I was sure he was right. And after he spoke, my memory seemed to conform to his version of the story. I was at the top of the tower with Captain Kid. The captain was looking through the telescope, trying to find the Upwards Facing Door. William came up the ladder, both hands on the rungs. No Cokes. No bottles. No bottle caps. Just his hands gripping the rungs of the ladder. If he had a water, he must've left it in the shuttle.

"Man, that's weird." I rubbed my forehead.

Then Ozzie sprang into the hall. Here was another musketeer, but this one's poncho was brightest yellow. So were his boots, and his pants were dark green. He patted his chest. "They had my team colors." He looked down at himself. "Even had the shirt-thingy with an elephant on it—like the A's mascot. Cool, right?"

William eyed me. "Ain't all there, is he?"

Instead of a baseball bat, now Ozzie had a sword, much the same as William's, but Ozzie's had a monkey crouching on the pommel rather than a lion's snarling muzzle. He whipped out the sword with startling efficiency. The blade seemed to hum. The only word I could use to describe it was *eager*.

"I bet that thing's sharp," I said, having no doubt it was.

Ozzie drew circles in the air with the point. "You wouldn't even believe. Like a scalpel."

It was my turn. But why would I even bother changing outfits if I intended to go home? *Oh yeah,* because I wasn't going anywhere besides the Red Realm, in search of lost fairies and more adventure.

I stood. Would I emerge from the armory dressed like my friends, or like something else, in the knight's armor or maybe like a samurai? I had always favored samurais. But I knew better; I was to be the third musketeer. Was that coincidence or by design? And if someone had designed it, who?

I stepped into the armory. The room was dim, cold, and smelled of oil and gun smoke. There were two of the Blue Skull guards waiting for me. One was the man who led us into the basement. The other was a woman. Unless I was mistaken, she was the same woman we'd ridden with in the van. Only now, her helmet was off.

She was lovely with black, wavy hair and dark eyes. Beneath her cloak, the collar of her shirt was upturned so the stiff fabric punctuated her chin at hard angles. She looked like a warrior assassin from a movie, or a comic book, not somebody you'd ever meet in real life.

With the wave of her hand, she guided my attention away from the peculiar beauty of her face toward a selection of costumes set out for me. There were four, each displayed on wooden mannequins. The first was a military uniform, both shirt and pants covered in green and black camouflage blotches. The outfit came with boots and a hat. If I was traipsing around in the woods, it would be the perfect thing to wear. However, I didn't know where I was going or what I'd find when I got there. Besides that, Jacksonville was a Navy town, so dressing up like an army man didn't seem like the best fit.

The second was a knight's armor etched with eagles and fleur-de-lis. It came with a green and white striped cape, a broadsword, and a helm of polished steel. It looked amazing, but like William said, it would be too heavy to wear for long.

Next was a samurai suit. The samurai had their own type of armor, completely different from the European knights. This example had a helmet with horns and a red mask, not a skull like the palace guards, but a scowling demon face. Over the shoulders and hanging around the waist were armored platelets linked by small iron rings. From the chest-plate hung pendants, and the whole suit was held together by intricate ribbons and embroidered garments. It was just my size, but so was the knight's armor and army outfit.

I looked to the last set of clothes. Draping a wooden mannequin was the festive livery of a musketeer. This set had an orange, forward-charging triceratops stitched onto the chest that looked like a sports mascot, much like Ozzie's elephant. I fingered the silky fabric and soft leather gloves. By a country mile, this would be the most comfortable. Yet, the strange red face of the samurai seemed to call to me. I felt like I was being tempted, like Jesus in the wilderness when the devil was trying to convince him to change rocks into bread. Where had that conviction come from? I wasn't sure, but it was as real as the heat building in my black tennis shoes.

"Have you made your choice?" the woman asked. She came to my side, her feet moving across the floor with padded scuffs.

I turned to her. "I guess I'll be the triceratops."

"Very well," she said and stepped around me to unhang the costume from its mannequin of wooden rods. With the clothes arranged on a table, she turned her back to me.

The other man was still watching through the dead eyes of his skeleton mask. "Get dressed," he breathed.

I pulled off my shirt. Then, trying not to think about the awkwardness of it, I loosened my belt and dropped my pants. There I stood in three-day-old tighty-whities, not as white as they used to be. The masked man looked at me with burning silence.

Moving to the table, he rudely scooted out a chair with his foot. He pointed to me. Pointed to the chair. No words needed. *You, idiot, sit. Get dressed.*

I sat, hastily pulling on the tights. They looked like suede or a weird blend of leather and fabric. Whatever they were made of, they were the most comfortable pants I'd ever worn. Next, I slipped the musketeer undershirt over my head. It was linen, long-sleeved, loose, and had ties to adjust the split opening at the neck. Not as comfy as the tights, but not bad. Then came the tunic, boots, and gloves. No hat, and I was glad for that. A hat would've likely come with a gigantic feather poking out the top.

Finally, I brought the belt around my waist. The belt was already laced through the loops on the scabbard. Even hanging at my hips, I could tell the rapier carried its weight high. The blade was light as a feather.

The woman wheeled a mirror toward me. "You look handsome," she said.

Maybe, but I felt like a total fraud, like I'd been shoe-horned into a marching band uniform, handed a trumpet, and told to play a solo in front of the whole school.

The man in the mask shoved the sword to hang the blade at an angle across the front of my left hip. "How does it feel?" he demanded.

At first, I didn't know what he was talking about, but then I reached for the grip, testing the position. "Good. I mean…"

"Try it," the man growled.

The blade slipped from its sheath with an irresistible physical satisfaction. The tension of metal sliding against the wood inside the scabbard felt important, humbling, awe-inspiring.

I looked from the etched blade to my reflection in the mirror. Oh, how I looked different. Not like a man, but not like a boy either. A background circuit of my mind started to question if I was taking on some of the captain's agelessness. A closer look at my reflected face revealed that wasn't the case. It was still me, Charles Miller, same as before. Only my clothes were different.

A startling white light flashed to my left.

Dawn was standing at the open door with her little disposable Kodak drifting away from her face. "Quite an outfit," she said.

I sheathed the sword. "Same to you."

She was wearing a dress, gold like the one worn by Katsuro's grief-crushed wife. Also, all the little tangles in her hair were combed out. She was stunning. There were a thousand ways for a girl to be pretty, but at that moment, hers was my very favorite.

"You're going with us?" she asked.

"I don't think I have a choice."

She held out her left hand, the same hand cut by the Destroyer Blade. A bandage wrapped her palm. My left hand wore similar wraps, but hers were new and unsullied. Her right hand rested on the hilt of her magic sword. There was something dreadful about that.

I went to her, taking her hand in mine, careful not to touch her injury. When we stepped together into the hall, the captain was there, clicking a switch on the side of his compass.

He showed it to us. "They fixed it," he said.

And they'd given it to him rather than Ozzie, just as I knew they would. With every successive click, the floating needle darted in a new direction.

The Blue Reaper stood beside him, his eyes wreathed in golden thorns and the painted red heart on his chin mocking the very idea of love. His gauntleted hand rested uncomfortably close to the revolver that killed King Katsuro.

Was he going with us?

Dawn handed the killer her camera. He was wearing her backpack over one shoulder. Her backpack was...

*Red like a...*

Nothing, just her backpack. At last, I was out. *Thank God for small favors.*

Lumbering down the hallway came the hunched form of the cyclops, the business end of his hammer bumping against the wall as he walked. With him on our side, the Blue Reaper seemed a less worrisome proposition.

The captain went to him. "That helicopter ready yet?"

The cyclops's massive voice filled the hallway. "They're fueling it up."

"Good." Captain Kid clapped his hands, admiring his companions.

Then the man from the armory jogged out carrying a canvas sack. "Your grenades, sir."

"Great." The captain took the sack, judging its weight with bouncing up and down motions. "How many is this?"

"Ten, sir." As the man's hands propped on his hips, the parting folds of his cloak revealed two things: a huge cowboy revolver in his gun belt and an assortment of merit badges sewn to the inner liner of his cloak. "God be with you," he said, "and God save the Patch Fairy."

The captain handed the grenades to me, then shook hands with the man. "God save us all. Thanks for everything." Then looking to his crew, "You didn't get dressed up for nothing. Let's see how fast that bird can fly. Not as fast as the shuttle, I bet, but good enough for our purpose."

I raised my voice. "Captain, will our next stop be the door to the Red Deck?" I knew it was—unless by some miracle he thought we could catch Castatine before she crossed over—but I needed to hear him say it.

He surprised me. "Oh, I think we have time for one more stop." His thumb pushed the selector switch on the side of his compass and the needle spun.

Dawn arched her queenly eyebrow. "Really, where to?"

The captain didn't answer but tossed the compass to Ozzie and turned on his heels.

# CHAPTER 31

# THE DOORWAY

We came out onto the helipad, all seven of us, including Dawn's new golden-handed tagalong. The palace staff came out to see us off, and many of the Blue Skulls and peacoat-attendants from the Presence Chamber, too. Most stood as couples, some with children between them. The children wore vests or jackets, all with patches. Some of the younger ones only had a few merit badges, but others had many.

One of the Blue Skulls, a young woman, rolled open the flaps of her cloak, showing us her knives but also the badges she'd collected. There were dozens of them sewn to the cloak's inside lining: squares, rectangles, diamonds, circles, and odd shapes in all colors. One patch bore the image of a teapot, another a lightbulb, another had a bow and arrow on it.

I stood chatting, forgetting about the bag of grenades in my hand.

Dawn turned to the Blue Reaper. "Have you earned patches from the Patch Fairy?"

The reaper's golden hand reached to his chest and pulled apart the folds of his cloak. A patch shaped like an open hand was sewn to his shirt. The hand was blue.

"What's that for?" she asked.

"Service to the Blue Deck," he rasped.

Dawn lifted her eyebrows. "That's very good. Is that your only patch?"

His dead face watched her. "No, but I am no longer a child. Most I've put away."

"But you kept them," she said.

He closed his cloak, looking to the helicopter.

Captain Kid darted over. He'd gone to the crowd of people, to shake their hands and receive well-wishes along with kisses from pretty girls in gold dresses.

With blushing cheeks, he said, "They all bid us good luck, true hearts, and glory."

Ozzie blustered. "You stopped there? *Geez-oh-man*, you could've had a girlfriend. I got a thing or two to teach you, Mr. Kid."

The captain tried to look stern, but his mouth spread into a smile. "Now's no time for girlfriends, First Assistant Engineer. We have the Patch Fairy to rescue."

With a knot in my throat, I said, "They all have patches, everyone, even the grownups."

"That they do." The captain regarded me with more compassion than I deserved. "The Patch Fairy means a lot to these people. Her badges are treasures. So is her love." He followed the Blue Reaper's dead gaze to the helicopter. "Time to go."

We approached the helicopter just as the huge rotors began to turn overhead. The vehicle was a rakish-looking beast, very angular with a matte black finish. It was military, no doubt about that, and maybe even stealth.

Climbing into the sliding door of the passenger compartment, we found aviation helmets waiting on our seats. They even had one for the cyclops, though, it wasn't big enough by half, and for him, the visor wasn't shaped right to accommodate the one eye in the center of his face. Also, I spotted our backpacks in a pile in the rear, secured to the deck by a webbed cargo net. I added the grenades to the lot, wondering if the captain's little crab was in there someplace. He had to be. We buckled in and the chopper took off amidst the roaring drone of engines and swirling wind.

The ride was terribly unpleasant. Aside from the noise, the vehicle swayed in the air unlike any commercial airplane I'd been on. Also, the seats were as firm as wood planks. Between the jerky ride and the weight of the helmet on my head, it was a miracle I didn't throw up or kink my neck.

We flew past the city limits, over smaller suburban towns and into farm country where rectangular patches of green divided the vast segments of land. I saw parked tractors and bulldozers, a large flat structure that had to be a high school judging by the size of the neighboring football field, and a huge water tower painted to look like a jack-o-lantern.

We flew over these sights, and they passed out of view. I thought for sure we'd keep on flying for hours, but less than thirty minutes into our flight, we slowed, easing closer to the ground. The helicopter rotated, circling above the trees, before letting down in a small clearing.

As the engines slowed, the cyclops unbuckled, ducking as he stood, and slid open the side door. Out my window, there was a barn in view, but little else. Not even a farmhouse or a pasture. The only sign of human habitation, other than the barn itself, was a dog that barked at us, upset by our rude intrusion on his playground. He was wearing a collar, so he must've had an owner at some point in his life.

When the mutt saw the cyclops climb out of the helicopter, he scampered off. The captain hopped out next. Dawn went to disembark, but the Blue Reaper's golden hand closed on her arm.

"Not you," he said, his crackling voice only slightly less cruel sounding now than it was in the Presence Chamber.

She considered the metal hand on her bare skin, then returned to her seat.

Captain Kid called out, "Charles, Ozzie, William—with me."

We exchanged shrugs that asked, *how am I supposed to know?*

None of us had the answer.

"Come on," I said, and we got out to follow our leader.

Captain Kid went to the barn, stopping by the open cattle door. The ground at his feet was worn into a shallow rut by the trudging hooves of cattle long since gone. Inside the darkened barn, tiny particles lit by sunlight drifted in the air. An allergic tickle irritated my nasal passages.

I sniffled and asked, "You want us to go in there?"

"I do," the captain said.

There was something altogether creepy about the building: its abandoned, dilapidated state; the forgotten collection of bladed, wooden-handled tools hanging on the wall; its complete isolation. In a movie, a psycho killer would love the place.

Yet, something else bothered me more.

In the shadows at the back of the barn, past the rows of empty stalls, between a stack of rotting hay bales and a machine full of toothy gears—*gears that looked ready to take a farmer's arm off at the elbow*—there was a metal railing with one side dipping down toward the floor. That could only be one thing. A stairwell. It was going down, not up to the loft above. Down there is where the killer would torture his victims. Anyone who'd ever seen a late-night movie on Halloween knew that.

I slid my rapier out of its slender scabbard. Behind me, I heard William and Ozzie doing the same.

"Go on," the captain prodded.

*Go on and face your fears,* is what he meant.

I stepped into the huge, open doorway, then across the bright line of falling sunshine into the dusky shadows. This was the part where a dove would drop out of the rafters and scare our pants off. Then we'd let our guards down. After that would come the true terror. That's how it always worked, right?

Not this time.

No birds. No mice scurrying between our feet. No snakes. And, as far as I could tell, no killers, either.

The smell of dirt and dust filled the room, and hay bales gave off a faint sour-sweet aroma, like grass if it's cut wet. I looked back at my friends. Here we were, the Three Musketeers, but we would've fit the scene better if we were dressed less flamboyantly. I thought of the Wonder Twins. William would have the power of the Pegasus embroidered across his jersey, Ozzie the elephant, and I... I confirmed the image on my tunic. A triceratops. Certainly, musketeers knew nothing of dinosaurs, so why was one on my costume?

I looked again into the shadows, the tip of my sword feeling the air in front of me. My feet moved numbly, carrying me closer to the stair rail. The trip seemed to take half-an-hour, although, it couldn't have been more than a minute. And then I was there, looking down into the hole in the floor, my friends coming up behind me.

"Why are we here?" I asked. My mouth was dry, and the dust settling on my cheeks and forehead, in my hair and up my nose, covered me with prickling irritations.

From the warmth of the sunlit doorway, Captain Kid watched us. "To go home."

"Home?" I repeated, looking again to the stairway. In the desert, he'd told us we had to use something manmade to go back down the deck. This was what he was talking about. *A stairway.* But, home? I'd almost given up on that idea.

I turned to Captain Kid. His combo boy scout-soldier ensemble looked less perfect than normal, his hair less combed, his face with a dimmer shade of inner glow.

"What if we don't want to?" Ozzie asked.

*Here it comes. The moment of truth. Stay or go home.*

Part of me wanted to run down the spooky stairwell, no more questions asked, but before I could make my final decision, there was one matter that had to be resolved. The basement-level workmen in my head had been busy sending up their strange intuitions like smoke signals, more closely related to instinct than deduction. At first, I thought their visions were telepathic warfare from the phantoms. Now, that didn't seem right.

So, what was my subconscious trying so desperately to show me?

I remembered King Katsuro spinning away from Dawn, his robes swirling around him in a shimmering blur of royal blue. The captain yelled at him—accused him of unworthiness—then pointed. He was pointing at blood on the Destroyer Blade, which could only mean one thing: Dawn was cut, and yet she lived.

Except, there was another possibility. There *had to be* another possibility because there was too much blood on the blade. Dawn's hand was sliced, not cut off, so why so much blood?

The answer was simple even if it didn't seem possible.

And the answer was Red.

*Too much blood on the blade.* The Smokers' Cabin seemed familiar—and more than just the cabin, but the whole situation—because I'd been on that bus before.

Ashes, playing cards, the familiar scent of cigar smoke in the air: those were just placeholder echoes in my mind, bookmarked sensations to make the déjà vu more real. The point of the vision was something else entirely.

With the phantom woman pressing her red high heel to my face, I'd looked back at my friends. Dawn was there beside me, so was Ozzie, but William was different. Not just different like he'd gotten a haircut—he was a different person.

In that brief glimpse, I'd seen a boy too similar to William to be his brother, but too different to be his twin. That one had given me a Coke. After popping the top, I'd stuck the bottle cap in my pocket. The version of William standing before me now had not given me a Coke, but I'd taken from him another bottle cap, also red, but that one was from his Howl soda.

The first boy was gone. *Yes*, but that was putting it too lightly.

The first boy was *dead*.

The Destroyer Blade gave up the secret when it slicked its shining surface with so much blood. In his timeline, he must've died in the Presence Chamber at the very instant Dawn reached for the blade.

In the shadowed interior of the barn, standing over a stairway that could take us away from this twisted, fallen world, I stared at William, my best friend, and wondered if I had the same close relationship with his brother.

A tear formed in my eye.

"What is it?" William asked.

*What is it? Oh, not much, only that last time we were here, that version of you didn't make it. So sorry, he was cut right out of time—as in, never even born. And now you're here, a little thinner with smaller ears, but with the same name.* I couldn't tell him that.

I groaned, covering my face with my hands.

Ozzie put a hand on my shoulder. "What's up, man? Tell us."

I peeked at him through my fingers, his dark hair more-or-less combed for the first time since starting this adventure. He wore a green, yellow, and white outfit that looked like a mashup between a musketeer uniform and a baseball jersey. On his chest was a grey elephant, and from Ozzie's lowered right hand stretched a beautiful, silver sword.

I tried to breathe, tried to still my pounding, aching heart. I lowered my hands, looking from him to our captain by the door. "We've been here before, haven't we?"

The captain walked into the dimly lit barn. I thought I could detect regret in his amber crystal eyes. He tipped back the brim of his cap to rub his forehead. "We haven't been to this barn before, but this is our second journey into the Attic of the World... *Although,* I'm interested to know how you figured that out." He looked at me with somber curiosity. "More on that later, I suppose."

William made a study of the captain's face. "What do you mean, this is our second time?"

"That is the question, isn't it?" Captain Kid stuck out his chin. "Charles, care to enlighten your friends?"

"No, I don't," I said, "but you should. You're our captain."

After an uncomfortable silence, he began.

The story he told was uncomplicated. He'd met Dawn, Ozzie, and I—a few of the other neighborhood kids, too—but not William. Instead, he'd met another boy. That's how he explained it, looking squarely into William's dark brown eyes, "Not you, *another boy.*" I suppose he was right. Telling him the name of the other boy would only confuse the matter because the two Williams were not the same person. The Destroyer Blade wasn't the world's ultimate do-over maker, it was a weapon, an *un*-maker.

Some little things had been different. The captain said he was pretty sure last time I was first mate, not Dawn. *Not so little of a thing, in my view.*

He shifted on his feet. "It's hard, ya know. This isn't like memory. It's like..."

"Déjà vu," I offered.

The captain looked at me meaningfully. He nodded. "Right. Like Déjà vu."

William was leaning on the rails, staring into the darkened mouth of the stairwell. "What happened to the other boy? He died, didn't he?"

"I'm afraid so." Captain Kid placed a hand on William's back. "He was taken by Katsuro's sword, but now you're here because the other one is not. That's why I had you stand away from Dawn in the Presence Chamber, because the other boy tried to stop her. And that's why Mr. Cyclops scooped you up, because you're brave like your brother."

William's shoulders slumped. "My brother..." His voice trembled. If he understood that the lost boy was not just a brother, but an odd sort of twin, I couldn't tell. William wiped his eyes. "If he tried to stop Dawn from touching the sword, he's a hero."

"Are you okay?" the captain asked.

William faced us. "I should be grateful in a way. At least I'm here and not...whatever I was before."

"I'm glad you're here," I said.

Ozzie threw arms around us. "Yeah, we're like the best friends ever." He looked at me with watery eyes, but he was grinning. "I'm having the best time of my life. And to think I almost chickened out."

"You did?" William puffed. "You were dying to go."

*Ooh, dying,* that felt wrong, but Ozzie pressed on. "When I went to pack my stuff, I almost didn't come out of the room, I was so freaked out."

I could relate. I'd gone to Tommy's bedroom, hoping to find courage in the company of my little brother. He was uninterested, caught up in his own miniature Star Wars fantasy.

The captain straightened his vest and hat, stood tall, and cleared his throat. "Gentlemen, if you want to go home, now's your chance. But if you care to see our quest through to the end, it would be an honor to lead such a fine company of knights."

William slipped the point of his rapier into the slotted opening of its scabbard and let the blade fall home. Then he stood with a hand on the gold and silver hilt. "You haven't been past this point, right? No more déjà vu?" He looked to me and the captain.

We both shook our heads.

The captain said, "This is all new. We're into the unknown, but I can't say I knew how it would happen before. That's not how it works."

William nodded, but his eyes focused on the open door of the barn where the cyclops waited. "It could be dangerous. One of us might die again."

The captain peered into the stairwell. "Dangerous, without a doubt. Quests often are. That's why I can't in good conscience take you into the Red Realm without offering you a way out." His tone regained a touch of its former good humor. "Here it is, boys, the Downward Facing Door. It will take you home if you want to go. No hard feelings."

*Home,* a tempting proposition. No more monsters, no more villains. At worst, there were a few kids at school I didn't like, but it was summer. School was over a month away. Aside from that, the only real problems in my life were chores from my mother. Compared to this place, that was pretty good.

But I had come to the Attic of the World with three of my earthly friends. Now there were only two. "What about Dawn?" I asked.

Captain Kid stepped toward the light outside. "She will go into the Red. She is among the Seven now."

*About that…I've been meaning to ask you…* But, like every time before when the Seven came up, this moment didn't seem like the time to ask. Now wasn't about asking questions and getting answers. Our arrival at the stairwell into the floor of this forgotten barn was about making choices.

I'd seen enough. To stay or to go?

Home would be nice. It would be so good to see my family, to let my mother smother me with kisses. And to get a bath and sleep in my own bed, not the ground or a narrow train-car bunk. My parents were surely worried sick. *Can't forget about that.* What would I tell them? What could I say that they would believe?

*We got lost in the woods.* That wasn't entirely a lie.

But even the savage misery of my parents, as sad as it was, could not outweigh whole cities and worlds of kids and grownups scared for the Patch fairy. Word of her abduction was spreading. Who would save her if not us? And what of the Patch Fairy's parents, the Blue King and Queen on high in the Rooftop of the World? Had they heard of the kidnapping? If so, they would be as sick over her plight as my parents were over mine. The only difference was—and it was a major one—we were on an adventure while the fairy was truly kidnapped.

I looked to the open barn door. The giant cyclops stood there, his silhouette carved into the day-lit countryside. Then I heard one of the captain's old questions echo in my mind, *if monsters are real, don't you want to know how many heads they have?* The cyclops only had one head, like normal, but only one eye… That was interesting.

Beyond the darkened figure at the door, I could see the tail of the helicopter, its vertical rotor a spinning, circular blur. Dawn was in the stealthy craft, left alone with the man in the blue mask. The *Blue Reaper*, as I'd taken to calling him. It occurred to me that I'd never seen his true face. I didn't like that—didn't trust him—and I didn't like him being left alone with my friend.

Sheathing my sword, "I want to continue the quest," I said. Then eyeing my friends, "If that's okay with you guys?"

Ozzie grinned wildly, but William's slowly nodding agreement seemed more conflicted. I was okay with that.

So was the captain. He shook my hand. "I was hoping you would say that."

Yet, with our palms pressed together, I had to ask one last time before committing ourselves to this mind-bending, trans-dimensional mission. "Is the fairy really worth it, worth the risks we're taking to save her?"

The captain released me. "Is her life worth more than yours?" He looked to my friends, to his *crew*. "Worth more than all of us combined if this mission should fail in the worst possible way?" He crinkled his nose. "I think one life is worth as much as another, and that's the heart of your question, if I'm not mistaken."

When I nodded, he said in his cheerful, casual tone, "Some folks are more important, nonetheless. I knew an ambassador once who won an entire war without firing a single shot. Saving someone like that is worth risking my little life."

*Little life.* If Captain Kid's life was little, mine was microscopic.

"Is the Patch Fairy someone like that?" I asked, already knowing she was.

"Not like an ambassador, but super important all the same. She spreads cheer everywhere. The people love her, as you've already seen, especially kids."

I remembered the people at the helicopter pad, the children at the terminal station, and the ones on the bus, many with patches. Then there was the captain himself, with his vest so proudly displaying the merit badges he'd received. To him, this was personal. Even Dawn's mysterious blue-skulled guard wore a patch from the fairy.

Ozzie, looking uncharacteristically respectful, asked, "Do you love her?"

The captain propped his hands on his hips. "I sure do. You will, too, if given half a chance."

They looked to me.

I smiled despite the fear constricting my heart. "I guess that settles it."

"Good." The captain puffed out his chest. "If you can curb your insubordination, I have an opening for a new chief officer. Would you be interested in something like that?" He was asking me.

"Sure," I said. "Who's gonna be your electro-techno-guy?"

Captain Kid thumbed over his shoulder. "Maybe the skull man." He shrugged. "Might not even need one now that we're through with the shuttle." He walked back out into the sunlight. "But I could use a navigator. Ozzie, switch the selector switch on your compass to the up position."

Ozzie took out the compass and joined him, fiddling with the settings.

"Captain," I called. "You said the Attic of the World is no place for grownups. Can we trust the Blue Skull?"

"I'm not sure, Chief, so keep an eye out." The captain jogged into the hammering wind beneath the propellers and boarded the chopper, signaling the pilot with a twirling pointer finger. *Time to roll.* As we entered behind him, he dropped into his seat and clapped his hands together. "Next stop Salicore, and there's no time to lose."

We were doing this, going on a mission to save a fairy from an evil unicorn. How was that real?

How, indeed? But it was, and into the Red Deck we would go, Captain Kid and his knights, along with Cyclops the Great, the Blue Reaper, and my beautiful friend, Dawn the Destroyer.

As the helicopter lifted from the ground, the barn was lost in a sea of trees, and with it, my way home, but for the first time on this journey, I wasn't ready to leave. Adventure lay ahead, and monsters in a whole new world. Besides that, the Patch Fairy needed our help.

Across from me, Dawn sat between her hooded guardsman and William. Her right hand rested on William's forearm. *Oh, jealousy.* And her wounded left hand was cradled in a bundle of the reaper's black cloak. *Oh, suspicion.* What was that man thinking? Was his mind on his new queen, or was he focused on the coming world? King Katsuro was right about one thing, what we were doing could start a war with the Red. The Blue Reaper had to know that.

Our flight carried us once more past Atsuma. Out the windows on my side of the helicopter, I could see the huge buildings cropping hard, geometric shapes in the glowing sky. So many people and the girl sitting across from me was the ruler of them all. Their queen. Did they even know? Probably not. Not enough time to spread the word. But word would spread and fast.

The Blue Reaper pointed with a golden finger. In the east, a fiery sun was setting over a distant ocean. "The Sea of Dreams," the masked man rasped.

The sky in that direction was lit with every blazing hue, fading toward us into the cool blue of twilight. In another few minutes, it would be dusk. Where was Castatine, I wondered. Was she at the Wall of Broken Hearts or had she crossed into the Red?

Oh, how cruel, to trap a gentle, generous fairy and steal her away to the darkness of the Red Realm.

As the engines of the helicopter roared, I put a hand to my mouth and breathed a secret prayer, catching it in my fist. It was risky to give God such a dangerous wish. What would he do with it? He'd already driven me from my entire world. If he had his way, who knew where I'd end up—*probably at Lord Nightmare's doorstep.*

But the fairy needed someone to rescue her. Who would do it if not us?

I sighed, staring at my fist, the prayer inside wanting to fly from my hand.

In my bedroom, I'd hid a prayer under my pillow, but there was no use hiding this one. Lifting my fist to the window, I opened my fingers. God would find the prayer, my secret wish, even in the Attic of the World.

*Because God can find anything. Even a Patch Fairy.*

I pressed my palm to the glass, looking from my hand to the land of mystery stretching over the horizon. Beyond my blue reality, new wonders awaited. That was a frightening proposition. What we might find, I couldn't imagine. I only knew one thing about the Red Realm, and it was bad news. The Red was ruled by the black unicorn.

Then the helicopter shook, rocking my head, and my helmet bumped against the window frame.

Seated across the aisle, Dawn smiled at me, folding her hands together in her lap. The Destroyer Blade rested between her and the Blue Reaper. The Reaper's golden-toothed grin and lifeless skeleton eyes never changed expression, but one message came through loud and clear: our troubles were just beginning. He knew it, and so did I.

So, what had I, that youthful, nervous version of myself asked for in that terrible, shaking, black helicopter?

It was the same thing I'd asked before: that Captain Kid would find his missing fairy...and that I could help him do it.

## ABOUT THE AUTHOR

Growing up with a father in the U.S. Army, Joseph Mazerac traveled extensively. He was born in Germany but quickly moved with his family to the United States where he spent his youth in Alabama, North Carolina, Alaska, Texas, Missouri, Florida, and Georgia.

After graduating high school, Joseph hit the road again, this time to California where he met his wife. While in California, he began his "day job" career as an Unexploded Ordnance Technician. That job sent him to remote locations across the U.S. and around the globe.

When he wasn't blowing things up, Joseph pursued a less dangerous but equally adventuresome creative life. He is a Royal Palm Literary Award-winning author, graphic novel illustrator, and podcaster—all of this despite his childhood battle with dyslexia! After many years with drawing as his first passion, he has traded the pencil for a keyboard. Now he uses carefully crafted prose to envision cowboys, phantoms, magic swords, and evil unicorns in a multi-layered reality overflowing with rich imagination.

Joseph is a husband, and father to four who prides himself in his family. He is also a dedicated person of faith and does not shy away from writing about faith as a normal part of the human experience. He cherishes time with friends and loves audiobooks, strong coffee, and scratching his dog's back.

While he still travels, he and his family have made Jacksonville, Florida their home.

Website: josephmazerac.com
Twitter: @josephmazerac
Facebook: @JosephMazeracAuthor

www.ingramcontent.com/pod-product-compliance
Lightning Source LLC
Chambersburg PA
CBHW030518020726
47494CB00004B/1140